THE MONGOLIAN MOONSTONE

An Ainsley Walker Gemstone Travel Mystery

J.A. JERNAY

PLOTWORKS PUBLISHING

ISBN (electronic): 978-1-960936-33-2

ISBN (print): 978-1-960936-34-9

CHAPTER ONE

As the train approached the border, Ainsley Walker slumped against the window, trying to summon the energy for a new assignment.

Problem was, she was still recovering from the last one.

North Korea.

Her escape from that horrific kingdom into China had been a minor miracle, with her name getting plastered all over the English-speaking media. Fortified by a glass of red wine, she'd foolishly typed her own name into a search engine. For the next twenty minutes, she'd read stories published about her escape. Some had been accurate, some bizarre. One website had even used her driver's license photo, the hideous one she'd taken back in college, with half-dyed hair and acne blotches.

Ainsley hadn't liked the attention, not one bit.

She'd quickly closed the browser, heart hammering against her chest. Name fame was okay, but face fame was about as desirable as a case of herpes, particularly for investigators.

So Ainsley had decided to lay low for a while.

It had been necessary anyways, since she'd lost her passport in North Korea. She'd had an interview at the U.S. consulate in Shenyang to apply for a replacement. The staffer had congratulated her on her escape, accepted her papers for the new document, snapped a photo, told her to wait fourteen days, then dismissed her with a curt thank you. His frosty attitude hadn't been a surprise. Ainsley hadn't expected to be treated like a returning champion; after all, she'd nearly caused an international scene. Plus, she'd felt lucky to have escaped the Hermit Kingdom alive.

Two weeks of thumb-twiddling. Two weeks of anonymity in an obscure city in northeastern China. Two weeks of breakfast alone in the hotel lobby, lunch alone at a noodle shop, dinner alone in her room. Then the media eye had swung towards the next shiny thing, and Ainsley had been forgotten once again. A small blessing.

The new passport had arrived on the same day as the new job. There had been a mysterious voice from an unlisted phone number. It had introduced itself with the name of Gantig. The voice had explained, in English, that an assignment awaited her in Mongolia. The voice had discussed a generous fee. The voice had been insistent on one point.

Ainsley had to get herself to Mongolia.

Fast.

That had been yesterday. Today, she was onboard the train, rolling through northern China, up steep wooded forest slopes, across bare orange hills. She could hear the diesel engine of the Trans-Mongolian straining under the effort.

Ainsley was on her way to Ulaanbataar.

A knock at the door. A room attendant entered, a humorless woman with rouged cheeks and pale skin. She was bearing a stack of folded sheets in one hand and a tray of teacups in the other.

Ainsley selected one stack of sheets and one cup of tea. The attendant swiveled and left as abruptly as she'd entered.

The rhythmic clicking beneath the floor slowed down. The train was decelerating.

Ainsley sat up. There were no scheduled stops. She wondered if Chinese authorities had decided to arbitrarily detain them.

She went out into the narrow corridor. Other passengers were milling about, mostly middle-class Chinese, the men in polo shirts and the women draped in Western brands. Nobody seemed too worried.

Hands touching the walls for balance, she made her way down to the restaurant car. She spotted a dapper elderly white man standing at the bar, a small glass of beer in his hand. He would speak English.

"Can you tell me what's happening?" she said. "I thought this train was going straight to Ulaanbataar."

He replied in a Hong Kong British accent. "No reason to panic. It is."

"But the train is stopping."

He sipped his beverage and dabbed at lips. "We're at the Mongolian border. They have to switch from Chinese gauge to Russian gauge."

"Really?"

The elderly man held up the fingers of one hand. "Chinese"—he widened the fingers slightly—"and Russian."

Ainsley exhaled in relief. "How are they going to do that?"

He nodded towards the window. Outside was an enormous hydraulic lift. Workers buzzed around as the forks of the lift slipped underneath the coach, then slowly jacked it up. Ainsley saw workers begin to manually detach the wheels.

"When the Soviets controlled Mongolia, they didn't want anybody rolling into their empire on their own lines, so they switched to an entirely different gauge from the rest of the world."

"Oh."

"Would you like something to drink?"

"Yes," she said, "thank you."

The elderly man gestured to the bartender, who poured her a small beer.

"Cheers," he said, lifting his glass. They clinked glasses.

"May I ask what you are visiting Mongolia for?" he said.

"For an assignment."

"Oh—what do you do?"

"I'm a gemstone detective."

He nodded as if he'd been expecting that very answer. "How interesting. You're definitely headed to the right place."

"Why is that?"

He made a *tut-tut* sound. "They don't call it Mine-golia for nothing."

Ainsley hadn't known anything about that. In fact, the only image she had of Mongolia was the one that everybody had—horses, crossbows, hordes of soldiers, and Genghis Khan.

"But it's not a wealthy country, is it?"

"Most definitely not," he replied, "but if the government would let the mining companies in, everybody would get rich." The elderly man leaned forward. "There are enough minerals and gemstones in Mongolia to turn every one of its inhabitants into a multimillionaire. That's the truth."

Ainsley's eyes widened. "I didn't know that."

"Trillions of dollars beneath their feet. I've been there nine times." He drank his beer. "Anyways, you'll love the country, just as soon as you get out of Ulaanbataar."

"Why?"

He pointed to a mobile oxygen tank on the floor near his feet. Ainsley hadn't noticed it before. "The air quality is so terrible that I have to carry this filthy tank around." He sighed. "I don't advise entering old age. It's quite overrated."

Ainsley was intrigued. This man was a repository of information.

"I'm going to sit right here," she said, "and you're going to tell me everything you know about Mongolia."

"My goodness," he said, "now you'll never get me to shut up."

He patted the bar stool next to him.

Ainsley felt a thrill go down her legs. This was the feeling she always experienced at the start of every assignment—the excitement of stepping into the unknown.

As she took a seat on the stool, the train entered Mongolia.

CHAPTER TWO

Twenty-four hours later, Ainsley was in the backseat of a BMW. Ahead, through the windshield, the boulevard was a line of taillights.

It was a traffic jam. In downtown Ulaanbataar.

This was ludicrous. A traffic jam in one of the most wide-open, empty, remote nations on earth.

Yet here she sat.

Ainsley looked at the back of her driver's head. He'd met her at the railway station, her name printed in block letters on a large card. He hadn't spoken a word of English.

Once inside the vehicle, he'd handed her a file folder with her itinerary. They were headed to the Hilton, where she would check in, then meet Gantig in the lobby at eight o'clock for dinner.

Gantig Batsuuri.

She knew next to nothing about Mister Batsuuri except that he was paying good money for her sleuthing services. He could be an insufferable egomaniac. He could be a humble family man. He could be a cunning criminal mastermind.

Ainsley would just have to find out.

The luxury sedan jounced through the uneven streets of the Mongolian capital. Outside the window passed the familiar logos—the green mermaid offering her coffee, the colonel hawking his fried chicken. Part of Ainsley felt reassured to see those corporate brand names here.

The car turned into the portico of the Hilton. Ainsley exited, and the driver following her inside, handing her bag to the porter.

At the front desk, she gave her passport to the clerk. Next to the front desk was a small shelf of books about Mongolia in a variety of languages. Before she could scan them, the front desk clerk handed her the keycard and directed her to the elevators.

With the porter, Ainsley arrived at the fourteenth floor, found the room, and went inside.

It was a king suite. The porter set down her bag on the dresser and went out. The door softly clicked shut behind her. She stood there, breathing in the luxury. She ran her hand across the turned-over corner of the bed linen. It felt like high thread count.

This was new Mongolia.

Then she saw it. On her bed lay a designer gift box. She approached it warily. Her name had been written upon a card on top.

Ainsley opened the card.

Miss Walker, a welcome gift for you. - Gantig

Her curiosity piqued, she lifted the lid. Inside lay a beautiful purple coat. She lifted it into the air and admired it. It had been embroidered and cut in a traditional Mongolian style, with long wide sleeves and lots of gold trim.

She held it up to herself in the closet mirror. This was a hell of a gift. It could mean that her new employer was somebody powerful and tasteful. Against her better judgment, Ainsley felt herself starting to wonder about him in a decidedly non-professional manner.

Feeling a flutter of excitement, Ainsley went into the bathroom, turned on the shower, and took off her clothing.

After thirty hours on a train, making herself beautiful was going to take some work.

CHAPTER THREE

At eight o'clock, Ainsley emerged into the lobby of the hotel.

She was wearing a simple dress, the only one that she had carried with her, a demure but form-fitting black number. On her feet were a pair of cheap heels she'd bought at a market in Shenyang, using nothing but pointed fingers and grunts.

Her hair was pinned back because she had nothing to fix it with. On her face she'd applied the smallest touch of mascara and lipstick, both purchased from a salesgirl who'd been pushing a cart up and down the aisle of the train.

In the lobby, Ainsley walked over to the bar and ordered a lemon-lime soda from the bartender. Nothing strong, not right now. She was still tired from the journey. A single cocktail would knock her back on her heels faster than an uppercut from a Russian welterweight. She needed to remain as sober as possible.

The bartender slid the fizzy drink across the bar on a napkin. "Room number?" He spoke with an Australian accent.

"Fourteen seventeen."

The bartender entered the number in the system. His eyes flicked up to her. "Ainsley Walker, correct?"

"Yes—why?"

"Mister Batsuuri left a message for you. It says that he's been delayed. He will arrive as soon as possible."

It was thoughtful of him to let her know. Ainsley thanked the bartender, then turned away. Her eye fell upon the shelf of books next to the front desk.

She perused the shelves, found an English-language book, and carried it with her to a red midcentury egg-shaped chair. Soda in hand, Ainsley sat down, crossed her legs, and looked through the book.

It was a history of the empire of Genghis Khan.

Ainsley had known that Khan's reach had been wide, but she hadn't known just how staggeringly wide. At the beginning of the thirteenth century, he and his horde had blazed across all of Asia, all the way to Hungary. They'd benefited from unusually heavy rainfall that fueled the growth of grass, which fueled their massive horse army.

In a single lifetime, he'd created the biggest land empire in the history of the world.

Through his ordered violence—the only accepted method of creating order back then—Khan's empire paradoxically stabilized Central Asia, which had been violent for centuries. Later, his descendants organized a massive postal system, instituted religious toleration, and set the foundation for the Pax Mongolia, a golden age of trade. The Silk Road, the adventures of Marco Polo, the trading alliances with cities as far away as Genoa, Italy—all of it was born from him.

Because of Khan, it was said that a young virgin with a tray of gold on her head could walk unmolested from the Pacific all the way to the Mediterranean.

Ainsley rolled her eyes. She doubted that, but the meaning was clear.

A half hour later, Ainsley finally set the book down, signaled to the bartender, and lifted her glass. "One more, please."

The bartender's eyes glanced behind her. "Maybe you want to wait."

"Why?"

"Because I believe Mister Batsuuri has just arrived."

Ainsley turned around. A young man was moving towards her across the lobby. He wore a stylish gray suit with no tie, and carried himself with confidence, his shoulders rolled back. A stylish passenger bag was slung over his shoulder. He would look perfectly in place strolling down the sidewalks of Williamsburg or Soho.

The young man stuck out his hand. "Ainsley?"

"You're Gantig?"

He nodded. "Thanks for waiting."

His voice took her aback. Gantig spoke with an easy American accent. It wasn't the voice of a professional, either. It was the voice of an American kid in sweatpants and flip-flops who'd just shown up late to his nine o'clock a.m. sociology class.

She shook his hand. "Thank you for the traditional coat. It's lovely."

He nodded briefly. She studied his face. It was smooth, the skin clear, the angled cheekbones sharp enough to open cans. Still, Ainsley felt her spirits fall. He may have been good-looking and draped in a nice suit, but he was still a kid.

"Thank you so much for coming. We have a lot to talk about. Are you hungry?"

Her tiger of a stomach pounced at the idea, but Ainsley cracked the whip and forced it back. "Let's talk here first."

Gantig sensed her hesitation. "What's the problem?"

It was difficult to put into words. "I mean, I don't really

know you yet. So it's a little soon to be getting in a car together."

Gantig looked at her. "Well, I don't know you either, so we're both taking a risk."

"No, there's something else." She took a deep breath. "How old you are, Gantig?"

"I'm nineteen."

Ainsley stammered, searching for the right words. They turned out to be the obvious ones. "You're only *nineteen* years old?"

"Yeah. Why does it matter?"

"I've never worked for someone so young."

His eyes found hers. "I've never hired someone so old."

Ouch. Twenty-nine years old, and Ainsley was already on the proverbial shelf. "Where did you learn English?"

"I go to school in the U.S. I'm a junior at USC."

Her mind raced through the possibilities. Evidently he saw her confusion. "University of Southern California. Have you heard of it?"

Ainsley wanted to wrap herself in a shroud and bury herself in the earth. Yes, of course, she'd heard of *that* USC, but she hadn't thought that anybody from this distant country would stand a chance of being admitted there.

"Before we go anywhere, I have a lot of questions. Because I don't know *anything* about you, or even about this country."

Gantig shrugged. "Is this really necessary? I mean we're going to talk later."

"Yes it is. I want to do it now before we go any further."

He sighed, checked his watch. "Okay, but we only have ten minutes."

The nineteen-year-old motioned to the bartender for a drink, then seated himself, legs splayed out as though he'd been called into the provost's office to discuss his behavior.

Ainsley lowered herself into the chair opposite him and pulled a notebook from her bag.

CHAPTER FOUR

Ainsley and her youthful client faced one another across the small cocktail table. Two beverages rested between them, one soda, one vodka. Wet rings formed on the cocktail napkins beneath each.

"So where do you want to start?" said Gantig.

Ainsley uncapped her pen. "Start with your background. Tell me where you come from."

"I grew up here."

"Ulanbataar." She jotted it down. "And your parents?"

"My dad is in business."

"What does he own?"

"Beverages, grocery, and gasoline."

"What's the name of his company?"

Gantig looked like he didn't quite understand her. "He owns all of them."

"What do you mean *all of them*?"

The young man grew slightly impatient. "I mean, he owns those three sectors of the economy."

Ainsley leaned forward, making sure she'd heard him right. "He owns *all* the beverages, *all* the grocery, and *all* the gasoline in Mongolia?"

"Yeah."

"That's wild."

He shook his head. "Here, it's normal."

Gantig explained. Following the collapse of the Soviet Union in the early nineteen-nineties, Mongolian society had been thrust into capitalism. The entrepreneurs who had jumped early had seized the first-mover advantage, and they became the tycoons. Ainsley realized that the word *monopoly* hadn't yet become a sin. A single individual was free to dominate the market.

Ainsley blew air softly out of her mouth. "So your family is wealthy."

"Yeah," he said.

He appeared uncomfortable, and she regretted bringing it up. People born into wealth never liked to talk about it, so Ainsley quickly changed the subject. "I'd also like to know why you brought me here. What do you need from me?"

"Hold on."

The bartender approached the table, and the two spoke in a rapid stream of Mongolian. The language was hard to describe, unlike almost anything Ainsley had ever heard before. It sounded a little like the snuffling of a horse. That wasn't meant to be an insult, either—it was kind of beautiful. She wondered if it wasn't a coincidence that the most equestrian culture on earth would develop such a pronunciation.

The bartender brought him a fresh vodka and went away. Gantig studied the glass, turned it with his hand. Without lifting his eyes, he said, "Have you heard of Zhakorum?"

"No. Who is that?"

Gantig reached into his passenger bag and produced a map of Mongolia. He pulled another cocktail table over to their own, then laid it out, smoothing the paper with his hands. Then he pointed to an area in the middle western part of the country.

"It isn't a person. Zhakorum is a village, located here." His finger pointed to a spot in west-central Mongolia. "It has maybe two or three hundred people today. Very cold. Life is hard there."

Ainsley squinted at the map, taking more notes. "Let me guess—this village has a gemstone?"

"No," he replied, "it's *missing* a gemstone."

"What kind?"

"A moonstone."

Ainsley nodded. The moonstone had been used in Roman jewelry for nearly two thousand years, and for even longer in East Asian cultures. In India the moonstone was a traditional wedding gift, with a special significance for lovers. Its popularity reached a peak during the Art Nouveau period, when the stone became the preferred choice among jewelers, particularly French designer René Lalique, who adored it.

But Ainsley knew the moonstone mostly as "the traveler's stone". Because of its association with lunar powers, wearing one at night supposedly provided protection from bandits. Back home, she had a moonstone ring in a drawer but rarely wore it, and definitely not for protection. A can of pepper spray or a switchblade worked much better.

"Can you describe what it looks like?" she said.

Gantig made a cylindrical shape with his hands. "It's like a short tube. A weird shape, you know? It used to be stored in the forehead of a statue of Buddha."

Ainsley scribbled every word into her notebook. She'd never heard of such a strange shape.

"But now it's gone," she said.

"Yeah."

"Do we know who might have stolen it?"

"It wasn't stolen. It was *buried*."

Ainsley lifted an eyebrow. "Buried by who?"

"A Buddhist monk."

She jotted that down too. This assignment was sounding more interesting.

"Can we talk to this monk?"

Gantig shook his head. "He died a long time ago. He buried the moonstone just before they killed him. I do have one picture of the jewel." He reached into his passenger bag and pulled out a small black-and-white glossy photo. The quality was poor, but she could make out an oblong gemstone with six sides. It looked like an Allen wrench.

"Hexagonal tube cut," she said. "That's unusual. How long is it?"

"They say it's four centimeters in diameter and eighteen centimeters long. Supposedly it took the monks over three months to cut."

Ainsley whistled to herself. There was no telling what something like this would sell for on the international market, given its size, its cut, and its history. Even if it were cloudy or somehow damaged, she guessed that the sky was the limit for asking price.

"Look at this," Gantig said. He pulled out a second black-and-white photo of a small but magisterial structure on a hilltop. Its stone terraces looked peaceful and inviting. "That was the monastery of Zhakorum, before it was attacked."

"When?"

"In 1922. There were almost twenty Buddhist monks living there. Then the Soviets rolled in."

"They killed the monks."

"Always. The first thing the Soviets did when they invaded a country was to kill the religious people and the intellectuals."

Ainsley studied the photo. "So these monks knew the end was coming. And that's why they buried the moonstone."

Gantig nodded. "So the Soviets wouldn't get it."

"What was this monk's name?"

"Cholsaiban. Here's a photo of him."

He handed her a third black-and-white glossy. The broad face that looked out at her from across the centuries was intelligent. A hard squint in the corner of Cholsaiban's eyes told her that he hadn't been any pushover, either.

"After they killed Cholsaiban," said Gantig, "they threw his body into a mass grave with the bodies of the other monks. Nobody escaped that monastery alive."

Ainsley thought about that. "But if all the monks were killed, how do we know that Cholsaiban buried the moonstone?"

As Gantig started to answer, a commotion broke out from the other side of the lobby. They watched as security guards dragged a pair of drunken men across the floor and literally threw them out the doors onto the street.

"Nice hotel," said Ainsley.

He shrugged. "It is. The men in my country are ... different."

"So my question."

"It's a good one. One of the professors at the National University of Mongolia did research in Moscow in the mid-nineties, after the end of the Soviet Union. He found a document describing a monk named Cholsaiban. The document said that another monk had cooperated with the Soviets to save his own hide. He had told the Soviets that Cholsaiban had buried the gemstone somewhere on the grounds of the monastery. The Soviets tortured Cholsaiban for a week, but he wouldn't break. Eventually they killed him."

Ainsley chewed on her lip. *Buried treasure.* This sounded like a pirate story, except that the pirates had travelled over an ocean of grass.

"So you want me to find buried treasure," she said.

"No," he said.

"I'm confused."

Gantig gathered the three photos together and stuffed them into his passenger bag. Then he swallowed the rest of the vodka in a single gulp and wiped his mouth with the back of his hand.

"Somebody," he said, "has already found it."

At last, the first rays of understanding dawned in her mind. "Ah. So my job is to find the person who found the moonstone—"

Gantig interrupted her. "No, we don't need the person. We just need the moonstone."

Ainsley tapped her pen against her teeth and studied him. "Can I ask why you and your family need this moonstone so badly? It's been buried for more than a century."

The young client clamped his lips tight. Then he said evenly: "There's more to this story than you can believe."

That was music to Ainsley's ears. "Well, I've got time."

Gantig rose to his feet. "It's been ten minutes, Ainsley. Are you coming with me to dinner?"

She sighed. "I guess so."

"Do you eat meat?"

She nodded. "Why?"

"Because that's all we serve in Mongolia." He offered a hand. "Come—we'll talk more on the way."

Ainsley reluctantly allowed him to help her to her feet. She didn't totally trust Gantig, but her gut hadn't sounded any alarm bells yet either.

CHAPTER FIVE

In the back of the Mercedes, Ainsley stared at the driver's hair. It was salt-and-pepper, thick and wiry. It was the same guy who'd picked her up from the train station.

"I hope you don't mind me saying this," she said, "but you must be rich if you have a private driver."

Evidently that was the wrong thing to say, because Gantig looked as though she'd just splattered him with a handful of mud. "He's more than just a driver, Ainsley. He helps us around the house."

"But you're nineteen. Don't you want to drive?"

Gantig thought about it. "No, not really. I can let someone else can do it."

They lapsed into silence until the car stopped in front of a restaurant with a modern glass facade. A team of black-clad valets stood at attention, waiting with hands clasped behind their backs.

One valet opened the door for Ainsley. She cautiously stepped out.

Gantig met her around the car. "Welcome to Sorak."

"You know this place?"

He grinned. "They know me. I come here all the time."

To underline his point, Gantig smacked one of the valets on the back. The black-clad man grinned, revealing a huge smile full of pink gums.

They entered the restaurant, and Ainsley studied the scene. Modern teak décor, hanging translucent globes, the hum of busy socializing—this place was modern, and packed to the gills with people trying to impress. She saw a lot of young executive types, and almost as many slender women prettied up to accompany them.

It may have been her first time here, but this restaurant somehow felt familiar. This same restaurant existed in different forms across the globe, wherever sophisticates gathered to make deals. It was the Sarrià scene in Barcelona, it was the Palermo scene in Buenos Aires, it was the West Loop scene in Chicago.

The moneyed elite.

A suave maître d' in a penguin suit recognized Gantig, greeted him, and led them through the restaurant. Ainsley admired the low crystal dividers that stood between the white-draped tables. Each was etched with a different frosted-glass image of a galloping horse, its mane blowing in the wind.

Their table lay almost square in the middle of the crowded space. That probably wasn't an accident. Gantig seemed like the kind of young rising heir to power who'd want a table with maximum visibility. The maître d' pulled out Ainsley's chair in an exaggerated display of courtesy. As she lowered herself into the seat, he pushed it forward towards her calves.

She and Gantig were now seated perpendicularly. Ainsley fluffed her thick linen napkin on her lap, sipped her water, and studied her young host as he settled into his element. He adjusted the cuffs of his shirt, tipped his chin up, and scanned the room, taking stock of the clientele. He smiled to one man, nodded to another, lifted a hand to a third.

Ainsley realized that he had brought her to this table because he wanted to be seen with her. She wouldn't complain. She was going to enjoy a proper expensive meal, her first in months.

The sommelier arrived. It was a woman in a conservative black suit and thick black heels, her black hair pulled back into a tight bun. She cradled a bottle of French wine in her left hand, the label turned outwards.

"Would you like to try it?" Gantig said, pointing at the bottle.

"Maybe," Ainsley replied.

"Yes or no?"

She couldn't decide. "I could be persuaded."

Gantig nodded to the waiter, who poured each of them a glass. "It's a Burgundy. I actually prefer Bordeaux but my father told me to try this one."

They toasted one another, and Ainsley looked at him over the rim of her glass. She was pretty sure that no other human in the world whose age ended in *-teen* suffix would know French wine varietals. She tried to imagine him in his frat house in the United States, ratty backwards baseball cap on his head, flip-flops, the scent of old beer everywhere, directing sorority girls towards the keg in the back kitchen.

She couldn't picture it. That didn't square with the young, wealthy sophisticate sitting next to her.

Gantig finished looking through the menu and sat it down. Ainsley cleared her throat. "We were talking about the reasons for recovering this gemstone."

He ignored her. "I'm having the lamb. You?"

"Listen to me."

"I am listening to you."

"You want me to find the person who dug up the moonstone."

"No, not the person," he replied. "We want the *moonstone*. We don't care who it was."

His eyes roved the restaurant, working the room from his seat. Ainsley rapped the table with her knuckles. "Hey, kid—over here. I'm asking you *why*."

Gantig sipped his wine, still not looking at her. "Because we're paying you."

"I'm serious."

His eyes slid over to hers. "I'm serious too. The reason isn't important."

"But it's important to *me*," she said.

Gantig rolled his eyes. She watched as he reached into his passenger bag and removed an envelope and pushed it towards her across the table.

"Here is your reason. This is half."

Ainsley peeked inside. It was filled with currency, mostly American hundreds. She estimated about thirty—which meant maybe three thousand dollars.

She slid the envelope back to him. "I may look like a mercenary, but I'm not. If I don't care about this job, I won't even cross a street to do it." Then Ainsley leaned forward and caught his eyes. "But if I care about the job, and if I feel the passion—I'll do anything to finish it. I'll crawl across a desert or swim across an ocean."

Gantig saw the intensity in her eyes. A brief expression of fright flashed across his face, and that's when Ainsley knew that she had him. This kid may have been worldly, but he was still nineteen years old.

"All right," he said. "You want to know the reason that my family needs this moonstone."

"Yes."

At that moment, the waiter reappeared at the table, hands held stiffly behind his back. The conversation paused while Gantig spoke in rapid Mongolian.

The waiter pivoted on a heel and disappeared. Gantig drummed his fingertips on the white tablecloth and avoided her eyes. "I ordered lamb for both of us."

"Great," she said, "now tell me the reason."

"They make it so well here."

But Ainsley's jaws had seized upon the knotted end of the rope. "For the moonstone, Gantig. The moonstone."

His lips sealed themselves together tightly. She'd backed him against the wall and now she waited for him to crack. At last his tongue snaked out of his mouth and wetted his lips. Then the words slowly broke out into the world like a baby crocodile slowly breaking out of its egg.

"Zhakorum," he said, "is sitting on half a billion dollars of buried minerals."

Ainsley bent an ear with an index finger. "Half a *what*?"

"Billion. With a *b*." He drew the letter in the air for emphasis.

"Do the people in the village know it?"

"Yes, they do. An Australian mining conglomerate has been talking with them for years."

"Australian company in Mongolia," she said, jotting it down.

Gantig glanced at her notebook. "The name is Excovane. It's the biggest mining company in the world. They already built a massive mining complex down in the Gobi Desert."

"Tell me about it."

He blew air out of his mouth. "What is there to say? It's so big that when the complex opened, the entire global commodities market was affected." His eyes communicated the rest.

"What's the complex called?"

"Muk Holgoi. And my father has seen their plans for Zhakorum. It will be even bigger." His eyes glanced at her scribbling in her notebook again. "Do you always take so many notes?"

She didn't look up. "Do you take notes in class?"

He thought about it. "I guess that makes sense."

Ainsley was starting to see the outline of the story, and it was an old one. A huge multinational corporation with almost unlimited resources swoops into a country of less than three million people, a majority of them unsophisticated herders. It dazzles the local government with promises of enormous wealth for everyone—but only if it, the outside company, could be granted access the people's natural resources.

Unfortunately, the story almost always ends the same way: The locals are exploited, used, or ignored. Sometimes even enslaved. They rarely or never see any of those riches.

"Now tell me about the deal."

"Which one?"

"The one that Excovane made with the Mongolian government." She caught his eyes. "They must've negotiated a contract, right?"

Gantig grew worried. His eyes flicked to the far corner of the dining room. "They have been talking for years, and what is coming out is ... not good." He lowered his voice. "That's been my father's role."

"What?"

"He's been fighting Excovane. For most of the last twenty years."

Ainsley lifted an eyebrow. "I thought he owned the beverage, grocery, and fuel sectors."

The young man's eyes flashed. "Yes, and he uses that money to protect his people." Gantig softly thumped the table with his knuckles. "Mongolians must be self-sufficient.

We need to own our national industry. Only then we can discuss outside investment. Not before."

This sounded like old-fashioned nineteenth-century nationalist talk. It also sounded suspicious from someone attending an expensive university for the children of the global elite. Still, Ainsley decided to keep that to herself.

The waiter delivered their dinner to the table. Ainsley tried not to gasp. Before her sat the biggest leg of lamb she'd ever seen on a plate. It was longer than her hand and forearm. A few roasted potatoes lay scattered around the meaty bone like an afterthought.

Gantig watched her. "I warned you."

"And you were right." She pointed at the potatoes. "Those look good too."

"Those are just for decoration. Mongolians eat meat and drink milk. That's it."

Meat and milk. This country would bring an army of vegans to their knees in less than a week.

Ainsley cut a piece of the lamb and lifted it to her nose. She caught the succulent scent of springtime clover. When she put it on her tongue, her eyes went wide. The meat was soft enough to melt in her mouth.

"So here's the big question," she said. "How does an Australian mining company have anything to do with finding this moonstone?"

The young client set down his fork. "You want the short answer or the long one?"

"Start with the short one."

He placed a finger on the tablecloth, then drew a circle around that finger with his other index finger. "Excovane has already obtained almost all the land around the Zhakorum area. But they don't own the village or its immediate surroundings, not yet."

Ainsley was scribbling again. "How much land does Zhakorum have?"

"A couple hundred square kilometers, not much. But they're key to the whole region—the river, the road, the microclimate. So now the Australians are really putting the squeeze on the people of the village. Showering them with gifts. I'm sure you can imagine."

"Yes, I can." Back home, Ainsley had friends who'd told her about the excesses of pharmaceutical conferences. The corporate world knew how to put on a full-court press when it needed to.

"So now the villagers are starting to change their minds. Last week they sent my father an ultimatum."

"Which is?"

"They're going to sign a contract with Excovane unless somebody presents the people of the village with a better option."

"When?"

Gantig held her eyes. "In two weeks."

Ainsley whistled low. "So now you understand better. Excovane will take over my country if we are weak. We have to put our foot down and stop the invasion."

"But what does any of this have to do with the moonstone?"

Gantig put his hand on top of hers. "It's a piece of leverage. If we can find the moonstone, and bring it to the people of Zhakorum, maybe we can end their negotiation."

Ainsley wiped her mouth on the napkin. "So the people of Zhakorum really do value this gemstone."

He nodded. "From what we know, it's their identity. They have this myth built upon the return of the moonstone. That's why we need it—and we only have two weeks." Gantig looked at her with probing eyes. "Are you willing to do it?"

Ainsley closed her notebook. "Maybe, but I need a contract first."

"That shouldn't be a problem."

"And I'd like to talk to your father, before I accept."

"Okay."

"When can I meet him?"

"We could meet him tonight." Gantig nodded towards a far corner of the restaurant. "He's sitting right over there."

CHAPTER SIX

Ainsley swung her head towards the distant corner. An older Mongolian man wearing an expensive gray British suit was sitting at a four-top table with three white men, each clothed in similarly expensive gray suits. Four snifters of post-prandial brandy sat on their table. It looked like a tense meeting had just concluded.

"You didn't say talk to him?" said Ainsley.

"Those are men from Excovane, and I can't interrupt. Image is very important to him."

As they watched, Gantig's father dabbed his mouth with the napkin, then stood up. The three white men followed suit. The group turned and began to cross the restaurant.

"They're coming towards us," said Ainsley. "Can you stop him?"

"Maybe."

The three Australian mining executives passed their table, exuding importance. Behind them trailed his father.

"*Aav*," said Gantig.

His father noticed him and stopped. He was a tall man, with a sharp look in his eye.

"What do you need?" He spoke in a deep baritone, and his English was flawless. His eyes glanced towards the three men walking ahead of him.

"This is Ainsley Walker," said his son. "She's the gemstone detective that we talked about."

Gantig's father turned towards Ainsley, then extended a hand. "I'm Elbegdorj. It's a pleasure to meet you. Thank you for coming."

Ainsley shook the hand. It was large and soft, an executive's hand. "It's my pleasure."

Gantig tried to catch his father's attention. "She would like a contract before she begins."

"Of course," Elbegdorj said in his baritone, "we'll make one tomorrow. Anything else?"

Gantig cleared his throat. He looked nervous in the presence of his father. "And she would like to speak with you at more length before she signs it."

Elbegdorj paused. "Yes, bring her around tomorrow night." He looked at Ainsley, his eyebrows lifted. "Is that okay?"

"Yes, thank you for your time," said Ainsley.

The Gantig's father dropped his head and lowered his voice even further. "I was told tonight that a man named Otgonbayar knows something about the moonstone."

"Where is he?" said Gantig.

"In the *ger* district. Go tomorrow." He nodded to Ainsley. "Take her."

Elbegdorj clapped his son on the shoulder and moved along. Gantig looked crestfallen.

Ainsley grabbed her notebook. "How do you spell that name?"

"Otgonbayar?"

"Yeah."

"I don't know. It doesn't really translate to English."

She scribbled it down the best she could. "And what's the *ger* district?"

Gantig smiled, cutting another piece of lamb. "Oh, you'll see."

Ainsley put away her notebook and drained her wine glass. The only thing she knew for certain was that tomorrow would be a day full of surprises.

CHAPTER SEVEN

Trailing Gantig up a well-worn path that zig-zagged up the side of a large hill, Ainsley found herself gasping for breath.

It wasn't from lack of sleep. She'd slept like a stone that night, entombed in her king bed in the hotel, the curtains shut tight against the bright summer morning light. It wasn't from lack of exercise either. She'd been in fighting shape for a few months now.

"How ... much ... further?" she said, lungs heaving.

"We're almost there."

They'd driven his Mercedes to the bottom of the foothills that ringed the basin of Ulaanbataar. That'd been almost two hours ago, and they'd been ascending without rest.

"This climb is killing me, and I don't know why."

Gantig stopped, turned. He swung an arm across the capital. "That's why."

Ainsley stopped and followed his gaze. The city of Ulaanbataar was spread out below them, and over the buildings hung a dark haze. That was soot, and it was the reason that her lungs were burning. It was also unexpected, given everything she'd heard about the open spaces in this country.

But it made sense. Across the world, sudden urbanization often resulted in an abysmal air quality reading. This one felt like it lay somewhere between Dickensian London and a thousand-acre forest fire.

"So this is the way to Otgonbayar?" she said, breathing heavily.

"Yeah."

Ainsley squinted upwards. "But there's nothing up there."

"You'll see. Five more minutes."

Putting one foot in front of the other, Ainsley carried on. The side of this hill was utterly barren, a scraped landscape of rocks and grass, with one exception—a few words written in white stones, large enough to be seen from a distance. It made her happy to know that Mongolians had the habit of scrawling on the sides of mountains, the same way small towns did back home in the U.S.

Up ahead, Gantig crested the final rise and stopped. "Here we are."

Ainsley arrived at his side and peered out. Here, a thousand meters above the city, was a rolling mountain meadow, stretching out left and right. It wasn't empty either.

"This is the *ger* district," he said.

Scattered through the meadow sat thousands of *gers*—the circular, transportable tents that the country's nomads had become famous for. Many Westerners know them better as *yurts*.

Ainsley shielded her eyes. "It's enormous. This must be fifteen kilometers across"

"And we can't even see half of it," Gantig replied. "There's another meadow beyond this one."

"How many people live here?"

"A few hundred thousand."

"Seriously? Don't lie."

Gantig turned to her. "I'm not. There are hundreds of thousands of people living here."

They descended to the meadow, and as they moved between the *gers*, Gantig explained their growth. In the last twenty years, traditional Mongolian nomadic families had been driven out of their traditional lives by environmental degradation. Many had sold their horses, moved in from the countryside, and formed these shantytowns just outside the capital.

"How do they make a living?"

Gantig shrugged. "Most of them don't."

It was a sad sight. Widely spaced, the *gers* exhibited signs of extreme poverty. On one, a ripped blue plastic tarp hung from the doorway. On another, broken pieces of wooden shipping crates had been hammered together into a grotesque imitation of a picket fence. Next to a third, a pile of excrement spilled out of a wooden box that sat parked uncomfortably close to the front door.

Nobody here seemed to have basic amenities—no running water, sewage systems, even basic heating.

"How do they stay warm in the winter?" she said.

Gantig pointed at a roll of aluminum that was poking out of the roof of one *ger*. A plume of black smoke was curling out of it and dissipating into the sky. "They burn coal."

"*Inside* their homes?"

"There isn't anything else, and coal is cheap."

Ainsley grimaced. "So that's where the air pollution comes from."

"Partly."

They were nearly halfway across the meadow when Ainsley remembered their purpose. "So you know where to find Otgonbayar?"

Gantig scratched his face. "I sent some text messages last

night. I found out that Otgonbayar's *ger* sits just below the script that reads *desert flower*."

He pointed at some writing on the side of a nearby mountainside. It was spidery Mongolian cursive. "That's it. Let's go."

———

Together they crossed the meadow, aiming towards the cluster of *gers* sprinkled at bottom of the mountainside.

"How are we going to know which one is his?" said Ainsley. "I guess we should ask someone."

Gantig shook his head. "No, that would raise suspicions."

"I don't see any addresses or postal boxes. It's our only choice." Ainsley pointed at a woman hanging a maroon wool blanket on a line strung between two poles planted in the earth. "She might know something."

The young client said nothing but followed her. As they approached, Ainsley got a better look at the woman's face. It was round and cherubic and her cheeks looked like someone had thrown a pair of soft red apples at her skull.

They stopped about twenty meters away. Gantig called out to her. She called something back. As the two went back and forth, Ainsley listened again to the language. It was virtually all consonants, the sounds curled up and slithered in the spaces of the mouth between the lower teeth and the gums.

The woman with the splatted apples on her cheeks gestured to the north and spat out a final syllable. Gantig turned to Ainsley. "She says Otongabayar lives that way, on other side of the goat heads."

Ainsley lifted an eyebrow. "Goat heads."

"Yes."

"Can't wait to see that."

They crossed a boggy part of the meadow and Ainsley found herself up to her ankles in black liquid.

"Gross," she said.

"It's a little drier over here," said Gantig. "Oh man, there it is."

Ainsley looked ahead. A pile of bleached goat skulls had been stacked up on the grass before them, two meters high. It looked like a grotesque scene out of a Joseph Conrad novel.

"At least we're going the right way," she said.

Ainsley carried on, the thick mud squelching beneath her boots. Soon they both spotted a *ger*, isolated a bit, set off from the rest of the community.

"I'm guessing that's him," said Gantig. "They said he doesn't like to associate with the others."

"Maybe we should have called ahead," said Ainsley.

Her guide looked at her. "Nobody calls ahead in this country. We just go."

A man was standing outside in his yard, smoking a pipe. He was about forty and his face and hands were covered with black smudges that looked to be coal. He looked like he hadn't bathed in weeks but nonetheless seemed very content.

Gantig stopped about twenty meters away and cupped his hands around his mouth, the way he had with the woman. "*Sain baina uu?*" he shouted.

"*Sain,*" the man replied.

Ainsley guessed that meant *good*.

"*Ta Otgonbayar guia mun uu?*" said Gantig.

The man took out his pipe and casually studied his visitors.

Ainsley tensed. "It's him?"

"Yes."

Otgonbayar slowly approached; Gantig did the same. Ainsley stayed a few steps behind and watched as they spoke together in low tones.

Gantig turned. "He says he won't talk to me while you're here."

"Tell him I can't understand him anyways."

"Let's make him happy. Would you mind stepping away for a minute?"

Ainsley scowled. "I seem to have missed the sign for the women's hut."

"Please, Ainsley." His eyes were pleading.

She fought the urge to snap back. But this wasn't her country, these weren't her rules. Ainsley was an interloper here.

Seething, she walked back across the meadow. Overhead, the clouds slid past in strange, unrecognizable shapes. She took a deep breath and found herself bent over, coughing.

She found a large, flat rock and perched herself cross-legged upon it and lifted her face to the sun. The breeze gently caressed her hair.

This was going to be a frustrating assignment.

She didn't know the language, couldn't begin to form sentences. She had no way of getting to this tiny village of Zhakorum, wouldn't even know where or how to begin. Currently their only lead was something this nineteen-year-old kid had heard from his father. And now that lead wouldn't speak to her.

None of this boded well.

Ainsley knew what she should do. She should end it here, before things went any further.

A moment later, Gantig came striding across the meadow. His walk was purposeful and assured.

"Great news," he said, "that guy told me exactly how to find the ninja miner."

"The *who*?"

"He says that the guy knows where the moonstone really is. He sells archaeological artifacts down at the market."

"Listen, Gantig," Ainsley said, "this is a bad fit."

"What do you mean?"

"I can't contribute here. It's too foreign."

He looked crestfallen. "No, Ainsley, please—"

"I'm serious. I want to go home."

Gantig rolled his eyes. "But you just got here. And we just got a lead."

Ainsley ticked off her list on her fingers. "I need money. I need independence. I need a phrasebook." She paused. "And I need a contract."

Her young client held his palms up. "I tried to give you money last night, but you gave it back."

That was true. "But the other things, Gantig—"

"You will get those other things." He went on. "Ainsley, I can't trust anybody in this country. People like to talk, and this task is sensitive. That's why I need you."

"Because I can pretend to be a tourist?"

"Yes, that's part of it. So don't quit yet, okay? Just wait a few more hours until we can talk to my father."

Ainsley sighed. She lowered her defenses. "Fine."

"Good."

She lifted her head. "I have a question."

"You have a lot of questions."

"What the hell is a ninja miner?"

Gantig jerked a thumb back towards the city. "Follow me to Naran Tuul, and you'll find out."

Ainsley hesitated, then followed him. She would give him a few more hours.

CHAPTER EIGHT

An ugly sea-green arch marked the entrance to the Naran Tuul International Trade Market.

As she plunged into the maze of open-air stalls, Ainsley began to sense the rough-and-tumble DIY ethos here. Boxy furniture for *gers*. Stacks of wooden latticework, to be hammered onto exteriors. Carts heaped with piles of colored felt, to be hung from doors or draped across beds or thrown onto dirt floors.

All of it made by hand.

She followed Gantig into the equestrian section of the market. It was a long row of practical vendors hawking bridles and bits, saddles and stirrups. Nearby, a row of imaginative vendors offered crossbows, breastplates, and helmets, mostly replicas, all modelled on the equipment used during the Mongolian Empire. Ainsley guessed that there were some killer Renaissance fairs in this country.

He slowed down to her side. "Okay, so a ninja miner is a person who digs small illegal mines. Or sometimes pans dirt for gold."

"Why are they called ninjas?"

Gantig made a curved shape in the air with his hands. "Because they use these big weird green bowls when they pan for minerals, and when they carry the bowls on their backs, they look like the Teenage Mutant Ninja Turtles."

Ainsley giggled. "It doesn't sound like a traditional job."

"No, it's not." Gantig went on to explain that recent winters had been especially harsh—known as *dzuds*—and that over one-third of the country's livestock had died. Many of the new herders had been forced to turn to ninja mining.

"So how many are there?"

He shrugged. "Maybe two hundred thousand. They make about five dollars a day."

"And this guy who found the moonstone is one of them."

"We're going to find out," he said. "But ninja miners search in places that everyone else says are unmineable. They learn a lot of secrets." He pointed ahead to a stall. "I think that's our guy."

Ainsley peered ahead. A small man with browned skin and a pair of white buck teeth poking out from his closed lips rested on a metal folding chair behind a metal folding table. On the tabletop lay an array of semi-precious stones. He watched the passersby passively with his legs crossed at the ankles.

"Does he have a name?"

"Otgonbayar thought it was Tsakhia, but he's not sure."

"What's his last name?"

"Some Mongolians don't have last names."

Gantig explained how it had been illegal to use family names for the seventy years that the communists had been in power. Finally, in 1991, President Ochirbat had issued a decree reviving those names, but the problem was that many people no longer knew their own family names. As a result, many invented names for themselves. Popular choices included eagles, crows, hunters, and Genghis Khan.

"So let's review," said Ainsley, "I'm a tourist looking for gemstones."

"And I'm your guide."

For cover, simple was always better, so Ainsley didn't object. "I'll ask the questions, and you translate. I'll bring up the moonstone last."

Gantig drove a fist into the other palm. "Let's do this. I'll pretend to be surprised."

They sidled up to the table. Tsakhia nodded at the visitors. His gnarled laborers' fingers were curled around a ceramic cup like the roots of an ancient oak.

While Gantig greeted him, Ainsley looked at the gemstones that had been spread out on the black tablecloth. The stones were all uncut. All tagged with labels written in three different languages—Mongolian, Russian, and English.

Her eyes scanned the collection. It wasn't a bad little collection of stones. She recognized aquamarine, topaz, jasper, gem beryl. A couple—goshenite, heliodor—were stones that she'd heard of but never seen before. There were literally a thousand types of gemstones that nobody outside of a handful of specialists had ever heard of, let alone seen.

Ainsley lifted a topaz up to the sun.

"Do you like it?" said Gantig.

She feigned indecision. "I'm looking for something more opalescent and lustrous."

The young client looked at her blankly. "I don't really know what that means."

"Just tell him we want something whiter."

Gantig translated, and the man uncurled a wizened finger and pointed to a beryl. He spat a short reply.

"He says that one," said Gantig.

Ainsley put down the topaz and picked up the beryl, dandling it in her hand. "It's nice. Now ask him if he has a blue lace agate."

When the man heard the translation, he shook his head. "He doesn't."

"Now ask him if he has a moonstone."

Ainsley watched Tsakhia's face closely during the translation. An odd spasm passed over it. Then the ninja miner shook his head and muttered something.

"He said he doesn't know about any moonstones in this country."

That was an oddly defensive answer. "Mongolia has every type of gemstone in the world. He must've seen a moonstone *somewhere*."

Gantig translated again, and Tsakhia crossed his arms and closed his lips over his buck teeth. The man's face drew tightly against his skull, his eyes bulging slightly. Then he spoke rapidly.

Gantig waited for the statement to end. Then he drew a deep breath. "He says that you must come from somewhere else to be asking such stupid questions. He says that no moonstone has been found in Mongolia for over a hundred years."

"Well, can you ask him—"

She didn't finish the sentence because Tsakhia leapt to his feet, swept all the stones into a sack, and cinched it tight. Then he picked up his folding chair under his arm and walked away.

Ainsley and Gantig found themselves standing at an empty table.

Gantig punched his fist into his other hand a second time. "That is not how it was supposed to go."

"It's fine," she said.

"But he just walked away!"

"That means that he knows something."

"But we just *lost* him!"

Ainsley tapped her impatient young client on the

shoulder with a finger. "Did you really think that you were going to enter a market, ask a stranger a single question, and have him suddenly hand you the moonstone?"

Gantig fell silent, a guilty look on his face. Part of him was still a nineteen-year-old boy—and they weren't known for their patience.

"I guess not," he said.

"This is just the first step," she said. "Sometimes you end up going down the wrong path. Sometimes you waste days, weeks, or months.

"That sucks."

"That's investigative work." She started back towards the parking lot. "Let's go. I have to get ready to meet your father tonight."

CHAPTER NINE

In her hotel room, Ainsley chucked the mascara into the bathroom sink, cursing under her breath.

She'd bought the tube that afternoon in an effort to pretty herself up. Some touch-ups were in order, if she was going to be presentable tonight.

But the mascara was ultra-clumpy. Correcting it was impossible, because it kept smearing across her eyelids. Three attempts, three failures—and now Ainsley gave up. She would go to the meeting with untrammeled eyes.

She thought about Gantig's father.

Elbegdorj Batsuuri.

Earlier, she'd typed his name into her browser and scrolled through the search results. The few English-language results were from Australian news outlets. In one, his name was briefly mentioned in the ninth paragraph of a decade-old article about Excovane. Another, however, did verify everything that Gantig had told her about him. Elbegdorj was one of the new class of Mongolian oligarchs.

Ainsley stepped out of her bathroom and took measure of

herself in the hotel room's full-length mirror. She was wearing a white ankle-length dress that she'd picked up in a boutique down the street from the hotel two hours ago. It was a tad shapeless but that wasn't a problem. On her shoes were a new pair of low white flats. Her arms were tan and her cheeks and lips had a spot of color too.

She was good to go.

Ainsley picked up her bag, spun around once more in the mirror, and headed downstairs.

———

As she waited near the front window, a black Mercedes SUV pulled up before the front door. She saw Gantig's driver, the man with the salt-and-pepper hair, emerge from the front seat. He spoke to the valet, who pointed at Ainsley.

Ainsley's finger found her sternum. *Me?*

The valet nodded.

She stepped outside and the valet opened the door for her. She slid into the cool leather interior. A bottle of spring water waited for her in the cup holder. This was unexpected. She'd assumed that Gantig would be picking her up.

The driver slowly slipped the vehicle into traffic.

Ainsley watched the city flashing by her windows. The modern cafe with tables beneath colorful umbrellas. The looming Soviet-era block building, painted a lurid blue. The Louis Vuitton outlet facing a pair of *gers* set up in the lot across the street. The fashionable slim women in five-inch stilettos stepping past the homeless country bum swaddled in shapeless dark blankets.

Ulaanbataar was a place of enormous contradictions—and in that, it was no different from any other modern city in the world.

Then the commercial district abruptly disappeared. The traffic died away, and an eerie calmness settled upon the city like a funeral shroud.

They stopped at a traffic light. Outside the window, all was quiet. Then the silence was shattered by the sound of glass breaking somewhere in the darkness, followed by the deep-throated roar of a group of men. She pictured a gang of rough young bucks with toothless grins and trouble on their minds.

Ainsley was relieved when the driver hit the gas and the Mercedes began to move again. Sometimes it was a relief to be the Western woman all dolled up and safe behind glass.

But something told her that it wasn't going to stay like that for long.

————

Soon they were passing through a wealthy residential district. Ainsley knew that the foothills had drawn close because she could see the lights of the houses perched high up on the hills on either side. Without warning, the driver abruptly turned into a pair of double gates, stopped, pressed a button in the visor. The portal slowly opened.

As the car passed onto the long driveway that led across the grounds, Ainsley peered over his shoulder through the windshield. Ahead sat a small mansion on a low hilltop. It was a modern architectural jumble, with bits of Greek, French, and Italian design all mixed together. Its only saving grace was that it had been lit better than an aging actress.

This was the Batsuuri residence.

The Mercedes moved up the entrance drive and stopped under the portico. The driver opened the car door for Ainsley. She felt the wind leaping at her like a pack of hungry dogs.

She stepped out of the vehicle. The driver silently held open the door of the mansion.

Drawing a breath, Ainsley went inside.

She found herself in the foyer. It was opulent in an old-fashioned European way. A curved staircase with a balustrade. A black-and-white chessboard tiled floor. A cherub spitting water into a fountain.

It wasn't surprising. Across the world, people decorate in this way when they first run into big money. It doesn't require any imagination.

A short man in a gray suit appeared discreetly at her side. He was the kind of person who made a room quieter the moment he entered. She assumed this was the *major domo*.

"Miss Walker," he said, "you stay here and wait for Gantig."

He gestured to a small library, just off the foyer to the right.

"Okay," she said.

Ainsley entered the room. Bookshelves lined the walls, floor to ceiling, each holding firm beneath a row of stiff brown leatherbound titles. Ainsley looked at the spines. She was certain that not a single one had ever been cracked.

The *major domo* stood in the doorway. "Something to drink?"

"No. When will he arrive?"

"Soon."

He disappeared. A large oaken desk dominated the middle of the room. Ainsley leaned against it, drumming her fingers on the surface. Minutes passed. She stuck her head out of the library. The foyer was empty, the short man in the gray suit was nowhere to be seen.

The Batsuuri house was quieter than a mouse fart.

Curiosity got the better of her. Ainsley slipped off her shoes, hung them from her fingers, and moved silently across the foyer. She entered the kitchen, which was spacious and contemporary.

It was empty too.

She slipped across the foyer and into the main living quarters. It was a large living room, filled with formal sofas and chairs that had been scattered around the room as if a Parisian salon had just been ransacked. Ainsley dragged a finger along the back of a sofa and felt the pretension slime up her arm.

Back to the foyer. The balustrade staircase called to her with the sultry eyes of a princess reclining on a chaise lounge. Ainsley didn't resist it. She quietly stole up the curving steps. She was grateful that it'd been made of stone—no squeaks.

On the second floor, she found herself at the head of a long hallway blanketed in thick green woolen frieze carpet. Brown wainscoting crawled along the walls at hip level, punctuated only by a series of doors on each side. These were presumably the bedrooms. The silence was thick and heavy. Her breathing felt labored.

At the end of the corridor, a rhomboid piece of yellow light fell out to the hallway from an open door. Ainsley decided to investigate and softly footed her way down the carpet.

As she drew closer, she spotted something leather on the floor beneath the lintel. It looked like a pair of wingtip oxford shoes. Ainsley wondered why someone would've dropped a pair of men's dress shoes in a doorway.

Drawing closer still, she saw that the shoes weren't empty.

They were tied onto a pair of feet.

And those feet belonged to a man. He was wearing a blue pinstriped suit and was laying on his side on the floor. His arms had been flung wide to the left and the right. At first she thought that he was performing a yoga pose.

Then Ainsley saw the white spume of foamy saliva that had spilled out of his mouth, tracked down his face, and pooled on the green carpet.

Finally, she recognized the man.

It was Elbegdorj Batsuuri.

CHAPTER TEN

Ainsley backed away, clamping a hand over her mouth. The man had been dead a short time. There were still bubbles in the froth on the floor, still some color in the cheeks.

She looked around. Nobody was here to witness her discovery. That meant that there was nobody to defend her either.

Then a horrible suspicion occurred to her.

Maybe she'd been set up.

The more she thought about it, the more she realized that it was entirely possible. Gantig had asked her to come to Mongolia, put her up in the finest hotel, literally wined and dined her. Then he'd taken her on a very suspicious fact-finding mission into the *ger* district, during which time she wasn't allowed to hear his conversation with Otgonbayar. Following that, he'd taken her to a market and played along with her little game.

All the while plotting something awful.

Like ... murdering his own father.

Ainsley didn't have the slightest idea how or why, but it wasn't that far-fetched. The more she thought about it, the stronger the idea grew in her head, and the surer she became.

The moonstone had never existed. The village of Zhakorum had never existed.

It was all a lie. She was a patsy.

And now the patsy had only one thing to do.

Run.

Panicked, Ainsley fled back down the hallway. She flew the stairs and crossed the foyer and pulled open the front door and ran under the portico and out into the night.

Clutching her shoes in her fingers, she ran barefoot down the front drive, cutting straight across the switchbacks, until she reached the front gate. There, a BMW was pulling up to the gate. Its headlights swept across the lawn and strafed across her body.

The vehicle stopped, and the driver's window rolled down.

It was Gantig. "Ainsley, what are you doing?"

Without a word, she ran past him and out into the road. She heard his voice shouting again, but she paid no heed.

Another vehicle was coming down the street, this one an Audi. Ainsley stepped directly into its path and lifted her hands. It slammed to a halt, tires squealing. She ran to the passenger side door and opened it and climbed inside. She didn't ask permission. She didn't care who was driving. All she knew was that she wanted to get away.

Behind the wheel was a young woman, about her age, dressed in a shimmery miniskirt and drapey red bedazzled top. Her face wore an expression of surprise. From the speakers played loud Mongolian rap.

The woman's fingers turned down the volume. "English?"

"Yes, English," said Ainsley. "Let's go, quickly. I'll pay you."

She fumbled in her purse for money. The girl looked at her with a disgusted expression on her face. "I don't want your money." Then her eyes roved up and down the strange hitchhiker, taking in her reddened eyes, her grass-stained feet, her trembling hands.

Ainsley looked at her. "Should I get out?"

"No," she said.

Nearby, Gantig had reversed his car. Ainsley clicked on her seat belt. "Hurry, I'm trying to escape that guy."

"Why?" said the girl.

"I'll explain if you go fast."

Ainsley noticed that the girl was barefoot too. She punched it into first gear, and the Audi leapt forward like a horse out of the gate. Ainsley gripped the handle above the door.

"This is a fast car," Ainsley said.

"Yes, it is very fast. Where are you going?"

Ainsley thought about that answer. She couldn't go back to the hotel, because that was the first place that Gantig would check. She peered inside her small bag. Inside were her wallet and her passport. Thank God she had brought both.

"The airport," she said.

"That's on the other side of the city."

"If it's too far, then just drop me somewhere in the city center."

The driver looked into her rearview mirror. "That guy is following us. Really fast."

"He's nineteen years old," said Ainsley, "they all drive like bats out of hell."

"What's a bat out of hell?"

"Never mind. Where did you learn English?"

"Television," she said. "And I used to give tours to Westerners with my father's company. I'm Erdene."

"I'm Karin."

It was a lie, but a necessary one. Ainsley wanted to minimize the record of her presence in this country.

"You want me to lose him, Karin?"

"Yes, please."

Erdene floored the accelerator and Ainsley felt herself sink backwards into the seat. The Audi tore forward, recklessly leaping left and right across lanes, between cars. She looked over at Erdene. The girl had a tight expression on her face and her arms were sinewy and strong as her hands gripped the wheel.

Then she turned left onto a side road, shot down it, turned right, took another side road. Ten minutes of this, and Ainsley was totally lost.

"I don't know where you're going," she said.

"Neither does your guy. We've lost him."

"He's not my guy."

"Who is he?"

"He hired me to help him."

"Doing what?"

Ainsley rubbed her eyes. She couldn't summon the energy to think of a cover story at the moment. "To find a gemstone."

A few minutes later, the Audi had arrived at the city center. Erdene pulled to a stop alongside a plaza. Ainsley opened the car door.

"Are you sure you don't want anything?" the girl said.

"Positive."

"Thank you, Erdene."

"I hope everything works out for you, Karin."

Ainsley paused. "Me too." Then she left the car and shut the door.

CHAPTER ELEVEN

An hour later, Ainsley entered the Chinggis Khan International Airport.

The marble felt solid underfoot. Overhead, the large dome was striped with running lines and sodium lights. A row of Frederique Constant clocks on one wall gave the time in Tokyo, Seoul, Beijing, Moscow. People buzzed in all directions, like transit centers everywhere.

She looked at the brand names of the airlines behind the counter. Turkish Airlines. Korean Air. Air China. MIAT Mongolian Airlines. Plus a few more that served local routes.

Ainsley would talk to all of them. She prayed that somebody spoke English here.

She stood in line at the Turkish Airlines counter, the nearest one to the door. There were five people ahead of her. Each of them looked at her with interest. She guessed that it wasn't often anybody saw a Western woman in a long grass-stained white dress arriving at an airport with no luggage.

Then it was her turn to approach the ticket counter. The man looked alarmed as she laid her passport down. "Talk in English?"

"Yes, please."

He searched for the right response. Ainsley knew how hard it was to switch languages on command. She imagined that it was even more difficult when switching alphabets.

"What can I help?" he finally said.

"I need a ticket out of the country."

"To where you go?"

"Anywhere."

"Anywhere?"

"It doesn't matter. I just need to go."

A look of surprise spread across his face. Then he looked down at his computer screen. "There is flight to Seoul leaves nine o'clock tomorrow morning."

"Is there something tonight?"

His eyes scanned the screen. "There is a flight to Tokyo at five-thirty in the morning."

"I will take that. How much?"

He typed on the screen. "Only first-class available."

She scowled. Only a few decades since the end of communism, and Mongolians had already learned how to force an upsell. That hadn't taken long.

"Fine."

He tabulated the total on a calculator. Then he lifted it up and showed her a number. "One million two hundred thousand tugriks."

Ainsley blanched. That sounded like a big number, and she hadn't done any research into exchange rates.

"How much is that in dollars?"

His eyeballs scanned the ceiling while he did the exchange rate in his head. "Five hundred fifty."

"Okay."

"May I see your passport?"

She dug into her purse, removed the passport, and laid it on the counter—

—when a man's hand landed upon it. She looked up.

It was Gantig.

———

He'd known she would come to the airport. He'd tailed her, lost her, then guessed her destination. Now he'd trawled the concourse until he'd spotted her.

She leaped back. "Leave me alone."

"Don't give that man your passport," Gantig replied.

She looked at the boy's face. It was tight and severe, seeming old beyond his nineteen years. Suddenly she knew that Gantig knew about his father.

"I can't stay here. I don't know you, I don't know this village of Zhakorum, and I certainly didn't kill your father, it's all just too much—"

He cut her off. "Ainsley, I don't know who did it, but it wasn't you."

"I'm not going to be set up—"

"You haven't been set up."

That stopped her. He was breathing heavily, staring at her.

"The problem is that your name has already been fed to the police. And you may not think much of my country, but we do have computer networks here."

To emphasize the point, his knuckles rapped on the top of the airline agent's computer terminal. The agent's mouth hung open, spellbound.

"So, if you want," he said, "go ahead and give your passport to this man. It could mean spending twenty years in Mongolian prison. Do you want that?"

Ainsley turned to the airline agent. His eyebrows had almost lifted off his head.

"I won't be needing a ticket," she said.

He nodded, then pushed the passport back towards her.

Ainsley hightailed it towards the airport doors, her lips pressed so tightly together that they'd turned white. She felt like a bug caught between a pair of pincers.

Gantig followed at her heels. "You have to listen to me."

"No," she said. "I'll get out of this country some other way."

"How?"

"I'll walk."

She burst out of the automatic doors and into the night air. The smog threw itself around her head like an abductor's sack.

"Ainsley, please stop," he said.

They were on the sidewalk outside the small terminal. She saw wealthy Mongolians stepping out of expensive automobiles, designer luggage in hand.

"Ainsley—"

She finally turned. "Gantig, I have one question for you."

"What is it?"

"What the hell are you doing chasing after me? Three hours ago, I walked into your home and found your father murdered in his upstairs bedroom. Shouldn't you be with your *family*?"

"I will," he said, "but keeping you in this country is just as important."

"That's horseshit."

He held up a warning finger. "Horseshit is valuable in Mongolia. We burn it for warmth."

"I can't believe you're making jokes right now."

The young man's face drew tight and severe again, and his voice lowered. "My father knew he was going to be killed."

"What do you mean?"

"He warned us about Excovane. He knew they would be coming for him."

"Who is they?"

"I don't know. He wasn't specific. But he did prepare us. He told us to treat every day like it was his last." Gantig paused, a tear appearing in his eye. Ainsley softened.

"I'm sorry—"

"The funeral is going to take days, maybe weeks. And we can't afford to lose that much time. We only have *two weeks*. This has to be started immediately."

Ainsley shook her head no. "I'm still the wrong person."

"No, you're the right one."

She started to walk away, but Gantig caught her by the wrist. Ainsley allowed it. She also allowed it when he turned her around to face him again. "You have no options, Ainsley. Think about it. You can't register for a plane or a train ticket. You can't rent a car. You can't even get a hotel room."

Ainsley did think about it. If what he was saying was true, he was right. She'd come here at his request, and now she was at his mercy. Like it or not, she'd hitched herself to Gantig— and that's the way it would have to be, until this thing got resolved.

She threw her hands into the air. "Fine, I'm trapped. What's the next step? Tell me."

"No, I'm not going to tell you the next step," he said.

"Someone has to."

A silver Audi pulled up to the curb. It looked familiar. The door opened, and out of the driver's seat emerged Erdene, still wearing her red bedazzled dress. She stood alongside Gantig.

"She will," he said.

Stupefied, Ainsley looked at the two of them. "There's something you guys aren't telling me."

"Ainsley," he replied, "meet my cousin Erdene."

CHAPTER TWELVE

Ainsley felt the surprise clogging her throat like a piece of gristle in a windpipe. For a moment, she couldn't breathe.

Finally she managed to choke out an obvious response. "So you're related."

"It was quite a coincidence that she was coming along when you stepped in the road," said Gantig.

Ainsley scowled at her. "You pretended not to know that it was your cousin pursuing me?"

"I wanted to see what you would say about him," said Erdene. "And besides, I wasn't the only one who was lying —*Karin*."

Ainsley lowered her head. She'd been busted.

Gantig put one arm across each of their shoulders. "Here is what is going to happen. Are you both listening?"

Ainsley nodded.

"I have to stay here, obviously. Ainsley, Erdene will take you to Zhakorum. Erdene knows the village because of her work in tourism. Together, you will learn everything you can about the identity of the person who found the moonstone."

Erdene caught her eye. "We will play the role of tourist

and guide. The people of Zhakorum might reveal more to us that way."

Ainsley glanced at Gantig. "This sounds familiar."

"It does. Are there any questions?"

"Yes. I need payment."

"I'll get it to you tomorrow."

"I want half up front."

Gantig was unfazed. "I already tried to give it to you."

That was true. "Sorry."

"Erdene will bring it for you in the morning, when you leave."

"That would be fine," she said quietly.

"She will also take you back to your hotel," said Gantig. "And she'll help you make arrangements for the travel."

"Why?"

"This journey isn't going to be easy. The steppe is difficult to travel across. People die, if they're not prepared."

The irony was a clown dancing before her eyes. She couldn't be ignored "Let's talk tomorrow."

Gantig nodded, shook her hand, and walked away. Then she turned to Erdene, who was studying her with that other-worldly face of hers.

"You will be ready tomorrow at six o'clock in the morning," she said.

Ainsley nodded. "I don't have much of a choice, do I?"

CHAPTER THIRTEEN

As the silver Range Rover bounced along the road out of Ulaanbataar, Ainsley circled her fingers around the safety bar above the passenger door.

In the driver's seat was Erdene, hands gripping the steering wheel. The road had been paved until the city limit, then had fallen away to a wide stretch of dirt.

It'd been a busy morning. After a sleepless night at her hotel, Ainsley had been picked up by Erdene. She'd given Ainsley the envelope with half the fee, exchanged into tugriks. It was a substantial amount to hand to a stranger. Gantig apparently figured that Ainsley was trustworthy—or, more likely, that she couldn't skip out on the job while trapped in a car with his cousin in the middle of the steppe.

They'd spent an hour at an outfitter's store, loading up with basic necessities—sleeping bag, hiking shoes, outdoors pants, waterproof parka.

Erdene had held up a *deel*, a traditional coat with wide sleeves, a wide flap that is folded on the chest, buttons on the right shoulder, a high collar, and a fabric belt around the waist.

"Do you want one of these?"

"Why?" Ainsley had said.

"It's good if you're planning to ride any horses."

Ainsley had shaken her head. She hated horses, ever since a supposedly docile mare had bucked her in middle school, shattering her arm. Today, she could barely look at them, much less ride them.

Now they were barreling out of the city at highway speed over a road that was definitely not a highway.

"Look," said Erdene.

She pointed straight forward. Ainsley peered through the windshield. About two hundred meters ahead, the dirt road ended—and beyond lay a seemingly endless expanse of low green grass.

"It's the end of the road," said Ainsley. "Literally."

"And the beginning of the steppe."

Ainsley felt the car hit the grass, and the sounds changed beneath the vehicle. The skittering pebbles that had been kicking up against the undercarriage vanished. They were replaced a constant hum, punctuated by the occasional low thump of a dislodged stone.

"From here," said Erdene, "we make our own road."

Ainsley looked out the window. Off in the distance she spotted a thin ribbon of dirt. "There's a road over there."

"There are a few," explained Erdene, "but nobody uses them. They're full of holes, and if you hit one, you have to wait hours and hope that somebody comes along to pull you out."

"So the roads are more dangerous than the open grass."

"Usually."

She peered in the rearview mirror. The brown cloud of pollution that hovered over the capital city was receding from sight.

Ainsley watched the green fields ripple outside. Then she felt herself gripped by a strange sensation.

Exhilaration.

It always arrived when she least expected it, that feeling of elation. It was wild, the type of untamed feeling that leaps out from the sky and wrestles with your soul. It emboldened her to speak and loosened her tongue.

"I have to say," said Ainsley, "Gantig didn't seem all that shaken up by your uncle's death."

"They weren't close. He was sent to a boarding school in Switzerland for almost ten years. We only saw Gantig in the summer, but even then he was often in France or Japan."

Ainsley paused. Her initial analysis seemed to be spot on: the worldly son of a sophisticated family.

"So you don't want to be at the funeral?"

She shook her head. "I was adopted at age sixteen. I barely knew him. It was a legal thing that didn't have anything to do with me."

"That probably makes it easy."

"I just think it's unfortunate that the mining company went to such an extent."

Ainsley looked at her. "You think Excovane was really behind this?"

Erdene nodded. "They're bastards."

"I thought they wanted to benefit the Mongolians."

"That's what they *say*." Her sideways glance indicated that the truth was quite different.

Ainsley sighed. "I just feel kind of useless here. I don't speak the language. I don't know the people. You could be doing this job without me."

"No, you're our cover story," she replied. "You can say the things that we can't. And all our questions can be diverted to you."

Ainsley understood. "Gantig and I did that at the market. I pretended that I didn't know anything and asked Otgonbayar the gemstone merchant if he had any moonstones."

"What did he say?"

"He lied and said there aren't any in Mongolia. Then he swept all his stuff into a bag and walked away."

Erdene looked pensive for a moment. "That means he knows something."

"Yes, he knows the ninja miner who apparently found the moonstone. But he wouldn't talk about it."

"Maybe we should've gone there first," she said. "We could've forced him to talk."

Ainsley understood the subtext. She already knew just how casually violence could be used around the world, and this was another example of it. "No, you don't want to do that."

"Why not?" replied Erdene.

"Because it's bad karma. It's what the Soviets did to your own people."

Erdene didn't say anything for a while. Then she said, "Do you trust me, Ainsley?"

"You lied to me the first minute we met."

The Mongolian woman laughed. "That's a good point. Let me ask it a different way. Do you trust me to help you find the moonstone?"

"I don't have much of a choice," Ainsley said, "and we've got two days in the car together. Let's play nice."

"Deal."

CHAPTER FOURTEEN

By midday of the second day of driving, they'd reached the edge of the village of Zhakorum.

Twenty-four hours on the steppe, and Ainsley noticed that Erdene hadn't struck out into the great wide open. Instead, she'd kept the vehicle speeding alongside a well-worn cat track at the foothills of the Altai mountains. It was like a boater avoiding open water, instead circling the lake by staying close to shore.

The previous night, they'd unrolled their sleeping bags on the open grass a few meters from the parked Land Rover. Erdene had made a small fire out of a few sticks of wood that she'd stacked in the back of the vehicle, and they'd heated up instant pasta in a flame-scorched pot.

Afterwards, Ainsley had laid out beneath the stars and felt the immensity of whatever lay stretched out overhead. She'd turned to look at Erdene. The Mongolian girl was stretched out on her sleeping bag too, a small glow on her face from the mobile phone in her hands.

"What's the wifi password?" Ainsley'd said.

Erdene hadn't even looked over. "Tour guides hate that joke."

"Sorry."

They'd fallen into silence, and then into sleep.

The next morning, Ainsley had woken at dawn with her face in the earth. After a quick breakfast of snack bars, she and Erdene had rolled up their sleeping bags, piled back into the Range Rover, and continued driving.

Now it was noon, and Ainsley was still unwashed, but she didn't feel dirty. It was hard to describe. She felt closer to the earth—not in a hippy-dippy patchouli oil way, but in a deeper, grittier way. It would be possible to live like this, at least for a few days.

As they descended the bumpy road that led to the village, Erdene slowed the car to a crawl. Ainsley peered through the windshield at the village, which from this height and distance resembled a smattering of forty or fifty tiny white cubes sprinkled on a vast putting green.

"So this village is unusual," said Erdene.

"Tell me why."

"Well, it's permanent. There are no *gers*. Maybe you already know that there aren't many permanent settlements because we Mongolians have a long tradition of nomadism."

"So why is this one different?"

"Because of the monastery," the guide replied. "It was the anchor of the region, at least until it was destroyed."

"Which happened in 1922."

"You have a good memory," said Erdene. "In the village, the first thing we're going to do is visit the museum. It's dedicated to the treasures of the monastery."

Ainsley found it hard to believe that there was a museum in this tiny, distant corner of the world. Still, she put aside her skepticism as they parked on the edge of the settlement.

She stepped outside of the car and took in the scent of the air. It was cool, pungent, laced with fresh green herbs.

It made her feel alive.

She followed Erdene into the village proper. Zhakorum itself was nothing more than a single road lined with mostly concrete bunker-like structures. The Soviets had left their thumbprints here, that much was for sure. A group of three elderly men chatting over a shared thermos of tea nodded at them. A stray goat wandered past, the irises of its other-worldly eyes glancing at the visitors.

"It's not too bad, in the summer," said Erdene.

"And in the winter?"

"It's different."

"How so?"

"You know, they keep each other company. And they drink."

Ainsley followed her finger towards a waist-high heap of empty vodka bottles piled beneath the window of one of the concrete houses. Ainsley admitted that that was probably the best recreation option when the temperature was cold enough to kill a yak.

They passed pitiful concrete structures that looked like changing rooms at a public beach. One store, however, was brand new, with fresh white aluminum siding and a real door. Inside stood several shelves bearing bottles.

"That's the liquor store," said Erdene.

"It's the nicest building in the village."

"Yes, because Excovane paid for it."

Ainsley thought about that while they trudged onwards. Finally, Erdene stopped before a ramshackle structure, four concrete walls and a piece of canvas for a window that rippled and flapped in the wind. In the doorway, a man leaned slovenly, a cigarette dangling from his lips. His left hand was plunged into his pocket and his right hand was holding a mobile phone. A small sliver of belly dangled below the hem of his t-shirt.

"Here we are," she said.

"Where are we?" said Ainsley.

"At the museum."

"But it's a shack."

Erdene stiffened. "This is the museum, Ainsley, and he is the guard."

She explained further. The owner of the museum was a man named Tsiltsin. He'd personally dug up half the buried treasures of the monks, then rejected offers from art dealers around the world to purchase them. He'd built this structure in the hopes of turning Zhakorum into a major tourist draw.

Ainsley crinkled her nose. So far the plan hadn't worked.

"It's a shed," said Ainsley.

"Tsiltsin can't afford an alarm system," said Erdene, "so he and his friends just take turns watching the building. This is one of the regulars."

They approached the man at the door. Erdene spoke a few words. He answered brusquely.

"What did he say?" said Ainsley.

"Nothing worth repeating."

"So can we go in?"

"Yes."

Ainsley had no patience for this. She moved past the guard and pulled the door open and entered.

Inside, she stopped and studied the place. It was a single bare room, ringed with hand-chopped wooden boards that had been carefully laid across waist-high gray rocks. On the makeshift boards law an assortment of minor treasures—a silver chalice, an amethyst pendant, a wooden bowl inlaid with mother-of-pearl, a book whose cover was encrusted with lapis lazuli.

In one corner sat a Buddha statue. It was about a meter

high and was a solid piece of stone. Ainsley wouldn't haven't wanted to try to lift it. It looked like it weighed a quarter-ton.

She peered at the object. That's when she saw the empty hexagonal space in the forehead. She knew what she was looking at.

Behind her, Erdene said, "That's where the moonstone belongs."

"This is the Buddha," said Ainsley.

She nodded. "The monk Cholsaiban pulled the moonstone out of its head and buried it before they arrived to kill him."

"Gantig told me the same story. And finding that stone is the key to getting the people of the village to cooperate."

Ainsley looked again at the statue, its rounded belly, its upturned palm, its slanted eyes, its look of repose. It honestly didn't appear any different from the millions of other Buddhas in the world.

Erdene stepped into the room and placed her hand upon the Buddha's head. "The moonstone is supposed to give this ordinary statue special powers. Or so the people believed."

She shrugged. Ainsley didn't comment.

"So we need to find this Tsiltsin."

"Sometimes he camps near the ruins. We can go find him this afternoon."

"Does he know who found the moonstone?"

Erdene shrugged. "Maybe. Maybe it was Tsiltsin himself. But we have to ask." She paused. "Just so you know—he's a character."

"You've met him before?"

"Only once."

"Will he remember you?"

"He's a strange man." She cocked her head towards the exit. "Come on, let's go."

They turned around—an discovered that the guard had filled the doorway. He barked something in Mongolian.

"He wants money," said Erdene.

Ainsley felt her pockets. "I left mine in the car. What about you?"

"Me too."

"Shouldn't he have asked for money before we entered?"

Erdene switched over to Mongolian. The guard shook his head no and stuck out his hand.

"He wants something right now," she said.

Ainsley reached into her coat pocket and found a small complimentary bottle of conditioner that she'd swiped from her hotel.

Impulsively, she held it out to him.

"Here," she said, "for you."

The guard took the small bottle and studied it. A broad smile spread across his face. He spoke a few sentences in Mongolian, then leered at Ainsley. He stepped aside from the door.

Erdene took Ainsley's hand and pulled her outside. As they walked through the village back to the car, Ainsley asked, "What did he say?"

"He said he would give it to his wife," replied her guide, "and that if she didn't like it, he would divorce her and marry you instead."

"Lucky me," said Ainsley.

CHAPTER FIFTEEN

An hour later, they stepped out of the Range Rover in the parking lot at the base of the monastery. Ainsley looked up at the towering hill in front of her. Its green slopes and blue sky and white puffy clouds reminded her of something. Then she realized what.

"It looks like a screen saver," she said.

Erdene was pulling a jacket out of the trunk. "You're not the first one to say that. Here, catch." She threw Ainsley her parka. "It's going to be a bit of a hike."

"There's no driving up there?"

"Tsiltsin prefers that visitors leave their trucks and approach the ruins of the monastery on foot."

"How old fashioned," said Ainsley.

"This is a sacred place."

The hike was up an old sheep trail. Ainsley felt the earth beneath her feet, the clean air in her nostrils. The trail wound up and around a hillock that rose out of the land like a camel's hump.

Then, half an hour later, they cleared the top, and Ainsley got her first look at the monastery of Zhakorum.

"Oh wow," she said, stopping in her tracks.

The monastery stood before her, two hundred meters long and crumbling, as gorgeous as any European ruin. Ainsley looked over the scene and noticed signs of a violent architectural death. Two walls lay flat on the earth, shoots of grass sprouting up around their edges like wild hairs of fire. On the western end of the complex, a rambling stone terrace lay broken and angry. The pavers looked as though the stones had been unnaturally forced up years ago.

"Not many Mongolians make it out here," said Erdene. "They believe this site is filled with dead spirits."

Ainsley thought about that as she fell in step behind the guide. They crossed the broken patio, making their way to the stone walls that stood forlorn, the roof of the structure having long ago fallen to the ground. Hearing the wind whistle high and ghostly through the spaces between the stones, Ainsley still felt a chill go down her spine.

"Once again," said Erdene dragging a hand across the walls, "the Russians destroyed all of this when they slaughtered all the monks."

"Gantig said that they always killed the religious people first," said Ainsley.

"University students too," added Erdene.

They passed into the open meadow on the back of the ruins. It was covered in a gorgeous carpet of grass.

"And this is where the bodies were left to rot," said Erdene, swinging a practiced hand. "Old people don't like to come here."

Ainsley squinted. On the far edge of the meadow was a small *ger*. As they stood there, the small, mournful sound of a stringed instrument left the round tent and drifted across the meadow. Ainsley winced. It had a scratchy tone.

"Tsiltsin is in," said the guide. "Let's go meet him."

"What is that instrument?" said Ainsley.

"A *morin khuur*. He's always playing it."

"He sounds unusual."

Erdene's eyes told her that she'd hit the target. "Let me warn you, it will not be a normal conversation with Tsiltsin. He talks a lot. And if he talks enough, maybe we will hear the thing that we have been waiting for. But maybe we won't hear it at all."

They crossed the meadow slowly, towards the lilting melody, the soft, spongy soil giving way beneath her feet. Ainsley imagined the decomposed corpses whose flesh had made the soil so rich. It almost made her gag.

Twenty meters from the *ger*, Erdene stopped and cupped her hands over her mouth. "Tsiltsin!" she shouted.

The musical instrument stopped. The front flaps moved, and a man stepped out. He was medium height, dressed in exotic caftan, red and orange and yellow. He wore his hair in a long ponytail. A short goatee decorated his oval face. A wild messianic look in his eyes.

This was Tsiltsin.

In his hands was an instrument like a homemade guitar, except that it only had two strings and the body was shaped like a square.

"That's a *morin khuur*," said Erdene. "It's very traditional. It can make camels cry."

They exchanged words in Mongolian. Erdene moved forward and introduced them.

Ainsley wasn't sure how to greet him—whether to shake his hand, hug him, bow theatrically, or whatever. In the end, it didn't matter. Tsiltsin merely nodded at her, then began lovingly running his hands up and down the neck of the instrument.

"He speaks a little English," Erdene said.

"A little," he said.

"Tell Ainsley your favorite saying."

Tsiltsin looked up, took a breath, and said in a voice high but clear as a bell. "Sky is endless. Wisdom is endless. Stupidity is endless."

Then he began to giggle. It started as a small sound in the back of his throat, then quickly grew to a full body-shaking laugh.

Erdene said something in Mongolian. To Ainsley: "I just told him that you were on a cultural exchange from the United States."

He replied, and Erdene translated: "He wants to know the reason you came to visit him."

Ainsley cleared her throat, looked him in the face. "Tell him that I was in the village of Zhakorum today, and I want to know what happened to the moonstone that used to be in the head of the Buddha statue."

Erdene translated, and immediately Tsiltsin's face brightened. He began speaking animatedly, with strong gestures. Erdene translated. "He's telling the story of Cholsaiban."

The man began strolling across the field. Ainsley and Erdene followed, looking at the places where he pointed. Then he entered the ruins, the odd caftan trailing behind him. His fingers dragged along the stones, a continuous stream of words pouring from his mouth.

"What's he saying?" said Ainsley.

"Everything you could want to know about this monastery." Her eyes gave Ainsley a knowing look. "I told you it wouldn't be a normal conversation."

They followed the museum owner onto the broken century-old patio, where he picked his way lightly over the jagged pavers, the narration never stopping. Ainsley was pretty sure that he didn't care if Erdene was translating or not. He just liked to hear himself talk.

They came to the lookout. Far below was the Range

Rover, and beyond was the village of Zhakorum, a tiny point in the vast sea of green.

There was movement caught her eye. Ainsley squinted. Coming up the road was another vehicle. It pulled alongside their Range Rover and parked. As Tsiltsin continued talking, Ainsley watched a figure step out of the vehicle.

Finally Tsiltsin paused for breath. Ainsley whispered, "Remind him of the moonstone."

Erdene did so. Ainsley watched her hands make the shape of the Buddha's head. The museum owner shook his head.

"If he could answer that," Erdene translated, "his village would have its spirit rejuvenated."

"Tell him that I heard something about it in Ulaanbataar, and that I'd like to compare information."

Erdene translated. Tsiltsin was silent for a moment, even bowing his chin into his colorful caftan.

Then he lifted his head. In English, he said: "Moonstone is gone. Long time."

"I want ... to help ... your village," Ainsley said slowly.

Ignoring them, he began humming to himself, his hands conducting an invisible orchestra.

Erdene looked at Ainsley and lifted her eyebrows as if to say, *I told you so*.

Then Tsiltsin's eyes suddenly lit up. His index finger pointed down to the ground. "You stay here. This night."

Ainsley looked at Erdene. "Do you want to cancel our hotel reservation?"

"Ha," said the guide. "I'll get the sleeping bags from the car."

CHAPTER SIXTEEN

"Do you know where the matches are?" said Erdene, digging through her backpack.

They were in the back meadow, a short distance from the ruins. Ainsley was sitting cross legged on a broad flat rock, swaddled in heavy Mongolian blankets, peering up at the rapidly darkening sky. It was a sheet of black vellum—and the stars crossing that sheet were an army of dead souls, each carrying a candle.

"No idea," said Ainsley.

She touched the grass beneath her, feeling the blades tickle her palm, the soft soil beneath. Her imagination ran free, picturing the murder scene a century earlier. The hacking. The screaming. Then the silence. A hundred holy men cut down by the sickle of communism.

"Found them!" said Erdene. The scrape of flint on rock caught Ainsley's ear, then an orange flare caught her eye. A moment later, a small fire sprang up between them.

Ainsley felt a shiver run down her back. The fire was calling to her. She stood up and carefully picked her way through the meadow towards the flame. Erdene had begun to unpack a few slabs of meat that had been packed in ice.

"That looks fresh," said Ainsley.

"It is fresh," the guide replied. "It is fresh from the supermarket in Ulaanbataar."

Ainsley laughed. "Let me have my illusions."

"Okay. I killed the sheep myself."

"With your hands."

"Exactly."

Ainsley watched her guide set up three long sticks in the earth, checking that they leaned securely over the fire. Then Erdene stuck a chunk of mutton on end of each stick. The smell of sizzling lamb reached Ainsley's nostrils. Her stomach erupted into a full-on rumble.

"This is how Mongolians usually eat," said Erdene. "Out in the country, it's meat and milk."

"No vegetables?"

Her guide shook her head. "The ground is frozen most of the year."

She was right. Ainsley realized that she hadn't seen so much as a single apple tree or berry bush.

She looked around. "Where's Tsiltsin?"

"He went to scare off some ninja miners. That's mostly why he stays up here. They would have already stripped everything from this site if he weren't here."

Tsiltsin's moonish face appeared at the edge of the fire, his eyes twinkling. He'd thrown a heavy insulated jacket over his caftan and a red winter's cap on his head. It read Chicago Bulls. In his right hand was a bottle of clear liquor with a Russian label.

"Tonight's gonna be a good night," he sang, "a good good night—"

Ainsley smiled at the lyrics. She watched him pour the clear liquor into three small plastic cups. He offered Ainsley the first. She accepted it and threw it straight back down her throat. The clear spirit was rough but it warmed her all the way down into her gut.

"Vodka," he said, "is only good thing Russia give Mongolia."

"There is Mongolian vodka," said Erdene.

He shook his head. "No, Russia better."

The mutton fat dripped into the fire, flaring brightly, and Erdene turned the meat to roast the other side. Ainsley watched her. "Aren't you upset to be missing your uncle's funeral?"

"We're Buddhist," explained her guide. "We don't worry too much when someone dies."

Ainsley guessed that she would pay her respects later. "So Buddhists don't believe in death."

"Of course we do. The difference is that we just accept it better than you do. Plus we believe that we come back in a different form."

Ainsley wondered if those slaughtered monks had felt the same way. A moment later, Erdene removed the meat from the fire and handed her the mutton on a paper plate. "No knife or fork tonight."

Using her incisor teeth, Ainsley tore off a small piece of the roasted meat. The mutton carried a strong gamey flavor that made her think of healthy animals grazing in a field of yellow buttercups. And the texture was so soft that she barely had to chew. The meat fell apart in her mouth.

"What do you think," said Erdene.

"I think," said Ainsley, "that even a vegetarian would be tempted by this."

A sharp sound cracked out of the darkness. It was the sound of stone skittering across a bigger rock.

Erdene grew stock still.

"What was that?" whispered Ainsley.

"I don't know," she replied.

Tsiltsin had stopped chewing too. He was listening, his eyes rounded and alert. He looked like a cartoon.

Ainsley lowered her meat. "I remember seeing a car pull up this afternoon, but I assumed the person had left."

Then came the muffled sound of footsteps sliding through grass.

Tsiltsin leapt to his feet, crouched low, ready to spring. Ainsley and Erdene did the same.

"Hello?" said a voice from the darkness.

It was a female. And she was speaking in English.

Ainsley shot up. "Yes! Can we help you?"

A figure materialized at the edge of the fire. She was a white woman, short and gaunt, with a faintly freckled face. She wore an unzipped blue outdoors jacket, two different layers of dirty sweaters, stained khakis, and some beat-to-hell hiking boots. Her blonde hair was twisted into a sloppy pony-tail and slung over one shoulder. One look told Ainsley that she was well acquainted with life far from civilization.

The woman looked at her. "You're American?"

"Yes," said Ainsley.

"I'm Harriet. I'm from Leeds," she said. After a pause: "Leeds is in England."

Ainsley kept a straight face. "That's a long walk."

"I didn't walk from England," Harriet said, missing the humor. "I've been here in Mongolia for a few months."

"Which is why you didn't get my joke," said Ainsley.

"So here's the problem. My rented car broke down here, and unfortunately I haven't a clue how to fix it and have nowhere to go. May I join you?"

Erdene nodded. "Of course. Please stay."

Ainsley had already seen Mongolian hospitality up close, and this was yet another remarkable example of it. The

Englishwoman wriggled out of her coat and dropped to the ground. Everyone scooted a little, making room for her.

Erdene noticed the woman's eyes staring at the lamb. "Would you like something to eat?"

"If you don't mind," the Englishwoman said. Her nose twitched and a look of hunger suddenly passed over her face. Erdene speared another chunk of mutton on a stick and set it over the fire.

Tsiltsin sat down again, paying no attention to the guest.

"We saw you arrive today," said Ainsley.

Harriet grew embarrassed. "Oh, yes, that's my truck, such as it is."

"Can I ask what are you doing here?"

Harriet's voice grew more formal. "I'm a naturalist, and my job is to track wolverines."

"That sounds exciting," said Ainsley.

Tsiltsin handed Harriet a cup of vodka. She held it tightly in her hands but didn't drink it. "I have a grant through the University of Leeds. I'm specifically tracking migration patterns."

"Of course," said Erdene, as though it were only natural.

"They've been passing across this land for a few days, so I was up here trying to get a better look at them."

"Where have you been staying?" said Erdene.

The naturalist shrugged. "Wherever the wolverines take me. I was with a host family in their *ger* for about two weeks. Then my hosts decided to move to better grazing lands, and the wolverines decided to head the other way. So I've been wandering alone since then."

Erdene handed her the speared meat. The woman devoured the mutton, turning away to preserve her dignity.

They lapsed into silence. Ainsley thought about how easily she and Erdene had accepted this strange woman out here in the vast wilderness of central Asia, in the same easy way that Tsiltsin had accepted them a few hours earlier. Ainsley thought that it was evidence of something primal inside humans, the ancient need to survive in groups. You couldn't see it in an urban apartment building, but you sure could see it on the steppe.

Then Tsiltsin stood up. "I go to get something."

"Have fun," said Erdene.

They listened to him pad away into the darkness. Then Ainsley said, "Tomorrow, where do we go?"

Erdene set down her stick and wiped her mouth. "I was hoping that Tsiltsin would offer more information about the moonstone. But no luck."

Harriet perked up. "You're looking for a moonstone?"

"We are," said Ainsley.

"I believe that I heard someone mention a moonstone," said Harriet. "About three weeks ago."

Ainsley froze with excitement. Her eyes grew large and fixed themselves on this strange visitor. "You heard them talking about a moonstone ... in Mongolian?"

"Yes."

"You speak Mongolian?" said Erdene.

"*Tiim*," she said. That meant yes.

Ainsley set down her meat and edged herself closer to Harriet. She was trying to contain her excitement. "So would you mind telling me, who were these people?"

Between bites of mutton, Harriet explained. "It was a herding family. They were staying near the family I was staying with. The two families visited one another for one night. I overheard the father talking about a gemstone that somebody wanted. It was confusing because I think they were talking about Buddha too. But my Mongolian isn't perfect."

Ainsley felt her eyes bug out of her head. "That sounds

like what we're looking for. Do you remember where this family was camped?"

Harriet thought about it. "Perhaps. If I consult my maps, I could show you exactly. It was about five hundred kilometers south of here. The father's name was Tungdik."

Tungdik. Ainsley committed that to memory.

"What if they've moved on?" said Ainsley.

"They haven't."

"How can you be sure? They're nomads."

"This family had a reason to stay."

Ainsley looked at Erdene. "How long would it take for us to drive five hundred kilometers?"

The guide's eyes looked up to the galaxy as though searching for an answer. "A day and a half. Maybe one day if we leave early and drive fast."

Ainsley felt tingles of excitement. The tingles always arrived like this when there was a new lead. "Harriet, could I ask you to show us to this family of herders?"

Harriet looked up at them. "Maybe. What do I get out of it?"

Ainsley crinkled her nose. Harriet knew the rule that a person should never give away for free that which will be paid for.

"I'm open to barter," Ainsley replied.

Harriet took another bite of meat. "Obviously, I need someone to help me fix my car."

"I can do that," said Erdene. "I was trained in auto repair."

"She was a tour guide," explained Ainsley.

"Oh," said the Englishwoman, "how fortunate."

Erdene passed. "What kind of vehicle is it?"

"A UAZ 452."

Erdene suddenly grew even more confident. "We love

those. I drove one for two years. I even welded its axle in a rainstorm."

"I'm worried that it might be the transmission," replied Harriet.

"We'll take a look in the morning."

The flames played across their faces as the three women looked at one another.

"Well, this is working out quite well," Harriet said at last, wiping her hands. "Very well indeed."

"I'm tired," said Erdene. "We should all get some rest."

As they stood up, Tsiltsin returned to the fire. In his hands was the *morin khuur*. "I play for you!"

"Not now," Ainsley mumbled. "We're going to bed."

But he wouldn't be deterred. Erdene exchanged some words. "He said it's a goodnight song."

As Ainsley crawled into her sleeping bag, the eccentric monastery caretaker began to draw the bow across the strings.

Laying on the cold ground, Ainsley plugged her ears with her fingers. It was going to be a long night.

CHAPTER SEVENTEEN

Just after dawn, the distant sound of a revving engine woke Ainsley out of her sleep.

She cracked an eyelid. A couple meters away, the cold, black embers of fire lay on the ground like pieces of black charcoal dumped out of a bad child's holiday sock.

She sat up and peered around. Of the group, she was the only one still in her sleeping bag. The others were nowhere to be seen.

Ainsley unzipped the bag and got to her feet in the brisk air, shivering. She tied on her boots and stumbled in the direction of the sound of the engine. She came to the edge of the hill and looked down.

In the parking area far below, the small figure of Erdene was buried deep inside the guts of a truck. Harriet was behind the wheel. As Ainsley watched, they unsuccessfully tried to rev the engine once again.

Ainsley walked back to the camp and rolled up her belongings. Then she pawed through Erdene's food bag until she found some cheese and salami and crackers. It felt like a three-star Michelin meal.

The other women arrived, Erdene looking downcast.

"It didn't work," she said. "I think it needs a new, how do you say it—starter cap?"

Ainsley nodded. "That's should be easy to fix."

"Not here," replied Harriet. "It can be quite difficult to find parts." She sighed. "I'm sure it will turn out all right. I've had a lot of good luck. The spirits of the steppe are watching over me."

"Is that so?" said Ainsley.

"Yes." The scientist's eyes told Ainsley that she was quite serious.

"We've asked Tsiltsin to help," said Erdene. "We gave him the keys, and he's going to ask people in the village for help. It's going to take a few days, at least."

"Can you trust him?" said Ainsley.

Erdene paused. "There is a fifty percent chance that he completely forgets."

Ainsley looked at Harriet. "So now you're free to accompany us."

Harriet lifted her chin. "I've not been officially invited."

"Consider it official."

The naturalist looked at Erdene, who nodded.

"Then I accept," she said.

To her surprise, Ainsley felt a small rush of excitement. She was always happy to have another English speaker, particularly one who carried knowledge and didn't outwardly have too many problems. It made sense that she would accompany them anyways, since Harriet had already met the herders in question. But there was one problem.

"But aren't you supposed to be tracking wolverines?" said Ainsley.

A small dark cloud appeared over Harriet's head. "I told you that I've already lost the pack. This wasn't the first one.

I've already lost three so far this trip." Her narrow shoulders slumped. "Maybe I'm just not a very good in the field."

"Nobody has to know," said Ainsley. "It's not like the wolves are going to tell."

"Fair enough."

Erdene slung her bag over her shoulder. "Are we ready to go?"

"I think so," said Ainsley.

As the three women descended from the ruined monastery, the sound of Tsiltsin's *morin khuur* drifted down from the hilltop.

Ainsley took a final glance backwards. It hadn't turned out to be such a dead end after all.

———

In the back seat of the Range Rover, Ainsley idly watched the green hillocks flashing by.

Harriet was in the passenger seat, the map on her legs, occasionally commenting on the terrain. She and Erdene got into a spirited discussion about wildlife.

Ainsley tried to relax. It was impossible. The jouncing on the rutted dirt track jarred her spine every few seconds. She was going to need a chiropractor after this. Plus Erdene was playing Mongolian rap on the radio. Ainsley hadn't even known there *was* such a thing as Mongolian rap. To her ears, it sounded about as good as American rap, which wasn't saying much at all.

"Can we change the music?" said Ainsley.

"You don't like it?" said Erdene.

"No."

Harriet grew suddenly philosophical. "Life is suffering, and suffering builds character. Right?"

Ainsley frowned. "My character is already built."

The naturalist was off on her own world. "It's the Four Noble Truths. They're really quite profound."

Ainsley was only half listening as she explained. *Life is suffering. Suffering is caused by desire. To escape suffering, end desire.*

"That's great," said Ainsley, "but I have a desire to change the music, right now."

Erdene laughed and turned off the rap. Harriet shook her head. "Someday you'll see, Ainsley."

———

Just before noon, Erdene slowed down and stopped the car in the middle of the dirt track.

"It's lunchtime," she said.

"You're not going to pull off the road?" said Ainsley.

"No. Why?"

Ainsley admitted that it made sense. There was no reason to pull off the road for other traffic, since it was barely a road and there was no traffic.

Outside the car, Erdene handed them some dried meat. Ainsley leaned against the rear of the car, chewing on it, when Harriet walked a few paces away.

"Don't look," she said.

"Okay," replied Ainsley.

A moment later, she glanced over. Harriet had her pants around her ankles and was squatting on the grass, a stream of yellow running out from between her legs.

"Oh, come on," Ainsley muttered, glancing away.

Harriet laughed. "I told you not to look."

"That's the way it's done here," said Erdene.

Ainsley sighed. She hadn't yet grown used to dropping trousers wherever you happened to be.

"How much longer do we have?" said Ainsley, keeping her eyes averted.

"It's a few more hours yet," Harriet said. "I do hope we'll get to Tungdik by nightfall."

Tungdik. Ainsley thought about it. "His name sounds Turkish."

Harriet buttoned her pants and stood up. "You have a good ear. Mongolian and Turkish are both Altaic languages. They're cousins."

"Was that because of Genghis Khan?"

"Yes. Khan left more than just bastard sons as he swept across Asia."

The climbed back into the car, and the conversation turned to Khan himself. Harriet noted that there were only three people in the history of the world who had conquered an entire continent in a lifetime—Alexander the Great, Napoleon, and Genghis Khan. Of the three, Khan was by far the most unknown. His childhood had been a mystery, much of his adulthood had been a mystery, and his death had been a mystery.

"All we know is that he was buried up in the mountains in the north," said Harriet, "but beyond that? Who knows."

The English naturalist went on to explain that even Genghis Khan's gravesite is a mystery, since he left orders that every man who accompanied his body to his funeral would then be killed, so that no enemy would ever know the location of his grave.

The newest discover, Harriet explained, was the fact that a large injection of Mongol DNA had been found in the Hazara people of Afghanistan and the Uighur Turks. Using modern tools, genetic scientists traced the arrival of this DNA back precisely twenty-two generations.

"If you go back twenty-two generations," said Harriet, "guess what time period you arrive at?"

"Genghis Khan's," said Ainsley.

"That's right."

"He went all the way to Europe," said Erdene. "There are many European people carrying Mongol blood."

"Especially the Hungarians," said Harriet.

"I don't believe it," said Ainsley.

Harriet explained that Genghis Khan's westward sweep ended nearly half a world away, in modern-day eastern Europe. Many of the horsemen who made it that far had elected to stay. Today, there is still a large population of people in Hungary who preserve Mongolian traditions.

"So what's left of Khan's empire?" said Ainsley.

Erdene's eyes found hers in the rearview mirror. "Physically?"

"Yes."

"Nothing. There is nothing left."

Harriet corrected her. "Not nothing. Every few years, some team of archaeologists will announce that they perhaps have found the remains of, say, a tiny thirteenth-century military outpost. But nothing ever comes of it."

Erdene puckered her mouth into a tight knot. "We never constructed many buildings. We never wrote much down." She shrugged.

"If a tree falls in a nomadic empire," said Harriet, "is anybody there to hear it?"

Ainsley chuckled. Just then, the Range Rover lurched over another large bump in the road—

—and suddenly slammed to a halt.

"Shit," said Erdene.

Ainsley leaned forward and looked out the windshield. They'd plunged headfirst into a patch of mud. Erdene slowly pushed her foot down on the accelerator. The engine revved higher and higher, but the car didn't move.

"You're going to redline," said Ainsley.

"Let me try reverse," said Erdene.

She shifted. The wheels spun helplessly. The acrid scent of burning rubber filled the vehicle.

"Oh dear, we're stuck," said Harriet.

"It's only temporary," said Erdene. "I'm going to need your help. Both of you step outside and go behind the vehicle."

Ainsley opened her door, stepped out, and sunk up to mid-calf in mud.

"This is awful," she said.

Harriet leapt clear over the mud. She offered Ainsley a hand. "Come on, it's just dirt and water."

Ainsley accepted the outstretched hand and tried to pull her leg out of the bog. It came free easily—minus her boot.

Hopping one-footed, Ainsley stared down at the patch of mud. There was a rapidly-closing hole where her leg used to be. "I can't believe this."

"Just reach in and pull it out," said Harriet.

Ainsley got down on her knees, leaned over, and plunged her arm into the hole. She found the boot and hauled it out of the mud. It was filled with sticky black mud.

"Holy smokes," said Ainsley.

"The stuff is like glue," replied Harriet. "I'm convinced it has a mind of its own."

Ainsley cleaned the boot and her arm on the grass, then pulled it back onto her foot. Then she went around to the back of the vehicle. Erdene handed her one of the vehicle's floor mats.

"Put this under one of the rear tires," Erdene said. Then she handed another to Harriet. "And you put this under the other one."

"This is to gain traction," said Harriet.

"Yes. Be sure to stand to the side when I shift in reverse."

Ainsley took the mat and quickly jammed it underneath the left rear wheel. Next to her, Harriet did the same to the right rear wheel.

"Good God, this is particularly nasty."

"Ainsley, help me."

She looked over. Harriet was standing knee-deep in the mud, both legs immobilized.

"What happened?"

"It was only a few centimeters deep when I stepped in. Now look."

Ainsley went over, squatted down, hooked her hands underneath Harriet's armpit, braced her legs, and pulled.

Harriet came out of the mud easily, more easily than she'd expected, and both women went tumbling backwards onto the grass at the side of the muddy track. They lay there for a moment, laughing.

"Oh God," said Harriet, "look, I lost both of them."

Ainsley looked down. The naturalist was in her sock feet.

In the car, Erdene said, "Okay, here I go—"

"Wait, Erdene, my boots—" said Harriet, but it was too late. Erdene had already thrown the Range Rover into reverse. The car rolled neatly backwards up the mats, over the mud, and back onto the small lump in the road.

The scheme worked. The vehicle was free.

Harriet and Ainsley ran back to the track. There were no leg-shaped holes left. No sign of any footwear.

There was nothing but solid, thick mud.

"Oh goodness, they're totally buried," said Harriet.

Erdene cut the engine and stepped out of the car. "What happened?"

"You ran over my boots."

She began pawing around in the mud with her bare arms. Ainsley could tell it would be hopeless. It was like using your arms to search through a huge vat of brown molasses.

The naturalist sat back. Her arms and even the end of her sloppy ponytail were caked with brown glops of mud. "I can't go anywhere without my boots. What do you recommend?"

"I have an extra pair in the back," said Erdene.

"Let me see them."

Erdene opened the back of the Range Rover and pulled out a pair of knee-high Wellington rubber boots. They were pink.

Harriet's face fell. "You've got to be joking."

"One of my clients left them behind," said Erdene. "They're all yours."

Ainsley stifled a laugh. "Try them on."

The Englishwoman took the boots and slipped them on her feet. "Okay, they fit. Let's go."

Ainsley patted her on the back. "You don't have anything to worry about, Harriet. The spirits of the steppe are watching over you, remember?"

Harriet cast her a warning look—then burst out laughing.

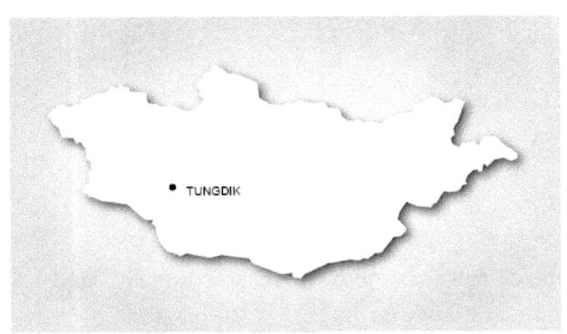

CHAPTER EIGHTEEN

The sun fell towards the horizon, washing the landscape in a bath of pink and orange hues.

The silver Range Rover idled on the dirt track near Tungdik's *ger*. The small round tent was colored a rich purple. It was nestled into the lip of a hillside.

Erdene looked over at Harriet. "Are you sure this is it?"

"I think so."

"I don't want to spend a night with the wrong family."

Harriet pored over the map in her lap. "I've doublechecked. This is the valley."

"Was it purple?"

"I don't know."

"Shouldn't we make a camp?" said Ainsley. "It's almost dark."

Erdene looked at her. "We're staying with Tungdik."

"But we don't know him. Only Harriet knows him."

The naturalist turned around in the seat. "Ainsley, it's customary in the steppe for nomads to accept all travelers."

"It's the Mongolian way," added Erdene.

"So we just knock on their door and ask for a bed?"

"Yes," said Erdene.

"Oh," said Ainsley. Approaching a stranger's house at sunset, knowing that that person would be required to accept you for the night, was going to require some getting used to.

Harriet folded the map. "I think this is it, Erdene. Everything seems to correspond."

Erdene shifted into first and turned the wheel. The vehicle rolled off the dirt track and onto the grass.

Ahead, the purple *ger* grew larger. A couple additional ones grew visible behind it.

When they were a couple hundred meters away, Erdene stopped the car. "Let's get out here and approach on foot."

They stepped out of the car. It was a glorious sunset and nearly as glorious a meadow. Around them stretched a carpet of wild grasses that gently sloped down to the edge of a blue lake about a kilometer away. On the other side of the flat blue water stood a small mountain range.

A sheep's bleat sounded distantly across the grass. Ainsley turned her eyes back to the land. It was sprinkled with livestock—cows, sheep, and goats.

Harriet came and stood next Ainsley. "What do you think?"

"It's gorgeous."

The naturalist sucked on a tooth. "I've seen better."

"You must be joking."

"No, I'm quite serious. There's even better land about a hundred kilometers west of here."

The three women crossed the grass. "Do you remember our roles here, Ainsley?" said Erdene.

Ainsley did remember. "This is a cultural exchange. I'm the tourist, you're the guide."

"What should I be?" said Harriet.

Erdene stroked her chin. "Didn't they already meet you?"

"Yes."

"Then just be yourself."

Harriet nodded briskly. "British naturalist, check."

———

At the *ger*, a nomadic herdsman was sitting on a small stool outside the front door. He was calmly stropping a knife on a piece of worn leather.

As they approached him, Erdene stopped and cupped her hands around her mouth. "*Nokhoi khor*!"

"That means *hold your dog*," explained Harriet. "It's the first thing you always say when you arrive."

The man stood and shouted something back.

"He said he doesn't have any," said Harriet.

"Is that Tungdik?" said Erdene.

The Englishwoman looked unsure. "I really need to get closer."

"If it's not, we have to back out right now, before he extends any hospitality."

Harriet looked the man. "Lord, I don't really remember. But he was missing a couple of his front teeth."

They moved towards the Mongol herder, and he moved towards them. The man was fairly large, and he wore a Western-style red parka with extra-long sleeves, a pair of blue jeans, and a pair of simple work boots. On his face, a smile struggled to lift up his sagging cheeks. Ainsley glimpsed a gap in his front teeth.

"That's him," said Ainsley.

"Yes," said Harriet. "He has a wife and a thirteen-year-old son who is a bit large for his age."

Tungdik shook each of their hands. His own was callused and ridged and felt like a plaster sculpture. He and Erdene chattered in rapidfire Mongolian, as if they were old friends.

Then he pointed towards the *ger* and gestured for them to follow him.

"Ready or not, we are now guests," said Harriet. "Is this your first time in a *ger*?"

"It is," said Ainsley.

She grinned. "Prepare yourself."

———

As she entered the small hut, Ainsley's eyes took in her surroundings.

It wasn't a large home by Western standards, but it was roomier than she'd expected, about ten meters in diameter. In the center of the *ger*, between the twin poles that held up the center of the roof, stood a wood-burning iron stove. On top sat a warming tea kettle; next to the stove rested a plastic bin containing a stack of thick white cakes. A hole in the center of the roof admitted the orange rays of sunset.

A middle-aged woman greeted them. She was large, like her husband, and she wore a simple blue pullover sweater with a long black skirt. A purple cloth beret sat perched upon her head, and her hair formed two long pigtails down her back. Her eyes were curious and friendly, and her puckered chin seemed to have a personality all its own.

Harriet and Erdene greeted the woman. Erdene introduced Ainsley.

"This is Norgema," said Erdene.

She shook the country woman's hand. "It's a pleasure."

The woman beamed, then pulled over a pair of stools.

Ainsley seated herself and took in everything. The walls, such as they were, consisted of a cross-hatched pattern of wooden slats covered with felt on the outside. To the left of the door was an area filled with cooking utensils and tools, plus a twin bed. Directly across from the door was a tall dresser with fourteen different drawers, topped by framed photos of grandparents. A small flatscreen television rested on a tall orange box that was covered in blue and white stenciling. Here, to the right of the door, was evidently the living area, with the stools, another bed, and a heavy carpet.

Overall, it was comfortable. In fact, it reminded Ainsley of her first apartment after college—sparsely furnished, smelling like livestock.

"All *gers* are set up the same," said Harriet. "It's the same pattern across the country. Guests are frequent and they always know where to go. It makes people feel comfortable."

Ainsley thought about that. As a young girl, she'd been exasperated by the standardized cookie-cutter design of homes in her suburban town. There'd been only three floor plans in her subdivision, which meant that she knew exactly what the other houses looked like without even entering. She'd complained about the developers, shouted about social conformity, then fled the town as soon as possible.

It turned out that Mongolian herders were no different from her own people.

"Have some tea," said Harriet.

Tungdik's wife was offering her a porcelain cup. Ainsley accepted it.

"Make sure to drink it all and ask for more," said Harriet.

Ainsley looked dazed. "This is all so strange that I've almost forgotten why we've come here."

"Well! Some kind of detective you are, forgetting about your assignment."

Ainsley rolled her eyes. "And some kind of naturalist *you* are, losing the very animals you're supposed to track."

"Touché. But you do realize that you would be lost without me."

"True."

The steppe breeze whistled around the felt walls of the

ger. Erdene and Tungdik had gone outside, their voices grown distant.

"Ask her about the moonstone," said Ainsley.

Harriet weighed the idea. "Maybe I'll bring it up later, when the time is right."

"But when? We only have two weeks."

"I don't know." The Englishwoman saw Ainsley's impatience. "You have to be patient. They don't know what it means to be in a rush."

Ainsley clenched her lips tightly. She knew that restlessness was her worst quality. And Harriet was right.

She would have to wait for the perfect moment.

CHAPTER NINETEEN

It was morning.

Ainsley woke up with a start. She felt something inside her arms. It felt like a human.

She cracked open an eyelid. It was Harriet, still dead asleep.

Ainsley disentangled herself from the woman, then sat up in bed. A small pain pounded between her ears. She couldn't remember what they'd all done.

The naturalist stirred and opened her eyes. "My, this is *lovely*."

Ainsley felt the hot feathers of shame tickling her neck. What had they done together? Ainsley didn't like other women in that way—and even if she did, Harriet would've been a poor choice. The naturalist stank worse than a week-old lamb carcass.

"I'm not sure I understand what you mean," Ainsley said.

The Englishwoman tried to contain her smile. "I'm talking about the *bed*. Do you know how long it's been for me?"

Ainsley breathed out in relief. "Where is everybody?"

They looked around. The *ger* was empty save for a pot of soup simmering on the stove. It smelled of meat and noodles. "Look at that," said Harriet, "Norgema's left breakfast for us. Let's have a bowl, shall we?"

They used a plastic dipper to pour themselves two bowls of soup. Ainsley sipped the broth and the ruminant flavor of mutton filled her mouth. She spotted a large chunk of dark flesh floating amongst the noodles.

Ainsley looked around the circular *ger*. It was tough to wrap her head around the fact that there was no line between guests and hosts. Everybody shared the most intimate of spaces here, without no boundaries. It was anybody's guess how husband and wife enjoyed their private time. She guessed that the herders had to be creative. There was no way they just rutted away in full view of children and guests.

Then she and Harriet stepped outside the *ger*. It was another bluebird of a day. The sun was already high above the eastern horizon, which meant they'd slept quite a while.

Nearby, Erdene was chatting with Norgema, who nodded towards the two visitors. When she saw them, she trotted over.

"So," said Erdene, "I have news."

"Oh dear," replied Harriet. "This sounds bad."

"I have to return to Ulaanbataar," said Erdene.

Ainsley felt a pit open in the bottom of her stomach. "When?"

"Now. Gantig called me this morning. We have an emergency about our family estate."

"Her uncle just died," explained Ainsley.

"Oh my," said Harriet.

Erdene picked up her bag. Ainsley hadn't noticed it sitting on the ground. "You two will be fine here. I talked with Tungdik and Norgema and they're staying here for several months."

"You're coming back?"

"Yes," she said, "I'll be back in a few days."

Ainsley felt a flash of panic. "Are you taking the satellite phone too?"

"Yes."

"So how are we supposed to reach you?"

"Tungdik has one. If you need to call me, just use his. And leave some money, of course."

Ainsley

"These people open their homes to strangers, but it takes a little more time for them to open their secrets. Now you have that time."

Ainsley felt a sense of panic. This woman, Erdene, was her only connection to Ulaanbataar, and by extension, to modern civilization. And now she was losing that connection. "No, please, I'm asking you, Erdene, don't leave without me—"

"I really have to," she said.

"But why?"

Her eyes searched the sky. "Because someone's trying to steal my uncle's business. The wolves are out."

"That," said Ainsley, "seems like a perfectly legitimate reason to leave."

"Really, it's nothing to worry about. It's just a twenty-hour drive. I'll come right back."

"Twenty hours is a lot," said Ainsley.

"Not in Mongolia," said Harriet. "That's like a quick hop to the corner store for a can of soup."

Erdene crooked her finger. "Harriet, follow me to the car. I have a few things to leave with you."

Ainsley watched the two women walk away. Then, after Harriet had returned with a box of items, Ainsley watched the Range Rover disappear into the grasses on the steppe.

She'd never felt so alone in her life.

That afternoon, Ainsley and Harriet followed Tungdik across the meadow. Ainsley tried not to snicker at Harriet's knee-high pink Wellingtons sinking into the sod.

At the second *ger*, the herder held the front door flap open so they could see inside. It was a tool shed. All the items needed by a livestock herder were piled inside—hooks, shovels, funnels, handplows, machetes.

Then Tungdik dropped the flap and led them up the incline towards the side of the hill where the herd was grazing. He talked the whole way, pointing out things about the landscape, with Harriet translating as best she could.

"He calls them the Five Snouts," said Harriet.

"What are those?"

She ticked them off on her fingers. "Horses, camels, sheep, goats, and yaks. The most common livestock." Tungdik started talking again, and the naturalist translated again. "He says that the family has been suffering a lot because of the last *dzud*."

Ainsley had never heard of a dzud. It must've showed on her face.

"It's the Mongolian word for a bad year of weather," Harriet said. "Last year was a hot, dry summer and a long, extra-cold winter."

"So this means that—"

"That Tungdik didn't grow enough grass in the summer to feed the animals through the winter."

"So that means they're dying," said Ainsley.

Harriet nodded. Then a small sound escaped Tungdik's throat. Ainsley noticed that a dark expression had come across his face.

"Oh no," said the Englishwoman, pointing ahead. "I think that yak just fell over."

They walked across the grass to the animal. It was on its side, feet twitching helplessly, its tongue lolling out of its mouth. Ainsley could see how distended its belly was.

Tungdik muttered something to himself. Harriet listened, then said, "Once it dies, he'll have to haul it back to the *ger* to burn it."

Ainsley felt a sudden rush of sympathy for this animal. They could save it, somehow. They were right here, looking at it.

"Tell him we can help. Tell him I'll help him drag it anywhere he wants."

Harriet translated. Tungdik grinned, exposing pink gums and crooked teeth, and answered.

"He said that it's too heavy for us to drag. He said something about needing the help ... of a bear."

Ainsley's eyes bugged out of her head. "A *bear*?"

Harriet spoke in Mongolian for a quick moment. Their host answered by lifting his arm over his head and spitting out a word.

"He said it's a ... honey bear," the Englishwoman said, "and we're going to meet the bear."

"I think you misunderstood him," said Ainsley.

"I'm *definitely* misunderstanding him," added Harriet. "But I know he said honey bear."

Ainsley shook her head. There was zero percent chance that she was going to accept an offer of recreation time with a Mongolian bear. She imagined an enormous grizzly tied to a stake, its sharp claws swiping through the air.

"Tell him I prefer not to meet the bear," she said.

"We have to be polite to our host," Harriet replied.

"How polite?"

The English naturalist caught Ainsley's eye. "Our lives are in his hands."

Before they could answer, though, Tungdik stepped

around the suffering yak and began leading them down the hill towards the lake.

"Seriously?" said Ainsley. "He's not going to try to save the animal?"

"What do you propose he do?"

That was a good question. Without food or veterinary services, there was pretty much nothing to be done.

They went down the hill to the edge of the lake. It was crystal blue and its flat surface was marred only by an occasional ripple from a gust of wind or a duck lifting off.

Tungdik swept his arm across the lake. Harriet translated, explaining that popular myth said that a city had once flourished here. It had disappeared beneath the waters hundreds of years ago.

Ainsley crouched and cupped her hand to drink the water. It tasted clean and fresh and sweet. "Do you know if that's true?"

"Well, they've found blue bricks and cast-iron tools at the bottom."

"An entire city right here," said Ainsley.

Harriet scratched the back of her head. "Well, back then, a city meant about two hundred people."

"So it was a settlement."

"Yes, probably."

They stood hypnotized, the way people sometimes do on bodies of water. Then a distant whine of an engine caught their ears.

Tungdik brightened up and said something.

"What did he say?" said Ainsley.

Harriet crinkled her forehead. "He said it's the honey bear."

They all turned. Arriving into sight on the edge of the hill was a small motorcycle. The man driving it, however, was absolutely enormous. He looked like a bodybuilder balancing himself on a single roller skate.

"That's Honey Bear," said Harriet.

Ainsley opened her eyes. "So Honey Bear is a person."

"*Khüü*," said Tungdik.

The Englishwoman looked surprised. "Oh. He said that Honey Bear is his son."

CHAPTER TWENTY

As they hiked up the hill to meet Tungdik's son, Ainsley had to rub her eyes to make sure she wasn't hallucinating.

Honey Bear was the largest teenager—or person—she'd ever seen in her life.

Well over two meters tall, and wider than a walk-in refrigerator, Honey Bear stepped off the motorcycle. His biceps bulged inside his blue vinyl bomber jacket. His thighs threatened to split open his brown sweatpants. Even his cheap sneakers looked near to exploding off his splayed feet.

On top of this mountain of flesh rested a cherubic face. It was the kind of happy fat little boy's face that begs you to excuse his mischief. Ainsley wasn't a mother, but that face brought out all sorts of instincts that she hadn't even known that she possessed.

"By God, he is *enormous*," she whispered to Harriet.

The Englishwoman nodded, almost alarmed. "Tungdik says he's only fifteen years old."

"I thought he was thirteen."

"Who knows. People don't keep track of that stuff here."

Ainsley shook his head. "He looks like a wrestler."

Harriet grinned. "Congratulations—you guessed it. Honey Bear goes to a wrestling academy in Ulaanbataar."

"It wasn't hard."

"His father says he speaks some English."

"We will put that to the test," said Ainsley.

"Agreed."

They watched as Honey Bear took off his helmet and moved towards his father with lumbering, shuffling grace. He wrapped his father in an affectionate hug. Tungdik's hands moved around the massive expanse of his son's back like a pair of tiny infants crawling around a ballroom dance floor.

The father disentangled himself and introduced his son to the two women. "Your father says you speak English?" said Harriet.

Honey Bear's eyes lit up with joy. His fat fingers twinkled on his hands. "Yes! I speak it! I speak English!"

"You speak very good English," said Harriet.

"Yes, very good!"

"I want to introduce you to my friend Ainsley."

"Nice to meet you, Honey Bear." Ainsley put out her hand for a shake. What she got was a full-body tackle. The teenager pulled her into his massive torso, and she felt his meaty arms wrap completely around her back. It felt like being smothered by an enormous pile of bologna. He smelled of wood smoke and diesel gasoline.

"Nice to meet you too!" she heard him say.

Slowly she extricated herself from his suffocating hug. "Where did you learn such good English?"

"At the academy! I am wrestler!" Honey Bear was beaming with pride.

"Are you professional?" said Harriet.

His face fell. "No, I am not big enough. Not yet. I must eat more!" The mere thought made his face grow animated and happy once again.

"Well, okay then!" said Ainsley.

"Okay then!" he repeated, then thrust a fat thumb forward. Ainsley struggled not to laugh, then gave in. He bellowed right along with her. Then Harriet started giggling too. Even his father was sporting a broad grin.

"Why are we laughing?" said Harriet.

"It's because of him!" said Ainsley. "It's his face!"

Honey Bear reacted as though he'd been electrocuted. A high peal of laughter popped out of his mouth that sounded like a strangled yodel. His body shook violently. This reaction made Ainsley laugh even harder. She felt like she was a teenager again. Then she remembered that he really was a teenager.

"It is not *my* face!" he said. He stabbed a finger at Ainsley. "It is *your* face! *Your* face!"

Honey Bear made an insane facial expression—eyes crossed, tongue out. Then another bizarre peal of laughter soared out of his throat.

Tungdik, meanwhile, cleared his throat. He spoke quickly in Mongolian, pointing to the fallen yak. Honey Bear sobered up and grunted agreement.

"He's going to carry the yak over to the *ger*," said Harriet.

Ainsley was dumbfounded. "But that thing must weigh a ton."

"True. And he's going to carry it."

Ainsley shook her head. "No way. I don't think there's a human on earth who can lift that thing."

Honey Bear followed his father over to the dying animal. First, he took off his bomber jacket and tied it around his waist. Then he crouched down on his knees and slid his arms beneath the yak. Then he got his right shoulder under the weight of the animal. Tungdik strained to push the other end onto his son's left shoulder—

Five seconds later, Honey Bear rose to his feet with a ton

of dying yak draped across his shoulders. His face was twisted into an exaggerated pantomime of concentration.

Then he began staggering across the meadow.

"Holy shit," said Ainsley.

The Englishwoman admired the boy. "My God."

"I have a very important question. Where is he going to sleep?"

Harriet shrugged. "I haven't the faintest idea. Perhaps he'll fall asleep on the grass and they'll build a *ger* around him."

They followed the young wrestler across the meadow. His legs had already formed that tripod shape that appears in people with enormous upper body weight. Tungdik walked alongside his son, clapping and encouraging.

Near the *ger*, Tungdik pointed to a spot on the ground. Honey Bear stopped ... and slowly toppled backwards. The yak hit the ground on its side. Then Honey Bear landed on top of the yak, and the animal emitted a pained bleating sound.

"I guess that's all she wrote," said Ainsley.

"It's still alive," said the naturalist. "Can you believe it?"

"Sure I can. It just got a free ponyback ride too. Hey, do we know if Mongolians eat yak meat?"

"They do."

Honey Bear rolled off the animal and lay flat on his back on the grass. A look of pure childish happiness spread across his face. "Ainsley, did you see me?"

"I did," she replied, "and you're *strong*."

"Very strong! Very strong!"

The young wrestler sat up and lifted his arms. They looked like a pair of fat pythons. His father patted him on the shoulder proudly and gestured for them to come inside.

"It's time to eat," said Harriet.

CHAPTER TWENTY-ONE

Sitting on the edge of the bed, Ainsley lifted the bowl of fermented horse milk to her face. It smelled like wet animal fur.

Tungdik had dipped a ladle into a plastic bin and filled several bowls of the frothy white liquid. He'd handed one to each of the two visitors. At first, Ainsley had caught the scent of purple lavender, but lifting it to her face had revealed its true character. It smelled exactly like the underbelly of a goat.

"It's *airag*," Harriet said. She explained that it was customary to offer the beverage to visitors.

Ainsley lowered the bowl to her lap. "It smells disgusting."

"It's rude to hesitate," said Harriet.

"This isn't hesitation. I'm not drinking it."

"You're insulting them, and you're embarrassing me." The Englishwoman caught Ainsley's eyes, then made a small circular *come-on* motion with her two forefingers. Then she lifted her own bowl to her face and swallowed deeply.

Sighing, Ainsley resigned herself to her fate. She took a deep breath, lifted the bowl of mare's milk to her mouth, and tilted her head backwards. She felt the liquid pour into her mouth. It tasted rich, creamy, fermented, and sour.

Tears nearly sprang from the corners of her eyes. "Ugh, it's awful."

Harriet wiped her mouth. "It's not so bad. But just imagine what they'd charge in Piccadilly Circus for a yak milk cocktail. Twenty quid, minimum."

"My God this is bad."

"Actually, you'll get used to it."

Harriet described the production of *airag*. How the mares are milked six times a day in the summer, how the fresh milk is mixed with yeast and traditionally left in a bag made of horse hide. How the best *airag* takes two days to make because it must be whirled a thousand times, how guests were usually expected to help shake the bag. How fresh *airag* is mild, how old *airag* is full of acidity and sourness.

"So this really is popular here?" said Ainsley.

"It's the national beverage."

"Good to know," said Ainsley, "but do I really have to finish it?"

"Yes. And then you will drink at least two more."

Ainsley's mouth fell open. "Why do we have to drink *three*?"

The Englishwoman shrugged in a what-can-you-do way. "It's tradition. To show appreciation, guests drink three bowls of *airag*."

Ainsley looked at the others in the *ger*. Tungdik, Norgema, and Honey Bear were all smiling at her, watching.

"So I don't have a choice then," she said.

Harriet shook her head. "Not if you want to find the moonstone."

Ainsley lifted the bowl to her mouth and finished the milk, trying not to choke. Then she mustered a weak smile and held the bowl out for more.

"I would like another," she said. Her mouth barely formed the words.

Norgema clapped her hands in delight and reached for the ladle.

———

Two hours later, Ainsley rolled her eyes as an impromptu karaoke party broke out.

After the bin of *airag* had been sealed up, Honey Bear had pulled out a bottle of vodka and begun pouring shots of the liquor and putting them into Ainsley's hand. Tungdik putting a plate of fried mutton into her lap too, and then more cups of vodka. It went on like that for while, mutton and vodka.

"I think I'm drunk," she said.

"The *airag* was mildly alcoholic," Harriet replied.

"How much?"

"Two percent."

"That must be why."

"It certainly couldn't be the vodka's fault," said the Englishwoman.

"It's never the vodka's fault."

Harriet threw back another shot. "Never never *never*."

Tungdik turned on a small portable karaoke machine that was in turn connected to the family generator just outside the tent. From the speaker issued a tiny beat and thin synth line that was evidently familiar to the family, because Ainsley saw Honey Bear's eyes light up. Then he took the small microphone in his hand and began singing a strange melody in a high, off-key voice.

It was a sight to behold. The boy's eyes were rounded and full of joy. He was an enormous ball of happiness.

Watching him, Ainsley hoped he'd always stay that way.

When he'd finished, Norgema took the microphone and

shooed her son away. Another song started up, and his mother began singing a schmaltzy love song that Tungdik seemed to love.

Meanwhile, Honey Bear crashed onto the floor at Ainsley's feet. "You're a good singer," she said.

"No!" he said, sitting up. "I am very bad! Very bad!"

"No, you're not," said Harriet.

"Very bad! But I can, can"—his fingers touched his chest —"feel what I want to do! I feel the ... spirit!"

"That is true," said Ainsley. "You have the spirit."

"I want talk," said the young teenager, jabbing a finger at Ainsley. He pointed to an open spot next to her on the bed. "I will sit there."

Ainsley braced herself. The enormous boy pulled himself to his feet, then lowered his rear end onto the bed next to her. The mattress sunk deeply beneath his weight, pulling Ainsley over sideways into his lap.

"Honey Bear," she said.

The boy put one hand on the back of her neck and lifted her back to a sitting position. It was like grabbing a cat by the scruff of the neck.

Ainsley arranged her shirt, then scooted a short distance away from the crater in the bed. "What do you want to talk about?"

"English!" he said.

She imitated his enthusiasm. "English—yay!"

"Yay!"

The boy started his infectious giggling again. "What do you want to talk about?"

"Why come my country?"

"You want to know why I came to Mongolia?"

Honey Bear nodded. This close, she could hear the slow wheezing from his nostrils as well as his stertorous breaths.

Nearby, Harriet caught her eyes and nodded quietly. That meant it was time. "I'm looking for something."

Honey Bear was listening closely. "What you look for?"

"A stone."

"Ohhh."

He didn't say anything else, so Ainsley described it further. "A moonstone." Her finger gestured to the sky. "Like the moon."

"Moonstone," said Honey Bear. It was clearly his first time hearing the word.

"That's right. It belonged to a monk. He buried it."

The boy's eyes looked at the wall of the *ger* as he repeated the words to himself. "*A monk he buried it. A monk he buried it.*" Then the meaning sunk in, because his face lit up again.

"I know this monk!" he suddenly said.

"You do?"

"I do! I do!" he repeated, growing excited.

Ainsley grew excited with him. "This monk was killed one hundred years ago."

"The Soviets! They kill the monk!"

Ainsley felt a thrill. Honey Bear had that detail down, and she hadn't even asked. "Yes, that's right! The Soviets killed him!"

Honey Bear shook his head animatedly. "Yes! I know him!"

"How?"

The boy's tongue snaked out to touch his lips as his eyes searched for the right words. "He was ... my family!"

"Really!" she said, scooting forward on the bed.

"Yes! He was my father father father father."

He counted each one off on his huge meaty fingers. That was four fathers. If he'd counted right, that meant the monk had been Honey Bear's great-great-grandfather.

"Do you know his name?"

Honey Bear nodded. "Cholsaiban."

Ainsley felt tingles race down her legs. That was the correct name. This meant that, unless Honey Bear was lying, this family was the descendants of the monk. But she doubted he was lying for two reasons. One, Cholsaiban wasn't a household name in Mongolia. He was obscure, almost lost to the sands of time along with the ten thousand other dead monks. Two, Honey Bear didn't have a dishonest bone in his body. A cherubic face like that couldn't lie.

"That's right," she said. "His name was Cholsaiban."

"So you look for moonstone?"

"Yes, but I don't know where it is."

Honey Bear looked at her, his black eyes dancing merrily inside the fat folds of his face. "I think my family have the stone!"

Ainsley felt an enormous hot lump form in her throat. She slowly repeated the statement. "Your family ... has ... the moonstone?"

"Yes, we have it!"

"Where?"

Honey Bear yelled out to his father. Tungdik shook his head no and motioned outside the tent.

The enormous boy's face fell slightly. "He say we don't have stone."

Ainsley felt her spirits plunge. But she managed to stay composed. It would be important to first verify that it was the correct stone so that this wild-goose chase didn't get any wilder or goosey-er.

"Honey Bear," she said, "can you ask your father what it looked like?"

The boy repeated the question in Mongolian. Tungdik held his hands a short distance from one another, then made a motion to indicate that it was long and narrow.

That was the same shape as the moonstone. Ainsley

struggled to control the rising excitement in her voice. Only her second day, and this was confirmation that she was on the right path. "Can you ask him where it is?"

Honey Bear asked the question, and Tungdik answered briefly.

"My father say he sell it."

Ainsley looked to Harriet, who nodded in confirmation.

"To who?"

Harriet translated this time. Tungdik waved off the question.

"He doesn't want to answer," said Harriet.

Ainsley's fingers picked nervously at the callouses inside her palm. She was so very close to finding this thing, and she wasn't going to rest until she learned it.

She was marooned with this family, and one way or another, she was going to make Tungdik spill the beans.

CHAPTER TWENTY-TWO

The next morning, outside the *ger*, Ainsley watched the reflection of the white clouds scudding across the blue surface of the lake.

It'd been a turbulent night. She'd dreamt of monks shoveling gems, of stone Buddha statues walking across the landscape, of enormous teenage wrestlers pinning her to a mat. She'd been relieved to wake up.

"It's an ugly day," said Harriet. Ainsley nearly leapt out of her shoes. The naturalist had appeared next to her without a sound.

"Please don't do that," said Ainsley.

"Don't do what? Make judgments on the weather?"

"No, don't creep up like that."

Harriet looked confused. "I track animals. Creeping up is what I do."

Recovering herself, Ainsley squinted at the clouds scudding across the heavens. "It seems like a normal day."

"Not here," replied the naturalist. "Mongolia has more clear days than any other nation in the world."

Ainsley noticed Harriet sipping a large mug of tea. "I didn't realize you were English until just now."

"Good heavens, of course I am," replied the naturalist. "Tea is seen as rather fusty but I don't care. It's these little bits of civilization I miss when I'm alone with the wolves in the field."

Ainsley couldn't disagree. Using her toe, she nudged a small rock out of its nest in the soft, springy grass. Nearby, a gopher stuck its head out of the earth, cheeped, and disappeared back underground.

"I have to get Tungdik to reveal the name of the trader," she said, "but I don't think he trusts me."

Harriet nodded. "You have to earn it."

"I know. What can I do?"

"Perhaps you could ask to accompany him on his work."

Ainsley looked back towards the *ger*. "What's he doing today?"

"I heard him say that he's killing goats."

Ainsley blanched. "Why?"

"Because he's a herder, dear. But in reality, there's another reason."

Harriet explained how the Mongolian countryside had been overrun in recent years with livestock. Using satellites, scientists at NASA had analyzed the landscape and found that seventy percent of the Mongolian grassland had suffered degradation due to overgrazing.

Ainsley was stunned. "In a country so enormous..."

"It's all economics," Harriet said. "After the end of the Soviet Union, poor people couldn't survive in the cities, so they turned back to subsistence herding. Now they've overrun the countryside."

"Tungdik's family is one of them," said Ainsley.

"And Tungdik's family is getting paid by the government

to cut their goat production in half. In return, they've agreed to stay on this land for the next five years."

"So that's how you know they would be here."

Harriet nodded. "You don't have to slit the animals' throat. But maybe you can do something. Let's go talk to him."

————

An hour later, Ainsley struggled to maintain her calm as the horse trotted beneath her.

Between her legs was a typical Mongolian breed, smaller and sturdier than Western horses. It had a large head, shaggy coat, and stocky legs. This was why the animal could survive winters on the steppe.

Inside, Ainsley was screaming. Her fear of horses had been well documented since the age of twelve, when she'd been bucked off a mare while at summer camp. Since then, the fear had only grown worse.

Still, she wasn't going to breathe a word to Tungdik, who sat astride his own horse, still wearing his red parka. He'd accepted her offer of help, though hadn't described what she'd be doing. Ainsley guessed that he'd probably been waiting for her to ask to help. After all, she was supposedly there on a cultural exchange.

Next to them, Honey Bear slowly puttered along on his motorcycle. He was wearing his sweatpants but had switched over from his bomber jacket to a black *del*. The traditional herder's jacket made him seem more serious. Sideways across his back rested a long pole, three meters across.

They were headed out to perform an unhappy task. Harriet had been right—father and son were culling the herd, on government orders.

After a period of trotting, they crested a small rise. About a hundred meters below them was a large grouping of goats.

Tungdik and Honey Bear both stopped. With effort, Ainsley managed to halt her horse as well, pulling back on the reins. The teenager stepped off his motorcycle, swung the pole off his back, and extended each end, like a telescope. Then he locked those pieces into place.

Full extended, it was almost ten meters long.

Tungdik handed the reins of his horse to Ainsley. He took the long pole from his son, laid it on the grass, and carefully affixed a rawhide loop to one end.

Ainsley could tell what that was for.

Holding the long pole, the herder walked towards the goats—then suddenly burst into a run, whooping loudly. The animals galloped away. Meanwhile, Honey Bear had revved his motorcycle and circled the group on the other side, corralling them back the opposite direction, towards the *ger*. Tungdik ran after them, batting at the ones who were getting out of line.

Ainsley held the reins of Tungdik's horse and watched the intricate dance. Tungdik yelled at Ainsley. He wanted her to follow him. She kicked her horse. It bolted fast—too fast. The reins of the other horse were yanked out of her hands.

"Crap," she said.

Ainsley slowed her horse down, wheeled it around. Tungdik's horse was wandering off in the wrong direction.

She rode alongside the animal, leaned over, and tried to snatch the reins. No luck. Tungdik's horse broke into a trot. She kicked her own horse until it broke into a trot too.

Ainsley came alongside the animal again, leaned over again, and this time took hold of its reins. She wound them around her wrist.

Now, with a set of reins in each hand, Ainsley pulled back on both.

Her own horse stopped, but Tungdik's horse refused and twisted away. Its reins tied to her wrist, Ainsley lurched sideways in her saddle, its reins wrapped around her wrist. She found herself strung out almost horizontally.

"Dammit—"

Ainsley felt her right arm starting to come out of its socket. This was the drawing before the quartering.

Finally, she dropped her own horse's reins and fell off her horse. She landed on the thick grass, on her right side.

She lay there for a moment, facedown, then lifted her head. Her own horse had wandered away.

"Come back, you bastard," she said.

She stood up, groaning. She tugged Tungdik's horse, but it wouldn't budge. It whinnied and yanked its head the other way.

"What is *wrong* with you—"

Then she noticed Tungdik and Honey Bear watching her. They didn't look pleased. Behind them, the goats were scattering.

"I need help," she shouted.

Father and son slowly approached. She saw the disapproving look on Tungdik's face.

She handed over the reins. If she'd wanted to earn this family's trust, she'd failed miserably.

CHAPTER TWENTY-THREE

She and Harriet were standing a short distance away, but Ainsley still couldn't take her eyes off the scene.

A minute earlier, Honey Bear had tied the animal's legs together. Its bleating had been awful to hear. Ainsley had been sure that it had known what was about to occur.

Now she watched through her fingers as Tungdik quickly pulled the knife across the throat of the goat. She gasped as the animal's lifeblood spurt into the plastic container beneath its neck. Her nostrils were filled with the tangy scent of hot blood.

"How terrible," she said.

Harriet was unmoved. "No, I think it's quite a humane death. You ought to see what the wolves do."

"I'd rather not," said Ainsley.

After the blood had stopped running, Tungdik sealed the container. Then he got down to business stripping the animal. Using a pair of knives, the father cut the fur off the animal's still-warm carcass, his hands moving with practiced speed. Honey Bear stacked the heavy flaps of fur on the ground.

Then Tungdik started the dissection of the goat's muscle.

That was hard to watch, but Ainsley knew that his nomadic family depended upon it.

"This is going to take a while," said Ainsley. "I feel useless just standing here. What do we do?"

"Let me ask," said Harriet. She said something to Tungdik. He looked at the two women, then pointed out to the hills and said something.

"He said that we could shoot some marmots," said Harriet.

"What are those?"

"Big furry rodents. They kind of look like fat squirrels. They're delicacies." The naturalist looked at Ainsley. "Are you up for it?"

"Sure, why not. Have you shot them before?"

"Oh yes, absolutely. They're not the most delicious thing I've ever put in my mouth, but one does get sick of granola."

"We'll need a gun," said Ainsley.

Tungdik grunted to Honey Bear, who reached into the waistband of his enormous pants and produced a pistol.

Harriet shook her head. "No, we need the rifle."

"Ahhh," said the huge teenager, recognizing the word. "Rifle is there."

Following his finger, Ainsley spotted the long barrel of Tungdik's rifle hanging off the side of his horse. She retrieved it, along with the small case of ammunition.

Harriet clapped her hands together in preparation. "Well, let's have a nice hunt, shall we?"

———

An hour later and several kilometers away, Ainsley was crouched on the grass behind a low pile of rocks. Her eye was peering down the long barrel of the rifle.

Through the crosshairs of the scope she saw the rodent pop his head out of the ground.

He's cute. Why did he have to be cute?

Ainsley hesitated.

Next to her, Harriet looked at her. "Do you have him?"

"Yeah."

"Don't dally. It's an easy kill."

Ainsley tensed her muscles, then pulled the trigger. Ten meters behind the marmot, a small cloud of black dirt and green grass erupted out of the earth. The animal squeaked and disappeared down the hole.

"God, I'm just awful," she said.

"It's because you tensed up before the pull," said Harriet. "The secret is to relax. Here, let me try."

Ainsley handed over the rifle to the naturalist. She'd never been particularly good at target practice, not with any instrument, not at any time in her life. During archery class at summer camp, her arrows had rarely reached the targets on the hay bales. They'd been shooting for over an hour now, one little fuzzy face after another popping up out of holes in the ground. It reminded her of playing whack-a-mole at the arcade, except with rifles instead of mallets.

On her belly, Harriet propped the rifle on the rocks and lowered her eye to the barrel of the rifle. She peered through the sight, paused, and squeezed the trigger.

Boom. No eruption of dirt. Ainsley squinted. "What happened?"

"I think I got him. Come on, follow me."

She trotted down the hill, Ainsley following behind. "Yes, it's right there—see it?"

Ainsley glimpsed the dead marmot. It was small and furry laying on its side.

"Nice shot," she said.

"You ought to see how the Mongols cook these things,"

said Harriet. "First they gut the animal, stuff it with charcoals, then they put the guts back inside and roast it for two hours. Then they scrape off the burnt fur—"

She was interrupted by a piercing cry overhead. Something large and fast and silent swooped over their heads. Both of them instinctively ducked.

The thing landed on the ground, next to the kill. It was an enormous bird. Its curved beak was meant for tearing flesh. And its two huge wings covered in spectacular golden feathers.

"Holy hell it's an eagle," said Ainsley.

"It is beautiful," said Harriet.

The eagle spread its wings and issued a single bloodcurdling shriek.

Both women quickly scrambled backwards on their hands.

When she'd reached a safer distance, Ainsley rolled into a crouch, hands on the grass. She was ready to run, or fight, if need be. Next to her, Harriet did the same, breathing hard.

"The message is made clear," said Harriet, looking at the eagle. "That is *your* dead marmot."

Ainsley couldn't help but admire the bird as it sunk its face into the marmot carcass. The eagle was enormous, its trunk the size of an athletic bag, and its golden plumage was thick and gorgeous. Still, as she watched it tear chunks of flesh off the marmot, its beak turning progressively redder, Ainsley was reminded of its savagery. This was an apex predator. It shouldn't be underestimated.

"Do you see what's on the ground behind it?" said Harriet. "Look closely."

Ainsley saw a couple of strips of leather trailing the eagle. They seemed to be attached to its legs. "Those are straps."

"No, they're leashes."

"What does that mean?"

"It belongs to somebody."

They stood there, watching the feeding. Ainsley finally broke the silence. "So I guess we wait for it to go away and then shoot another marmot?"

"There's certainly no shortage." The naturalist's eyes roved the landscape, then paused. "Oh boy. It seems we're not alone."

Ainsley turned and looked in the direction of her gaze. Running down the light brown slope of a nearby mountain, only a few hundred meters away, was a human dressed in black. It was wearing a red hat.

"I will bet my paycheck that's the owner," said Ainsley.

Harriet nodded. "I would say that is not a Mongolian either. Not with that hat."

"Maybe you ought to reload the rifle," said Ainsley.

"Perhaps," said Harriet, "or perhaps not."

As the individual approached them, Ainsley could see it was a man. He was wearing in a brocade black coat. His strange hat was red and lined with brown-and-white fox fur. It was turned up oddly on either side, almost like a pair of wings. From the hat a long red tassel hung down halfway down his back.

Most interesting was the thick brown leather glove that the man wore on his right forearm. It extended up to the elbow.

The man looked at the women, then nodded. His face was warm and friendly.

Then he looked at the eagle. The man approached the animal slowly, speaking in a strange language—it wasn't Mongolian, Ainsley could tell that much.

Three, two, then one meter—and then he was crouching next to the bird, stroking its head.

"What?" Ainsley said. "How is he doing that?"

"Unless I'm mistaken," said Harriet, "he's a Kazakh eagle hunter."

"For real?"

She nodded. "This is quite rare. There's only a few hundred, and they live only in this part of Mongolia, Bayan-Olgii."

"What is he doing here? I thought everything around here now belonged to Tungdik."

Harriet shrugged. "This guy has probably been a nomad his whole life. Who's going to tell him where he can or can't go?"

"Tungdik might have an opinion about that."

"He might."

As they watched him coax the animal onto his arm, Harriet explained that the Kazakh eagle hunters were famous. Theirs was an ancient art, and they mostly used the predatory birds to hunt foxes in the winter, when the brown of the fox fur was easy to see against the white snow. Recently the country of Kazakhstan had been trying to lure the hunters back to their ancestral homeland, but without much success. The high point of their year occurred every October, when they participated in the annual Golden Eagle Festival. A few years earlier, it had been won by a thirteen-year-old girl.

"How long do the hunters train the animals?" said Ainsley.

"A few years. Then they're released into the wild."

The Kazakh finally succeeded in luring the eagle onto his arm. The bird hopped up, its long talons gripping the thick leather of his glove like eight curved butcher knives. The man stroked the eagle gently on his back, the animal making several small cries.

Then, in a movement so swift that Ainsley barely saw it, the Kazakh slipped a small leather mask over the bird's eyes. It looked like a tiny leather aviator helmet from World War I.

"Wow," said Ainsley.

"That mask calms down the bird," said Harriet.

They walked over to the hunter, who was still standing over what little remained of the marmot carcass. Harriet opened the conversation with a salutation.

The man knew some Mongolian about as well as Harriet, and they began a slow, halting conversation.

"He said that he's still training this one," she explained to Ainsley. "He also apologizes for stealing our kill."

Ainsley tried not to smile at his apology. They'd been joking earlier about the hundreds of marmots burrowing around beneath their feet.

"Tell him it's okay."

The conversation continued. While he spoke, the eagle hunter stroked the majestic creature, occasionally glancing up to catch Ainsley's gaze.

"He said that he owes us," said Harriet. "He wants to make it up to us."

"That's unnecessary," said Ainsley.

"I'm going to ask where he lives." Harriet did so, and his response was to make a circle with his left hand.

"He said everywhere," said Ainsley.

The Kazakh eagle hunter explained something else. Ainsley had no idea what he was saying but she could see the warmth and passion in his eyes as he explained it.

"He said that you are very, very generous for having given your kill to his animal. He wants us to know that he is in our debt."

Apparently her easy-come-easy-go attitude towards the dead marmot counted for much more than Ainsley had thought. Truth be told, she hadn't really had a choice. She couldn't imagine fighting with an eagle over a dead rodent. She was pretty sure there weren't any tips in any traveler's handbook either.

"Tell him we'll collect some other time," she said.

Harriet translated, and his response came quickly: "He said that with friends you are as broad as the steppe. Without them you are as narrow as the palm of your hand."

The Kazakh eagle hunter smiled, made a small bow, and walked away. They watched him ascend the small hill, the eagle still resting on his arm, its leather ribbons trailing behind.

Soon both hunter and eagle disappeared over the ridge. Ainsley turned to her naturalist. "Harriet, did that really happen?"

"Yes, it did." The Englishwoman slipped another cartridge into the rifle. "Now let's pop another one."

CHAPTER TWENTY-FOUR

It was the end of day, and long red strips of dying sunlight reached across the green steppe.

Ainsley, Harriet, and their hosts had gathered around a small barbecue pit. Honey Bear was napping inside the *ger* nearby. Ainsley had noticed that the young wrestler slept a minimum of twelve hours a day. She imagined that it was pretty tiring to drag around that much mass. Plus, she kept reminding herself, he was just a teenager, even if he didn't look like it.

Tungdik used a shovel to dig the bloated, burned marmot carcass out of the ground. Two hours in the fire, and it had ballooned to the size of a basketball. He used a sharp knife to scrape the burned fur off the scorched skin.

Ainsley kept her eyes on her host. This man, a remote herder in a remote corner of one of the most remote countries on earth, held the key to finding the moonstone buried by a Buddhist monk a century ago. He was all she had. Whatever was locked inside his brain was her only filament of a thread of a clue that would lead her to the moonstone.

Tungdik finished stripping the burned fur. He sliced open

the black sphere of a dead rodent. Black coals and pink intestines spilled out. The smell of charred game meat singed Ainsley's nostrils. He cut a small piece of the innards and held it out to Ainsley.

She felt her stomach churn. It looked like a piece of undigested marmot shit. That was no exaggeration either—it may very well have been exactly that.

Norgema handed her a wooden bowl. Ainsley put the shit-nugget in the bowl and waited for it to cool. She forced a smile and a polite nod of the head. She would wait until both were distracted, then toss it in the grass behind her.

He offered the next piece to Harriet, who popped her piece into her mouth without a second thought.

"And the verdict?" said Ainsley.

She shrugged. "It's barbecued marmot. It never really gets better. Will you be eating yours?"

"It depends. How long will we be welcome with these people?"

"Well, they'll never kick us out. That's not Mongolian tradition. But eventually they'll give us subtle signals that it's time to leave."

"I see."

"Don't worry, we're not at that stage yet."

The purple flap to the *ger* parted, and Honey Bear's enormous mass stepped out. "Ainsley!" he shouted.

"What?" she shouted back.

His fingers made the shape of a telephone. "Telephone!"

"The satellite phone?"

"It must be Erdene," said Harriet. "Do you want me to come with you?"

"No, that's okay," Ainsley replied, pulling herself to her feet. No matter what the call was about, she was thankful to have an excuse to leave the horrible rodent roast.

Ainsley entered the *ger*. The satellite phone sat open on the side table, the receiver face up. She put it to her ear.

"Erdene?" she said.

A young man's voice said, "No, it's Gantig."

"Oh."

Ainsley had nearly forgotten about him since leaving Ulaanbataar days earlier. How many days it'd been, she couldn't be sure—days and night seemed to run together in a blur here on the steppe. She understood why the nomads measured time by seasons instead. It felt more natural.

She could hear the urgency in Gantig's voice. "Erdene told me everything that you've done so far. Did you get the name of the trader with the moonstone?"

"No, not yet," she admitted. "This herder family is tight-lipped. I've been trying to earn their trust."

"There's another problem," he said.

"What is it?"

His voice even more urgent. "You have to get out of there, Ainsley."

She felt sweat pop out across her body. Her grip tightened on the satellite phone.

"Why?" she said. The syllable came out like a croak.

"Somebody has been talking. Somebody at Excovane knows you're looking for the moonstone."

"Who?"

"Erdene says she thinks it was the guard at the museum in Zhakorum."

"So what?"

"They don't want anybody stopping this project." He paused. "Ainsley, they killed my father."

She paused. It felt like somebody had poured a pitcher of ice water down her spine.

"I ... understand. But someone is coming after ... *me?*"

"It's what we heard."

"How?"

"We have sources inside Excovane."

Her throat was dry. "What should I do?"

"Leave."

"How? I don't have any options here."

"Erdene said you picked up an Englishwoman. Can she help?"

"Her name is Harriet, and no. Her truck is getting repaired back in Zhakorum. We're marooned here."

Gantig sighed. "You're going to have to go somewhere. Just in case."

She peered out the flap of the *ger*. The herder family had circled together, sharing scraps of charred marmot. They looked happy together. It wouldn't be fair if anything untoward happened to them.

Ainsley would have to remove herself.

"All right," she said, her voice down to a mere whisper. "I'll just ... leave. I don't know where to go or how to get there."

"There's a couple of small cities near you. Find one and call us."

"I'll try."

"You've got the number of this sat phone, right?"

"Yeah."

"Ainsley, again, before you leave—*please* get the name of that trader. Pay them if you need to."

"Okay."

Gantig ended the call. Ainsley replaced the receiver and leaned against the family dresser and closed her eyes and sighed.

———

She trudged back to the small feast. Honey Bear saw her coming.

"Ainsley, I save it for you!" The teenager offered her a bowl filled with slices of charred marmot belly.

"Thank you," she said wearily, sitting down.

Harriet's eyes were on Ainsley. "Something happened?"

"I have to leave."

"Why?"

"It's complicated. I don't want to explain. But it could be dangerous if I stay."

Harriet grew pale. "Oh."

Ainsley added, "And I *really* need him to give me the name of the trader."

"Okay—"

"I need it *tonight*, Harriet."

"Well—"

"I want to offer to pay him. Can you translate for me?"

"You want me to ask him right now?"

"Yes," said Ainsley, "right now."

Harriet sat up, brushed off her coat, and cleared her throat. "Tungdik?"

The herder looked up from his bowl. His fingers were glistening with marmot fat.

Ainsley listened as Harriet explained the situation. The herder's face grew dark. He shook his head no.

"He said no," said Harriet.

"I can see that," said Ainsley. "Now tell him that I will pay him two hundred dollars."

Harriet translated, and Tungdik grew angry. He set the bowl down and spoke sternly, his face serious. Then he stood up and went inside the *ger*.

"What did he say?"

Harriet looked alarmed. "He said that you have been rude to offer money to your host."

Ainsley buried her face in her hands. "I know, and apologize for me, but it's urgent."

It was too late. The mood of the gathering had changed. Norgema and Honey Bear both stood, collected the bowls, and returned to the ger.

Harriet and Ainsley were left sitting alone.

"Now what?" said Ainsley.

"I'm guessing we sleep on the floor tonight."

"And what does that mean?"

"It will be a sign that we should leave."

Ainsley dropped her head, feeling ashamed. "This just feels terrible. Where are you going to go?"

The naturalist pulled her knees up to her chest. "I have to get back to Zhakorum to get my truck. Probably I'll hitchhike. I've done it before. You?"

"I don't know."

The sentence died away as the darkness engulfed the two women.

CHAPTER TWENTY-FIVE

Well before dawn, Ainsley woke up on a mat on the floor of the tent, her plan in mind.

It wasn't a particularly good plan, or an ethical plan, or a well-planned plan.

But it was something.

She lay still, listening. All around her were the sounds of sleeping—Norgema and Tungdik in their bed. She could see Honey Bear's hulking form in the other bed, a loud snore issuing from his nose.

Ainsley and Harriet had lost the privilege to that bed, just as Harriet had guessed.

Next to her, the Englishwoman snored, deep in sleep. Ainsley hadn't said a word to Harriet about the plan.

Because it didn't involve her.

All clear. Ainsley quietly pushed aside the blanket and rolled off the mat. She felt the dense carpet under her shoulder, and the coldness from the earth seeping up from beneath it.

No need to change. She'd gone to bed already wearing all her clothing. It was part of the plan.

Ainsley got to her hands and knees, slowly lifted herself to her feet, so slowly that it nearly hurt her bones. Even a small click from her knee might be enough to wake up the herder family.

And she couldn't afford that.

She tiptoed to the front door. The flap of heavy purple felt hung cold and thick against the outside weather. She dropped to her hands and knees again. She ever-so-gently nudged her head through the left side of the flap. The cold air was going to enter the *ger*; that was unavoidable. But if she moved fast and let in as little as possible, then she might get away with it.

Outside, the air was crisp and cold. Shivering, Ainsley quickly ran round the *ger* to where she'd hidden her bag. She'd put it there the previous night, after everyone was in bed.

To make an efficient escape.

Slinging the bag across her shoulder, she quickly walked across the grass to the family's second *ger*, the one used for storage.

There, she lifted the flap and went inside. All was pitch black. It carried the smell of fuel tanks and freshly cut grass. It wasn't unpleasant.

Ainsley fumbled inside her bag for a pack of matches that she'd pilfered from the family's dresser the night before. She lit one. It flared briefly, illuminating the interior—the hardware, the ropes, the knives, the buckets, the few remaining bales of hay.

And one more thing.

Honey Bear's motorcycle.

She walked over to bike. The keys were in the ignition, just as they'd been yesterday, and the day before. No reason to hide the keys out here on the steppe. The worst thing that could happen is that a yak might eat them.

Or a visitor might steal them.

It wasn't stealing, though. She reassured herself with that thought. This was going to be a sale.

Ainsley reached into her bag and pulled out the money that Gantig had given to her. She counted out a large portion of it, then tied it with a rubber band. She pulled an oily drop-cloth into the middle of the ger's floor and laid the money in the middle of it.

They wouldn't miss that.

Gripping the handlebars, Ainsley rolled the motorcycle out of the *ger* into the dark meadow. The sun was a sliver of purple on the far horizon. The moist grass wettened her ankles.

She popped the kickstand and checked the fuel tank. It was half full. She would need more than that.

Ainsley went back into the *ger*, found the gasoline can, and returned to the bike. She unscrewed the cap and began to fill the tank.

There was a movement in her peripheral vision. She looked up. Against the dark field was the silhouette of a dark figure.

Ainsley felt cold sweat spring out in her hands. The fuel glopped out slowly from the can, because it wasn't getting enough air from the valve.

"Come on, come on," she said under her breath.

At last the tank was filled. She lowered the can, screwed on the cap, and turned towards the *ger*—

—when she heard her name.

"Anshlee," said the voice.

Busted.

It was Norgema.

The mother of the herding family came into view. She was wearing a coat over her sleeping robe.

Ainsley stopped. Her hands on Honey Bear's motorcycle, a thief caught in the act.

They couldn't communicate, but Ainsley decided to try to come clean. "One minute," she said, holding up one index finger.

She went into the *ger*, replaced the fuel can, then picked up the money from the floor. She brought it back outside and pushed it into the woman's hands.

"This is for you. For the motorcycle."

Norgema didn't speak English, but Ainsley knew she would understand what was happening. The woman looked down at the money, then looked at Ainsley.

She flipped through the wad, counting it. Then she made a murmuring sound of approval.

Ainsley made a thumbs-up sign. "Good?" She lifted her eyebrows and nodded her head yes to indicate pending approval.

A beat. Then Norgema made a short, curt nod.

Ainsley felt her heart leap. That was all she needed. Norgema had agreed to the sale. It was no longer a borderline theft.

Then Norgema made a come-here movement with her hand.

Ainsley drew closer. The mother of the nomadic family looked into her face. She spoke one word.

"*Tumenbayar*," she said.

Ainsley squinted and tilted her head. "What?"

Norgema repeated the word. "*Tumenbayar … munstun*."

Tumenbayar, munstun. Ainsley was lost. This may as well have been in Chinese. Actually, Chinese might've been easier.

"I don't understand," she said.

"*Munstun*," repeated the woman, more firmly. Then her hands drew the shape of a cylinder, about a foot long. "*Munstun*."

Then it hit Ainsley. She was trying to say *moonstone*.

"Moonstone?" she said.

Norgema shook her head yes. "*Tumenbayar*."

"Tumenbayar?"

The woman puffed out her arms and cheeks and pretended to waddle across the grass. It was a funny pantomime.

Ainsley understood. "Tumenbayar is a man?"

Norgema nodded. "Man! *Tumenbayar* man! *Munstun*!"

Ainsley felt the excitement rising. It was possible that Norgema was telling her the name of the trader with the moonstone.

"Where?" said Ainsley. "Where is Tumenbayar?"

"Hm?" said Norgema, not understanding.

"Where is Tumenbayar?" Ainsley pointed to the north. "There?" She pointed to the south. "There?" She pointed to the east. "There?"

Comprehension dawned in Norgema's eyes. She pronounced the next two words very clearly: "Muk Holgoi."

"Muk Holgoi?"

The woman nodded. She pointed to the south. "Tumenbayar *munstun*."

"In Muk Holgoi."

Norgema nodded emphatically.

Then Ainsley remembered that name. Muk Holgoi was the enormous mining complex that Gantig had discussed with her. The one that Excovane had already opened, over the objections of many voices in the Mongolian government.

If she could trust Norgema—which she probably could— that was going to be her next destination.

"Thank you," Ainsley said, bowing to Norgema, hands clasped.

The nomadic woman smiled. Then she took the motorcycle by the handles and started walking it. She made a follow-me motion.

Perplexed, Ainsley followed Norgema across the grass.

They walked for almost fifteen minutes, as the sliver of purple turned into a rosy orange glow in the east.

At last they reached a small cat track in the meadow. Ainsley recognized it. This was the road that she'd arrived upon, with Erdene. Turning around, she saw the herding family *ger* far behind her.

Norgema pointed to the south. She was trying to send Ainsley off in the best possible way.

"Thank you again," said Ainsley.

The two women hugged one another. Then Ainsley slid onto the motorcycle, jumped down on the starter, and the engine roared to life.

She waved goodbye, popped the bike into gear, and rolled away.

Towards Muk Holgoi. Towards Tumenbayar.

Towards the moonstone.

CHAPTER TWENTY-SIX

It was no secret that Ainsley had always hated riding horses. But most people didn't know that she disliked riding motorcycles almost as much.

She knew *how* to ride one. Senior year in college, Ainsley'd had a boyfriend with a beat-up Indian Scout Sixty, a classic cruiser. Sometimes on Sundays they'd gone out to far country roads, where he'd shown Ainsley the basics of riding. It'd been easier than she'd thought, and she'd grown proficient. But she'd never taken a safety course or been certified for a license.

Ainsley was regretting that now, because this was tricky.

It was almost eleven o'clock, and she'd been riding for hours, alone. The cat track had petered out pretty quick, and since then, she'd continued across the open grass, averaging eighty or ninety kilometers per hour.

Slowly she'd been relearning the ropes—how to spot mud patches, how far to turn the accelerator grip, how to go over the smooth small hills rather than cut through the rough valleys. She was grateful that the motorcycle wasn't too heavy either.

But she hadn't used the brakes yet. On the steppe, there was almost no need, since there was literally almost nothing to stop for. She was like a swimmer who grew up in a lake and never learned how to kick-turn off the wall of a pool.

Kerchunk.

It happened before she knew it. The front wheel of the bike plunged into a hole and she sank deep over the handle-bars, elbows wide. Then she came up. But when the back wheel hit the hole, Ainsley was popped off the bike like a piece of popcorn off a frying pan. She was lifted a full meter in the air—

—she saw her life flash before her eyes—

—and she landed on prairie grass. It was as soft as a feath-erbed. Ainsley's body bounced once, twice, then settled in nicely on her back. Nearby, she heard the small clinks of the motorcycle. It had fallen over, wheels still spinning.

"Holy hell," she said.

Ainsley felt around on her body. Nothing seemed hurt or broken. She stood up, testing her legs. They were fine. She walked back to the motorcycle. She pulled out a water bottle from her bag and took a deep swig.

Then she took in the landscape, feeling the cool wind against her skin, one thought running in an obsessive loop through her mind.

Muk Holgoi.

The mining complex. She had almost no idea where it could be, other than south. She didn't even have a map; Erdene had taken that with her. All Ainsley knew was to steer herself to the south, which she was doing by the sun.

What she really needed was a place to stay tonight, since she'd left her sleeping bag in the nomads' tent. A settlement of some kind.

Then she saw a flash of light.

It was only for half a second, but it came from the base of

a small mountain range to the south. Her mind ran over the possibilities. It could've been a car. It could've been a pair of glasses. It could've been an empty beer bottle.

Whatever the flash was—it grabbed her attention, here on the steppe.

Ainsley remounted the motorcycle, started it up, and took off towards the flash.

———

Three hours later, as she crested the rise, the chilled air on Ainsley's face told her that a river was approaching.

She'd crossed a gently rolling series of gorgeous hills, passing over each one fast enough to feel her stomach lift, then settle again.

Now she slowed to a stop. In front of her was a swift ice-blue river. It wasn't very wide, maybe twenty meters at most, but it felt freezing cold. Her fingers were losing sensation just standing near it.

Ainsley was flummoxed. There didn't seem to be a way to cross this. Ainsley couldn't see the depth, but that didn't matter. A knee-high river would still flood the motorcycle's engine. Plus, it was moving fast. She picked up a handful of grass and flung it into the water. The blades were carried away and out of sight in almost an instant.

Then she spotted a light trail in the grass. It was barely visible, the merest suggestion of a path. It traced the edge of the river.

That was a good sign. Even if it ended up being nothing more than an animal track, she knew that other living creatures had faced this same dilemma. One of them must've figured out a solution.

She started the motorcycle again, wheeled around, and followed the track southeast, along the river's edge. Her face, cheeks, and hands quickly grew numb from the icebox flowing swiftly on her right.

A half hour later, she found it.

The bridge.

Ainsley parked the motorcycle, slipped off, and walked up to the edge of the bridge. It was made entirely of wood, and looked about eighty meters across—and less than three meters wide. Wooden beams had been set horizontally, in a long series of bands, like trestles of a railroad track. On top of those, on the far right and far left, lay two strips of wooden planks, stretching vertically from one end of the bridge to the other. Those, Ainsley guessed, were for automobile wheels. At each end of the bridge was a berm, a mound of earth providing elevation above the river.

There were no railings, no signs, no weight limits.

Cross at her own risk.

Ainsley stepped onto the bridge, testing her weight. It felt okay. She gingerly walked halfway across the bridge, testing its capacity. It didn't sway, creak, or crack. The wood was weathered but there were no broken slats.

Maybe crossing it would be safe. Maybe it wouldn't. She doubted that infrastructure inspectors would be coming out here.

Ainsley tapped her lips with a finger while she made her decision.

She would try it.

In second gear. That was a little faster than she should cross a wooden bridge with no railings, but at least doing so would keep the weight of the bike moving forward, not resting downwards. She would also drive on one of the vertical strips, which were meant to bear more weight than the horizontal bands alone.

There was no reason to delay any longer. The crossing had to be made.

She went back to the motorcycle, swung her leg over it, placed her hands on the bars, and took a deep breath.

"Do it, Ainsley," she said.

She started the engine, popped it into second gear, circled around, and drove towards the bridge. Her breaths were coming shorter and faster now. This was crazy, she was crazy—

The front wheel of the bike hit the berm. A second later, Ainsley found herself on the bridge. She steered the tires onto the left strip of planks. The wood made a horrible rumbling sound beneath her wheels. She could feel the cold of the river below her. It felt like riding over a glacier.

Stay focused, she thought. Ainsley concentrated on keeping the front end of her tire aligned in the middle of the vertical strip of wood.

Halfway across. The far end of the bridge was larger now. She was squeezing the handlebars so tightly that her hands felt like bird claws.

Just a few seconds more.

Then she saw it. A large dark object, in the left strip. It looked like a dead animal. Her front tire was headed directly for it.

She turned the wheel slightly to the right. The front end of the bike slipped down, off the left strip, and suddenly she found herself in the small valley between the two strips of reinforced wood.

Nothing between her and the water except a single row of horizontally-set wooden slats.

Passing the roadkill, she turned the wheel to the left, to get back up onto the strip. Her front tire hit the edge and slipped back down. The bike began to lose balance, so she turned the wheel back to the right.

This time, she overcorrected. Angled too hard, the bike

went up hard onto the vertical strip on the right. Panicking, she cranked it back to the left, too hard.

Now she'd overcorrected again. The greatest cause of motor vehicle accidents in the world.

In horror, Ainsley watched, in slow motion, as the front tire of her motorcycle flew over the edge of the bridge.

Ainsley instinctively threw herself clear of the bike. The river water rushed up to greet her—

—and she belly flopped into the river.

A half-second later she was underwater. It literally took her breath away. The current was an icy assailant that was carrying her away against her will. Ainsley burst out of the water, lungs convulsing, her mouth opening and closing like a grouper on the deck of a fishing boat.

She heard deep guttural sounds. They were coming from her throat.

Then she felt her foot touch the riverbed. It wasn't deep.

She turned her head and looked for shore. It was only three or four meters away. Ainsley managed to wheel her arms overhead, once, twice. This was the weakest freestyle of her life. After six strokes, her hand hit mud. She was at the shore. The water was only ankle deep, and soon she was pulling herself out.

Ainsley crawled up the low riverbank until she felt grass beneath her palms. Then she collapsed, her face in the dirt. Inside her chest, her lungs were performing a frenzied dance. She felt the sunshine on the back of her neck. She kept her face pressed sideways against the grass, focusing on her breathing, until she felt the hyperventilation slowly disappear.

Then she sat up.

The bridge was fifty meters away.

"My God," she said.

Ainsley stood up. Her clothing was soaked, but it had

been designed to dry quickly. Keeping body heat was vital out here on the steppe, and she didn't intend to lose too much.

Ainsley trudged back towards the bridge, her hair hanging like two wet sheets on either side of her head. Cold water squished in her shoes.

The motorcycle had landed on its left side in the shallows, not even two meters from the river's edge. Most of the machine rested above water.

It was possibly recoverable.

Without hesitation, she stepped into the calf-deep water, lifted the machine by its handlebars, and pushed it out of the river and up onto the bank.

On the grass, she put down its kickstand and inspected the machine. There was no visible damage. Her bag was still strapped to the back and had barely gotten wet.

She tightened her lips, made a fist. She'd almost made it across that ridiculous bridge. Just a few more seconds, and none of this would've happened. But she'd panicked.

Ainsley went back up onto the bridge and walked to the dead animal.

It wasn't a dead animal. She picked it up.

It was a black scarf. Somebody had dropped it here, days, weeks, months ago—and she'd driven off the bridge to avoid hitting it.

Filled with self-loathing, Ainsley stormed off the bridge and back to the motorcycle. She sat on the saddle, turned the key, opened the choke lever, and squeezed the clutch.

It didn't start.

She tried a second time.

Nothing.

She tried a third and a fourth time, swearing with every jump. The engine simply refused to start. Ainsley was no mechanic, but it didn't take a mechanic to guess that the engine had been flooded.

She stepped off the motorcycle and punched the air. She felt the tears coming to her eyes.

The universe was telling her that it was time to take a walk.

At last she untied her bag, slung it around her shoulder, and patted the motorcycle's leather seat.

"Goodbye," she said.

Then she started walking towards the flash in the mountains.

CHAPTER TWENTY-SEVEN

Six o'clock in the evening, and Ainsley felt something hard and flat beneath her boot.

It took her by surprise. She'd been walking across the open grasses for the last four hours, sometimes staggering, sometimes with eyes closed. While her clothing had dried, her wet shoes still squelched. Those would take another day to dry.

Ainsley looked down. Beneath her feet was a piece of concrete. She lifted her face. In front of her was a wide strip of concrete, maybe ten meters across. It evidently hadn't been used in years, because it had broken into pieces. It was over-grown with grasses that rendered it nearly invisible at eye level.

She followed the strip of ancient concrete. It was longer than she expected, stretching on for at least a thousand meters, until it hooked hard to the left, into a valley between a pair of small mountains.

Then Ainsley realized what she had stumbled upon.

A landing strip.

This meant that there could be an airport, or the ruins of

one, at the other end. Energized, Ainsley strode atop the broken concrete, around the hook, and into the small valley.

What she saw there took her breath away. It wasn't an airport.

It was an abandoned air base.

Ahead were eight old aircraft shelters, four on each side of the concrete, each made of what seemed to be reinforced concrete. Sealed tight behind pairs of heavy sliding doors, they stood thick, solid, and forgotten. Nearby lay the disintegrated frame of what seemed to be a large soldiers' barracks.

She drifted slowly through the ghost base, hearing the wind whistle in her ears. She got a weird tingling feeling in her backside. That had been Ainsley's warning signal all her life—*danger danger danger*—but it could sometimes be wrong. Occasionally she felt that just because she'd been left alone in an atmospheric place. She clutched her bag more tightly around her shoulder.

She arrived in what used to be a plaza. In the middle stood a decrepit fighter jet that had been repurposed as a sculpture. A steel base propping it beneath, it had been propped at a thirty-degree angle, as though it were preparing one final voyage into the sky. A red star had been painted on its tail. Ainsley approached the pedestal and noted some sentences etched into the stone. The letters were Cyrillic.

It was in Russian.

Suddenly Ainsley realized where she was. This wasn't just any air base. This was an abandoned Soviet military base.

Scratching her chin, she looked at the scrap and rubble scattered around the area. The Soviet Union hadn't collapsed until 1990, but this base already looked as though it'd been decaying for a couple hundred years. It was proof of nature's power, especially on the central Asian steppe.

A short, sharp whistle sounded to her left. Ainsley

whirled. It came from a long, plain, rectangular red brick building. It had no windows, but the walls were intact.

A man stood in one of the two front doorways, next to a faded mural of a hand wielding a torch. He was watching her.

Cautiously, she picked her way across the rubble on the ground. As she drew closer, she studied him. He was middle-aged, normal size, wearing a green parka with a pair of jeans and running shoes. He also was white—dirty brown hair, small hard gray eyes, and an oddly amphibious nose. From his cruel, plump lips dangled an unlit cigarette. It seemed like the kind of face that would always need a cigarette.

"Do you speak English?" she said.

Without a word, he stepped towards her. She didn't like the way he did it. She backpedaled three steps.

"Don't you *dare*," she hissed, holding up a warning finger.

He stopped to light his cigarette. His cruel eyes didn't even bother to watch her while he cocked his head to light it. That's how little of a threat he felt that she posed to him.

Ainsley felt the sweat pop out on her forehead. She reached into her bag for something to defend herself with.

Then she heard another voice shout: "*Molotov! Ne trogat!*"

She looked over. Another man, quite a bit older, had appeared in the doorway, his hands on his hips. He was wearing a Patagonia fleece, wire-rimmed spectacles, and a sunhat fastened to his chin by a strap. His stooped posture told Ainsley that he was too old to back up the strength of his voice.

Molotov sneered at her, then pivoted on one foot and headed back towards the abandoned building. He entered through the second door. The elderly man kept his eye on him.

Ainsley forced herself to breathe out.

"Do you speak English?" said the man.

"Oh, I was going to ask you that."

"You're American too?"

"Yeah."

The old man looked her up and down as though sizing up an unfamiliar insect. "What are you doing here?"

She shifted her weight. "It's a long story."

"There are no short ones. Nobody comes here by accident."

Ainsley felt her stomach rumble. "I'm sorry to ask this but—do you have anything to eat?"

The man's face softened with sympathy. "Of course. Oh, I'm Bill."

"I'm Ainsley," she said. They shook hands; his palm was soft but the grip was firm. "I had a motorcycle but it crashed into a river. I've been walking all day."

"Holy moly," he said. "This is not a part of the world where you want to find yourself alone without a vehicle."

"I know."

"Let's get you some food. Follow me."

Ainsley started to follow him into the ruined building, then stopped, one leg on the front step.

The old American turned around, seeming to read her mind. "There's nothing to fear, Ainsley. There's four people here."

Swallowing hard, she stepped into the building.

CHAPTER TWENTY-EIGHT

Ainsley followed Bill down the long gusty hallway. He kept a slow, steady, turtle pace. The corridor was lined with open rotted doorways, each revealing a different empty room, cluttered with pieces of brick, piles of scrap, broken furniture, and rat droppings.

"What *is* this place?" she said.

Bill turned his head. "It's where poor travelers stay while hoping for a ride. Those of us who don't have a *ger*, of course."

"How long have you been here?"

"Only a couple of days. I'm trying to get out east, back towards the capital."

"So you're waiting for a ride."

"Yes. There's always one, eventually. Believe it or not, this is a transportation hub for hitchhikers. Where are you headed?"

"Muk Holgoi."

"Ahhh. You'll want to wait for Yalgesh," he said.

"Who's that?"

Bill chuckled. "He's the only ride you've got. Don't worry, I've driven with him. He's one of the good ones."

That was reassuring. "When does he come?"

"I have no idea. Nobody really keeps to a schedule out here. Here's my room."

Ainsley followed him into what had once been sleeping quarters for Russian soldiers. A bunk bed with bare wires stood flush against the far wall, and Bill had rolled out his yellow sleeping bag upon the lower bunk. On the floor rested his blue waterproof backpack, zipped shut, as if he'd expected to leave at any minute. Next to the door was a dirty sink that hadn't seen water in decades. She noticed that Bill had set his toothbrush and toothpaste neatly atop it.

"I'm afraid it's not very homey," he said.

Ainsley surveyed the place, her hands on her hips. "You've done the best you could."

Bill reached into his pack and withdrew a narrow brown cardboard sleeve. "Today we have MREs on the menu. Let's see what this one is." He peered through his spectacles at the small print on front of the package. "Pasta primavera. How does that sound?"

"That would be great."

Ainsley watched him rip open the package and fill the chemical heater bag with water. After it had warmed up, he slipped the pasta package inside.

"Now we wait," Bill said, propping it upright against the leg of the bunk bed. "Seven minutes."

Ainsley sat down cross-legged on the floor. Bill did the same opposite her, groaning as he came to rest.

"Old man no like floor," he said. "I'm something of a collector of stories, Ainsley. I'd like to hear yours."

She wasn't ready to share just yet. "First, I'd like to know about that guy you called Molotov."

"Oh, I barely know him. Enough to know that he's really not someone you can trust."

Her eyes flashed. "Obviously. But what does he do?"

"I don't know. He's ... a parasite."

That seemed like the harshest word Bill could ever summon. Ainsley studied her host. The old man seemed to be one of those outwardly quiet-mannered people who hide an inner strength of conviction. In a prison, he'd be the soft-spoken inmate who would one day, without a word, shank a bad guy in the corridor.

"It sounds like you've spent a lot of time here," she said.

"Oh, I've been coming to Mongolia for decades."

Ainsley uncrossed her arms. "That is interesting. I have to ask why."

Bill nodded, as though he'd expected the conversation to go this very route. "I do genealogical research for my church."

"Which one?"

"I'm a member of the Church of Jesus Christ of Latter-Day Saints."

That explained it. Bill was a Mormon missionary. Unlike others, Ainsley didn't have any opinion about Mormons. Personally, she'd had decent experiences with them. They seemed like the usual mixed bag of humanity.

Bill reached into his backpack and withdrew a thin tablet. "I've been visiting nomadic families to educate them about how to record their roots. They really don't know much about their backgrounds. Many of them lost their family names during the Soviet era. So I've been showing them modern methods, how to scan their photos, how to put them up on Family Tree."

"It's going well?"

His face brightened. "Oh, they love it. The young ones especially."

Ainsley tapped her upper cheekbone with a couple of

fingers. "Honestly, I didn't even know Mormons were in Mongolia."

The missionary drew himself up straight. "Thirty years ago, my late wife and I were one of the original six couples to arrive here. Now there are ten thousand converts." He puckered his lips proudly. "That's pretty good for a country that's used to be one hundred percent Buddhist."

Ainsley couldn't share in his pride, but she admired his commitment to his goals. On one hand, you could fault Mormons for their strange restrictions—dancing, caffeine, and alcohol. On the other, you had to applaud their desire to change the world. Still, she wondered if Bill's decades of effort would've been better spent on something practical, such as distributing mosquito nets in Africa. She had always felt that it was better to save lives than afterlives.

Bill cast an eye upon her. "Now it's your turn."

She hesitated. Something about this situation was holding her back.

He moved the MRE away from her. "No food until you share your story."

His smile told Ainsley that it was good-natured. She decided to give him the abbreviated version. "Okay, I came here to find a gemstone. There've been a lot of twists and turns. I was told that the guy who has it went to Muk Holgoi."

He nodded sagely, as though that's exactly what he'd expected. "There are a lot of gemstones in Mongolia."

"This one is apparently very special. It's a moonstone."

"What's the trader's name?"

"I can't remember, but I wrote it down. The names here confuse me."

The missionary slid the packet of pasta over to Ainsley. As she devoured the food, Bill told her about Mongolian naming practices. In the twentieth century, when the people were still under the thumb of the Soviets, Mongols sometimes took Russian names like Alexander or Sasha. Occasionally they were given mixed names like *Ivaanjav*, which was a combination of the Russian *Ivan* and the Tibetan *-jav*. People with political passion might even name a child *Octyabr* (after the October Revolution) or *Seseer* (USSR).

"But the most amusing is the name *Melschoi*," he said.

"Why?"

"It's an acronym. It's the first letters of Marx, Engels, Lenin, Stalin, and Choibalsan."

"So nobody born after 1990 has that name," she said.

"That's right," Bill said. He was looking at her oddly. "Ainsley, do you believe in God?"

She paused. "I believe in a ... supreme being."

"Have you ever considered becoming part of the Church of Jesus Christ and Latter Day Saints?"

Ainsley smiled. "I haven't."

"I can tell you'd be excellent in the field."

"I'm not interested, but thank you."

Bill shrugged, as though he'd known the outcome. "Well, I had to try."

"Of course you did."

Ainsley set aside her empty pasta packet. Her stomach felt halfway sated for the first time all day. "So this man with the gemstone. His name is...." She reached into her bag and pulled out the small notebook where she'd jotted it down earlier in the day. "Tumenbayar."

"Tumenbayar."

"Yes."

The old Mormon thought about it. "Curious, I don't think I've heard that name."

A horn sounded outside. Bill craned his neck to see out the window. "It is your lucky day. Yalgesh has arrived."

———

Ainsley shot to her feet and went over to the open window and looked out. A muddy black Jeep had just pulled up. It looked like it had driven around the world four times.

A man in a sunhat had stepped out from behind the wheel. He was stocky and his mannerisms were intense. His back was held to her.

"That's the guy?" she said. "The one going to Muk Holgoi?"

The Mormon nodded. "Yalgesh comes by once a week. If you'd arrived even an hour later, you would've been stuck here for a very long time."

"That was lucky."

"Help me up, please, so I can walk you out."

The old man extended his arms, and Ainsley helped pull him to his feet. They went down the hallway and outside.

In the late afternoon sunlight, they approached the driver. He was bent over in the dirt, touching his toes.

"Yalgesh," said the Mormon.

The driver lifted himself up, revealing his face. Ainsley felt her breath taken away.

He wasn't Mongolian at all. He was Caucasian.

"Hi Bill," he said.

"I got one for you."

Yalgesh looked Ainsley up and down. "You're travelling to Muk Holgoi?" His voice carried a curious mix of accents that she couldn't pin down.

"Yes."

His eyes took in her bag. "Where's your luggage?"

"This is it."

He sucked his teeth. Ainsley noticed that his green eyes were sharp and intelligent. A forest of short bristles covered his face like a carpet of tiny spikes. "You have some money?"

"I do." Ainsley replied.

"How much?"

"How much do you want?"

Yalgesh grinned. "It's flexible pricing."

Ainsley crossed her arms. If he was going to play games, she would do the same. "How about a dollar an hour?"

That grin stayed put. "Ah, the special economy pricing. For that price, we tie a rolling chair to the back of the jeep."

Bill cleared his throat. "If I may share my opinion—"

Yalgesh turned to him. "Of course, Bill, I'm always waiting for you to interrupt."

"It's a sixteen-hour drive," said the Mormon.

"And overnight," added Yalgesh, holding a finger up. "That doubles the danger."

"Why do we have to drive overnight?" said Ainsley.

Yalgesh sprayed his fingers towards the abandoned structure. "Because who wants to sleep here? Not me!"

"What if she gives you fifty dollars?" Bill said.

He waved it off. "Pah. You know how dangerous it is!"

"We really could wait until morning," Ainsley said again.

Yalgesh ignored her. "I insist on one hundred dollars."

"No," she said.

Yalgesh pulled his keys out of his pocket. "I wish you a very pleasant day."

"Sixty," she said.

"One hundred."

"That's not how negotiations work, Yalgesh. You're supposed to say ninety."

He rolled his eyes. "Ninety."

"Seventy."

"Eighty," he said.

"Seventy-five. Plus dinner because I don't have any food."

The driver nodded once, a quick jerk of the head. The game had been played. "Well done, American."

They shook hands. He took Ainsley's bag and placed it in the trunk of his Jeep, between a pair of large blue coolers.

That's when Molotov strolled over with his backpack and threw it at Yalgesh.

Alarms went off in Ainsley's head. "Wait, he's coming too?"

"It seems so," said Bill.

"I don't trust him."

Yalgesh lowered his voice. "I don't trust him either. But he pays." He said something in Russian to Molotov. The skeevy guy thrust him a wad of cash.

"Is there anybody else?" said the driver.

"No," said Bill. "Me and two others are waiting to go east."

"Sorry. Maybe Kharjool arrives tomorrow."

Nearby, Molotov spat on the ground, wiped his mouth on his sleeve. Then the Russian wandered a short distance away and turned his back. Ainsley saw a yellow stream of liquid begin to hit the dirt at his feet. She quickly turned to Bill.

"You've been a big help," she said.

"That's because somebody helped me," the missionary replied. "Now you help somebody else."

Ainsley looked at him as though coming to a great realization. "That's how they do things here."

Bill raised a finger. "It's how things *should* be done everywhere."

"Thank you," she said.

They shook hands. Meanwhile, Molotov had slid into the front seat. Yalgesh chased him out with a rolled-up magazine. The skeevy Russian reluctantly entered the back.

"Please," said Yalgesh, gesturing to the passenger seat. "For the woman."

Ainsley glanced at the Russian in the backseat. His hard

little eyes rolled around in his skull until they fixed themselves on her. Then his face twisted into a sneer.

"Please don't remind him of that," she said.

Ainsley drew a deep breath, brushed off the front seat of the jeep, and slipped inside. She pulled the door shut. Behind her, the Russian smelled like old cigarettes and vodka. Ainsley discreetly placed her fingers over her nose.

Yalgesh slipped inside and started up the motor. A minute later, the vehicle jerked forward.

Ainsley looked in the rearview mirror. As the deserted airbase grew smaller behind her, she saw the missionary waving goodbye to her.

For a moment, she felt utterly alone.

CHAPTER TWENTY-NINE

Nighttime, five hours later.

Yalgesh drove with his right hand on the steering wheel. The left hand twiddled a coin between his knuckles.

The jeep rolled at a modest speed across the pitch-dark landscape. They were supposedly following a road, but it was more like the mere suggestion of one.

Ainsley had grown tired of staring at the high beam headlights strafing the small rocks and small ditches. She looked over at the driver. His face barely lit by the dash-board, Yalgesh's pupils flicked left and right, scanning the road.

"Do you want me to take over?" she said.

He sucked on the inside of his cheek. "No. Only I drive."

Behind them, Molotov was snoring loudly, passed out across the seat. Ainsley's fingers knitted themselves together in her lap. "Yalgesh, I thought you were Mongolian when I first heard your name."

"I'm Mongolian in my heart," he said. "You don't have to be born here to feel it. The steppe has always called me."

"Where are you originally from?"

"I am from twelve different countries. My parents were part of a religious group and we moved a lot."

"But originally what country?"

Yalgesh looked at her. "You have a lot of questions."

"We have sixteen hours together."

"So you're going to question me for sixteen hours?"

That was a good point. Ainsley admitted that he had the right to remain silent, if he wanted. Yalgesh was a driver, after all. He was probably tired of answering questions from tourists, week in, week out.

"Sorry," she said. "I'll be quiet."

"Thank you."

Yalgesh turned up the music. It was a pop song that had taken the world by storm the previous year. It should've been surprising to hear it out here, in the middle of central Asia, but it wasn't. Nothing about the modern world really surprised Ainsley anymore. It never seemed to make any sense.

The driver's hands beat a rhythm on the steering wheel, and his off-key voice reached in vain for the high notes. When the song ended, Yalgesh pulled a cigarette from his pocket and put it in his mouth but didn't light it.

"I'm was born in Afghanistan," he said, "and I'm not just a driver."

So much for silence. "What else do you do?" she said.

"I'm a trader."

"What do you trade?"

"I find fossils and sell them to the Chinese."

Ainsley ran her tongue around the inside of her mouth and looked out the passenger window. Trading fossils was related to trading gemstones. She decided to play it cool.

"That sounds fun," she said, keeping her voice flat and unimpressed.

"Yes, it is. Very fun. See, I find these things that are

millions of years old. Then I clean them, make some calls, and drive to the south border. There, I sell them for money."

Ainsley affected a bored demeanor. "So you must be really rich."

"No," he said, "that will only happen if I discover a whole skeleton. So far, only skulls."

"How much do the Chinese pay for a skull?"

"My biggest sale was nine thousand dollars. I lived on that for one year."

"You must know a lot of buyers."

"Oh, definitely."

Ainsley decided to cast her net. "I'm looking for somebody in Muk Holgoi."

He laughed. "There are two thousand people in Muk Holgoi."

"Oh."

They didn't speak for a while. "Tell me who it is," he said.

"I thought you didn't want to talk."

"No," he said, "you're right. I don't."

Yalgesh turned the radio back up. This time, it was a nineteen-eighties British New Wave tune. The singer was crooning how you want her, and she wants you, but no one ever was to blame. It took Ainsley back to old times.

The driver reached under his seat, removed a bottle of vodka, and took a deep swig from it. Then he put the bottle between his legs and lowered the music.

"I liked that song," said Ainsley.

"I want to know who you're looking for."

"Why?"

"No reason."

"Do you want to help me find him?"

"No."

"Then why do you want to know?"

"Because I'm curious."

"Look, if I tell you his name, and if you know him—then you have to help me find him."

Yalgesh shot her a dirty look, then turned the music back up. Ainsley looked out the darkened window. She knew it wouldn't take much longer. The fish was slowly reeling itself onto the boat.

Finally, he snapped the music off again. "Okay, I promise to help."

Ainsley tried not to smile. "I don't want your help, Yalgesh."

"Why not? You have too many friends in Mongolia?"

Ainsley shook her head. "I don't know if I can trust you."

He grew visibly upset. "You are driving with me, in the middle of the night, alone. If I wanted to hurt you, I could do it. Especially with him." He jerked a thumb towards the sleeping Molotov.

That was true. "Are you sure you want to know?"

"Yes."

She drew another deep breath, stretched out her hands on her thighs. "The man I'm looking for is ... Santaboryum."

Yalgesh thought about it. "I don't know this person. It doesn't even sound Mongolian."

"Correct. I made it up to see what you would say."

To her surprise, Yalgesh laughed. He shook a finger at her. "Very good, American. I like you."

"The man's name is Tumenbayar."

Her driver grew very quiet and serious. Ainsley realized that he was trying to look at her face.

"You said Tumenbayar."

"Yes."

"He is Mongolian."

"Yes."

"I know this man."

CHAPTER THIRTY

Ainsley heart leaped into her throat. "How?"

Yalgesh lifted the vodka to his mouth, took another swig, then put it back on the floor. "Tumenbayar is my competitor."

That was the best news Ainsley had heard in days. Two rival traders, vying with one another.

"Then it should be easy for you to find him."

"But I don't want to help you," he said.

Ainsley sank back into her seat. "So you are not a man of your word."

Without warning, Yalgesh suddenly slammed on the brakes. The jeep shuddered to a halt. Behind them, Molotov rolled into the back of the front seats, then mumbled something in groggy Russian.

"You," Yalgesh said, pointing a finger at the roof of the jeep, "did not let me finish my statement."

"When?"

He hitched a thumb backwards to indicate earlier. "When we were having the discussion."

That was ludicrous. Ainsley wasn't in the habit of cutting

people off, let alone the man who was singlehandedly driving her across the darkened fields of Mongolia while a leering rapist slept in the backseat. She was looking for allies, not enemies.

She feigned regret. "I'm very sorry for not letting you finish. Can we keep driving?"

He jabbed a finger towards her. "To get my help to find Tumenbayar, it will require something more."

A shiver ran down her belly, and Ainsley closed her legs. "What, exactly?"

He ran his fingers together. "Money."

Ainsley relaxed. She was expecting something much worse.

"Okay," she said, reaching into her bag and finding the envelope with the cash from Gantig. "How about fifty."

"Dollars?"

"Yes."

She handed Yalgesh a wad of bills. She watched him count them off.

"It's good," he said, pocketing the money.

There was a short, weird sound from the backseat. Ainsley turned her head. Molotov had thrust his hand out and his beady eyes were flicking between her face and her bag.

"No," she said firmly.

He lunged forward. Yalgesh whapped Molotov, over and over, with his right fist and elbow, all the while yelling the guy in broken Russian. The man shrunk back and covered himself in a blanket, hiding his face.

"Molotov is a dog," Yalgesh said, settling forward again. "You have to always be strong with a dog, or he take advantage."

Ainsley reached down and pulled her seat as far forward as it could go. "How much longer to Muk Holgoi?"

"Maybe eight hours." The driver took another pull from the vodka bottle, wiped his mouth, then shifted into first gear.

"Are you sure you should be drinking?" said Ainsley.

He looked at her as if she were stupid. "Of course I am sure. How else can I tolerate such a boring drive?"

"We could talk," she said.

"I don't like to talk with women."

He was trying to keep a straight face, but he couldn't quite manage it. "You're an asshole."

"Oh I know."

"I don't believe you anyways. You're a talker."

Yalgesh laughed. "You're right. I talk with anybody. I talk too much."

"Then talk to me about Tumenbayar."

Yalgesh thought about it. Then he handed her the vodka bottle. "Okay, American. Keep this away from me until we arrive."

Ainsley rolled down her window and tossed it out into the night.

"What?" said Yalgesh. "That was my vodka!"

"I know," she said. "But I just gave you fifty extra dollars, Yalgesh. With that, you can buy ten more bottles of vodka when we get to Muk Holgoi."

"But—"

She cut him off. "Now talk."

———

For the next half hour, Yalgesh treated Ainsley to a spoken autobiography.

Yalgesh had come from an odd family that had caravanned around central Asia for years. As a young man, he'd studied archaeology at Cambridge University, even doing part of a Ph.

D. before dropping out to pursue a more exciting life as a fossils trader in Asia.

Ainsley listened, waiting for the occasional place to interject. There weren't many of those. Yalgesh reminded her of the grad students that she had known back home. All would-be professors, every one of them, loved to run their mouths—especially the men.

He described for Ainsley how the traders worked. He described how he'd been busted in Western Europe for importing saber-toothed tiger skulls, which is when he went rogue. Yalgesh moved to Mongolia permanently, found work as a driver—which was the perfect cover—and began using the Chinese as middlemen.

"My dream," he said, "is not just to find the whole skeleton. My dream is to find ... the big one."

"What's that?"

"The T-Rex."

He explained that it happened more often than people thought. Bits of Tyrannosaurus Rex remains were unearthed pretty often in Mongolia. But millions of years of rainfall, earthquakes, alluvial flow, and other geologic events made finding a full skeleton nearly impossible.

"That's going to be a tall order," said Ainsley.

His reply was glum. "We all need to have dreams."

"What about Tumenbayar?"

Yalgesh explained that Tumenbayar had started out in the fossils game, but he'd switched over to precious stones and rare minerals. They were easier to transport and often more lucrative. Though the two were no longer direct rivals, he wasn't sure that Tumenbayar had entirely left the field.

"If Tumenbayar found a rare fossil," Yalgesh said, "I'm sure he would steal my contacts and cut me out. So, no, I don't trust him."

"Why is he at Muk Holgoi?"

"He works there."

"As a gemstone trader?"

Yalgesh shook his head no. "He's a geological engineer. He trades on the side."

Ainsley fell silent as Yalgesh continued describing the intricacies of the fossil trade. He only stopped talking when he noticed the snoring coming from Ainsley's side of the car.

CHAPTER THIRTY-ONE

Hours later, Ainsley jerked awake. They were on a road—not a semblance of one, but an actual gravel road. A large truck had just passed them heading the other way.

Behind her, Molotov was asleep, mouth open. To her left, Yalgesh smiled at her, bleary-eyed.

"What time is it?" she said.

"Eight o'clock in the morning."

"You must be tired."

"Very tired. But we are almost there."

Outside the window, a sliver of orange had appeared on the eastern horizon.

"There," he said, "look."

He gestured straight ahead. A small control tower stood at the side of road. A tall fence—the first Ainsley had seen in this country—stretched out to the left and the right. A pair of yellow arms blocked vehicles in both directions, and beneath each arm lay a set of nasty iron spikes.

Yalgesh came to a stop at the end of a line of vehicles waiting for admittance. "Always traffic here," he said.

Ainsley sat up in her seat, smoothing her hair in the visor mirror. "When was the last time you came here?"

"Two weeks ago."

"Maybe they tightened security since then."

"Mostly it depends on the guard that is working. I know all of them."

As they crawled towards the small tower, Ainsley spotted a sign posted in the ground that read *Muk Holgoi Mining Area: An Excovane Property*, followed by the usual warnings. Beneath, the same message was written in Mongolian, Russian, and Mandarin.

"Let me do the talking," Yalgesh said.

A small snort escaped Ainsley's nose.

Yalgesh looked at her. "Is something funny?"

"You were talking *for hours* last night."

The fossil trader looked hurt. "Yes. You even fell asleep while I was talking."

"It was three o'clock in the morning," she said.

At last they pulled up alongside the guard tower. A guard stepped out, dressed in a crisp quasi-military uniform. He was Mongolian. He and the driver exchanged words.

"He wants your identification," said Yalgesh.

Ainsley handed over her passport. Yalgesh slipped a few tugriks inside of it and handed it over.

The guard went into the tower, scanned the passport into some kind of device and brought it back and handed it over. His face betrayed nothing of the bribe.

In the backseat, Molotov rolled down his window and blatantly handed the man a wad of banknotes. The guard nodded and lifted the yellow arm.

They entered Muk Holgoi.

———

As they rolled onto the mining property, Yalgesh said, "Think of Muk Holgoi like it's an independent kingdom."

"So it's like the Vatican," said Ainsley.

"Yes, exactly."

"A state within a state."

He nodded. "Excovane makes their own rules."

Ainsley stared out the window. The flat, brown landscape was littered with piles of scrap and small hillocks of dirt. A row of twenty empty semi-trucks was arrayed at the side of the road. Just beyond that stood an enormous earth mover, its wheels as high as a two-story building. It was the same size and shape as the brontosauri that had wandered this land millions of years ago.

"Hold on," said the driver.

Yalgesh suddenly twisted the wheel and drove the Jeep off the road, over the flat ground, and up onto a berm. Ainsley tightly clutched the handle on the ceiling. The vehicle was flying along the top of the berm.

He rolled down Ainsley's window.

"Look!" he said, pointing down with his finger.

Ainsley stuck her head out the window and looked down. Below them was an enormous open pit mine. It was at least two kilometers across and was ringed in scalloped rows that resembled terraced gardens. An access road led down around the outside edge.

"The Oyut deposit!" shouted Yalgesh. "Copper and gold! It's one of the biggest in the world!"

"How much do they pull out?" she shouted.

"I don't know," he said, "but it will operate for over a hundred years."

He yanked the wheel back, and the Jeep dropped off the berm, rumbled across the landscape, and arrived back on the road in a spray of pebbles. He rolled her window up.

"You really didn't need that vodka," Ainsley said, relaxing her grip.

Yalgesh wiped his forehead. "You're probably right."

Ahead, on the horizon loomed a complex of industrial structures. "That is the main area," said Yalgesh. "We're going to stop at the visitors' office to get badges. Did you make an appointment?"

"No," she said.

"Then they might force you to take a tour."

The jeep rolled up to a Quonset hut. Yalgesh shut off the engine. The three of them stepped out of the vehicle and went into the structure.

———

Ainsley found herself in a small welcome room. At a modern welcome podium stood a young Mongolian woman dressed in blouse, skirt, and heels, one finger scrolling on her phone. Big washes of ambient chillout music played overhead.

She noticed the visitors and quickly stowed the phone inside the podium. A white toothy smile appeared on her face. "Welcome!"

Then she recognized Yalgesh. The smile vanished. "Yalgesh."

"Hello, honey."

She threw a yellow badge at him. Behind them stood Molotov. She spoke to him in Russian. He grunted a response. She threw another yellow badge at him.

Then she turned back to Ainsley. "From where do you come?" Her accent was light and almost singsong.

"The U.S."

"Oh I see. So the tour begins in a few minutes."

"I'd prefer not to take a tour," Ainsley said.

"I'm afraid you must."

Ainsley pulled out her biggest whopper and decided to see if it would float. "But I'm a journalist."

"Did you contact the public relations department?"

"Yes, but they didn't return my email."

The greeter shook her head. "Then you have to take the tour."

"Really?"

"Yes."

Ainsley reluctantly filled out the necessary forms. The greeter handed her a green badge and gestured to the middle of the Quonset hut. "We have an introductory video that will begin shortly."

"Thank you."

Ainsley turned to Yalgesh. "Give me your keys."

"Why?"

"I need to know that you're going to introduce me to Tumenbayar when this is done."

He looked disgusted. "No."

Ainsley instantly turned to the greeter. "Miss, I would like to report a crime. This man—"

Yalgesh shoved his keys into her hand. "Take them."

Ainsley smiled sweetly. "Thanks."

The greeter was a step behind. "There was a crime?"

Ainsley fumbled for a recovery. "I mean, it's a crime that you don't have more visitors. This looks impressive!"

The Mongolian woman relaxed. "Oh yes, thank you."

"What time will the tour finish?"

"At one o'clock."

Ainsley turned to Yalgesh and pointed her finger towards the floor. "Meet me here then."

CHAPTER THIRTY-TWO

The tour guide arrived shortly. He was an older Mongolian man with slumped shoulders, small potbelly, and tired face. He wore a red Excovane polo shirt and gray slacks and new boots.

In the waiting area stood a pair of Chinese couples. Ainsley watched how the two men stood with legs planted far apart in classic power stances. They seemed like professional colleagues. Their female spouses wore Coach purses slung over their shoulders and held themselves with spines erect. The quartet carried themselves as though they were kings and queens of the world. Ainsley knew why.

Their culture was rising.

Ainsley looked down at herself. She felt acutely embarrassed by her own dirty clothing, the sweaty filth that had dried under her arms, the stubbly hair sprouting on her legs. Her own condition could be explained, but she couldn't help but feel a touch of shame. She wondered if other people around the world sometimes felt this way in front of the Chinese.

But she hadn't taken this job to look pretty.

The guide greeted them, first in Mandarin, then in English. He distributed yellow hardhats, then led them outside to an official Excovane van.

Climbing into the back seat, Ainsley felt tired. The five hours of car sleep she'd managed to get wasn't going to cut it. Plus, she was hungry. Yalgesh had given her a few pieces of dried beef, but that had been nine hours ago.

Ainsley had no patience for this tour, but there was no choice. She'd been too tired to complain or think of a better way. She strapped on her seatbelt and hoped for the best.

The van carried them to the berm overlooking the open pit mine. The five passengers left the van and assembled at the lip of the massive excavation. Ainsley looked down once again on the concentric design, the tiny trucks climbing the spiraled rings.

The tour guide explained the site in Mandarin. Then he turned to Ainsley. "Mines like this one bring billions of dollars to Mongolian economy. The GDP increase fifteen percent every year. Inflation increase twenty percent every year. You know Ulaanbataar?"

"Yes, I do," said Ainsley.

"You see KFC, Louis Vuitton, Versace?"

"I did see them."

"Okay, so you know. But, I tell the problem. We need China to buy. It's because we have no ocean, no port, no big rivers, no infrastructure. China has that. So we sell to them." He nodded towards the Chinese tourists. The expression on his face said everything—respect mixed with jealousy.

Ainsley's stomach growled. "Excuse me, but are we going to eat?"

He shook his head. "We eat later."

"Is there a place to buy some food right now?"

"No."

They returned to the van. Ainsley couldn't disguise her

misery as they drove to another part of the tour. The guide must've noticed, because he stopped translating his thoughts into English. She guessed that he viewed her as a lost cause.

Next, they arrived at one of the mine's processing facility. The five tourists stepped out, donned their hardhats on command, and followed the guide into the plant. As they moved through the cavernous space, the guide explained the chutes and bins, the process of extraction. He occasionally translated into English, but stopped when it became clear that Ainsley was barely paying attention.

Ainsley paid no attention.

Outside the plant, the tour guide approached her. "Are you okay?"

"I'm just tired," she said. "And to be honest, I didn't really want to take this tour."

"Oh."

She felt bad saying it so honestly. At that moment, Ainsley noticed a group of horses standing in the dirt a short distance away from the factory.

"Horses?" she said. "You have *horses* here?"

"They belong to Excovane," he replied.

"Are they used in mining?"

The tour guide shook his head. "No."

"What are they used for?"

He shrugged. "Here, everybody has horses. We don't even think about it."

Irritable, Ainsley switched topics. "Okay, so where are we going next?"

"Tevan Tolgui," he said. "It's new pit. We extract the coal, the stoking coal. It is ingredient in steel."

Try as she might, Ainsley couldn't summon any interest in that. "Is it possible to let me finish the tour early?"

The guide grew curt. "No."

In the van, Ainsley slipped into the back seat again, miserable. When they arrived at the coal pit, she didn't even get out of the vehicle. She watched the four Chinese tourists follow the tour guide towards the mine.

Then she passed out.

Ainsley jerked awake an hour later as the others reentered the vehicle. She caught the scent of carbon clinging to their clothing.

She stayed silent as the van arrived at its final stop, a set of boxy gray office buildings with thin vertical slits of windows. It looked like a prison. "These are the Muk Holgoi offices," said the guide. "We are going to see where the engineers work."

Ainsley's ears pricked up. Yalgesh had said that Tumenbayar was an engineer.

The five of them exited the van and followed the guide into the complex. It was not at all different from a Western business office. Clean linoleum, overhead florescent lights, coffee machine. Very functional. A woman at the front desk greeted them.

Ainsley followed the guide through a large open-plan office filled with low cubicles. The engineers were mostly Mongolian, with a smattering of white Australian faces here and there. The workers wore rugby shirts with orange, black, and silver stripes. That was the only obvious sign of Australian culture in the building.

The tour guide explained the setup as they moved through the room. "In this place they calculate many things, very complicated."

"I have a question," said Ainsley.

"You do?" he said, surprised.

"I'm looking for someone who works here, a geological engineer. I want to know if he is in this room."

The tour guide looked unsure. "Maybe I know him. What is his name?"

"I don't want to meet him," she said, "but his name is Tumenbayar."

The guide nodded. "I know him. He's over there."

Ainsley followed his finger towards a lanky man in a rugby shirt sitting in a cubicle with low walls. He wore his long hair in a ponytail and a pair of expensive headphones over his ears. His eyes indicated that he was deep in concentration. On his screen was a three-dimensional model of a substrate complex. She could see columns of data analytics on the left and right sides of the screen.

Sensing that he was being discussed, Tumenbayar looked up from his screen. For a moment, he locked eyes with Ainsley.

She quickly looked away. "Thank you," she said.

The engineer's eyes followed Ainsley as she moved away and out of sight.

CHAPTER THIRTY-THREE

At five o'clock that afternoon, Ainsley and Yalgesh ventured into the Golden Yak pub.

There were four different pubs on the Muk Holgoi property, all of them run by Australians. Yalgesh had recommended this one, because it was known as the hangout for engineers.

"What are the chances we'll see Tumenbayar?" said Ainsley.

"The chances are high," he replied. "There is nowhere else to go after work."

Entering the pub, Ainsley let her eyes adjust to the dimness. It felt like walking through a portal to a different universe. Australian football and rugby played on the television screens. The walls were decorated with murals of boxing kangaroos. Mongolian servers passed them carrying plates of fish and chips and pints of yellow frothy lagers.

They were seated at a hightop table with a clear view of the door. After they'd ordered, Yalgesh turned to her. "So what did you learn on the tour?"

"That I hate tours," she answered. "But I already knew that."

He yawned and stretched. "I should get a job on this property. This place is a gold mine."

"Yeah, I'm sure it is."

"But I mean it literally. There are millions of ounces of gold under our feet. This will change the world's gold reserves, if they can get it out."

Their fish-and-chips arrived, and Ainsley tore into the plate like a woman dying of hunger. She hadn't seen a fish on a plate in weeks. It just wasn't served in Mongolia.

Yalgesh watched her inhale the food. "Hey, it's already dead. It's not going to swim away."

"I want another," she said.

"Then order one."

Ainsley ordered a second plate. His eyes on the door, Yalgesh lowered his pint of beer. "He's here. Behind you. Don't look."

Ainsley turned around anyways. The pony-tailed geological engineer had just entered the pub.

Tumenbayar.

With him were two other men, probably engineers. All three still wore their orange, black, and silver rugby shirts. She guessed there was no point in changing if there was nobody to impress.

Yalgesh waved him over. Tumenbayar walked over with a hint of a smile at the corners of his mouth. His long, loping stride made him look like a wolf ready to pounce. They greeted each other in Mongolian, slapped hands.

"We talk in English, okay?" said Yalgesh.

"Okay," said Tumenbayar. "I need to say something, you caused me so much trouble in the Dalkatkhan site."

"And yet who gives you the referrals?"

"But the question is, are you worth the trouble?"

Yalgesh smiled. "Only you can answer that question." He suddenly remembered his guest. "This is my friend, um—"

"Ainsley," she said, sticking out her hand.

The geological engineer looked her up and down. "I saw you today. You're a tourist? A journalist?"

"Something in between," said Ainsley.

He slowly shook her hand, his face a caricature of suspicion.

"Why don't you sit with us?" said Yalgesh. "We have a lot to talk about."

"My colleagues—" the engineer started to say.

Yalgesh waved them off. "No, you can see them tomorrow. This woman"—he gestured to Ainsley—"is only here for one night."

The engineer seemed embarrassed by the sexual undertones. Ainsley decided to look past the comment. She was laser-focused on talking to Tumnebayar, no matter what it took.

"First one is on me," she said, pointing at the selection of draft beers.

Those were the magic words. "Give me one minute," he said.

Tumenbayar went over to his colleagues, spoke briefly, then shook their hands. He came back, set his bag down, and took another stool. He and Yalgesh started talking shop.

Ainsley watched the two men as they chatted. Both traders, one in fossils, the other in precious metals and gemstones. She wondered how much their two sidelines overlapped.

"Did you hear about Shim-chi-soo?" said Tumenbayar.

"At the border two weeks ago?"

Both men started laughing. Ainsley waited for them to explain the inside joke, but they didn't bother.

"How's your business going?" said Tumenbayar.

Yalgesh hung his head. "Oh, you know, I have some leads over in Kazakh area, but it's been getting harder. So many ninjas now."

"They're destroying the countryside."

"And my trade."

The waitress brought Tumenbayar a beer. Sipping it, he turned to Ainsley. "So what's your story?"

There was no point in tootsie-footing around the subject. "I'm here to talk to you," she said.

The engineer was startled. "Are you a headhunter? I told the last one that I didn't want to leave MolTolgoi—"

"No," said Ainsley, "I'm a gemstone detective."

He looked confused. "You're a gemstone detective."

"Yes," she said, "I find lost or stolen gemstones."

Understanding dawned on Tumenbayar's face. "So you know my other job."

"You're a stone trader."

"And you are here to ask me about a gemstone."

"I have a lot of clients here," she lied, "and I'm looking for several different stones."

Tumenbayar steepled his hands on the table. "How many?"

"Three," she said. Another lie.

"Describe them to me."

"The first two are the ones I care about." Ainsley took a deep breath and started to invent stories. "First, I'm looking for a jade in the shape of an octopus. It was imported here from Korea in the nineteenth century and my client is a private collector who thinks his maid stole it."

Tumenbayar shook his head. "An octopus? In Mongolia? You must be mad."

Ainsley laughed. "I told my client she was being stupid."

"Next one."

"Okay, second, I have a client who is looking for a large

three-point-four carat ruby in a distinctive irregular hexagonal cut."

The geologic engineer shook his head. "I have two rubies, but they're uncut."

Ainsley blew air out of her mouth in an exaggerated fashion. "Well, that's it. I guess I can leave."

At that moment, the waiter set down her second plate of fish and chips. The engineer leaned forward. "But you said there was three."

With knife and fork, Ainsley began cutting her fish. "Oh yeah. Well, the third is a moonstone. It's long, like a cylinder." She used her utensils to illustrate. "That's all I know."

Tumenbayar's face lit up. Ainsley tried not to smile. She'd hooked him.

"The moonstone," he stammered, "I think—I think I have that."

Ainsley feigned more interest in her food than in the conversation. "Oh wow, that's great."

"Who wants it?"

"A client in Ulaanbataar. He sold it a few years ago and regrets it."

Tumenbayar's long fingers tapped the tabletop. "Well, he will not pay the same amount he sold it for. I need to make money too."

"Okay," Ainsley said, shrugging.

"What is he willing to pay?"

She made a show of thinking about the price. "I think he said two hundred dollars."

Tumenbayar leaned back and laughed out loud, the mirth rippling across the skin of his face. Then he took another drink of his beer.

"What's so funny?" said Ainsley, still playing the innocent.

"Two hundred? It's this long!" He measured fifteen centimeters between his two index fingers.

"Yeah," she said, "but is it cloudy? How is it cut? That affects the value."

Tumenbayar regarded her coolly. "I could bring it here for you to see."

Ainsley shrugged. "Sure, if you want."

"It won't take long. I'll be back in fifteen minutes. Will you still be here?"

Ainsley looked at Yalgesh. "Only if he orders another beer."

Yalgesh raised his hand, gestured to the waiter. Tumenbayar leapt to his feet. "Okay, I will come back."

"Sounds good," said Ainsley.

They watched him leave the pub. When the door had swung shut, Yalgesh looked at Ainsley.

"You're good," he said.

"What do you mean?"

"Don't pretend to be so innocent," he said. "How much is that moonstone really worth?"

"You want the truth?" she said.

"Yes."

"By itself, not much. But it's possible that little moonstone"—she twirled a finger in the air—"could cost this company billions."

"Does Tumenbayar know that?"

She shook her head. "He has no idea."

"And you just offered two hundred dollars for it."

Ainsley grinned. "Yep."

A broad smile broke out across Yalgesh's face, and he clapped his hands together. "Oh, I love screwing my friends. How can I help?"

CHAPTER THIRTY-FOUR

A quarter hour later, Tumenbayar arrived back at the pub, out of breath. Ainsley noticed that he'd changed into a khaki utility shirt and jeans. The better to play the role of an outdoor man of adventure.

"I have it," he said.

The trader sat down on the stool once again. Ainsley and Yalgesh waited with arms crossed.

"Let's see it," said Yalgesh.

Tumenbayar looked at him. "Are you involved in this deal?"

"I'm her driver. And I led her to you."

Ainsley waved it off. "Be quiet. Let's see the moonstone."

The geological engineer lifted his bag from his shoulder and set it on the empty stool next to him. "Not yet. I want to know more about you, Ainsley."

She willed herself to remain patient. "What do you want to know?"

"Are you an independent gemstone detective?"

"No," she lied, "I work for a jewelers' collective."

"Where is this collective?"

"It doesn't have a location. It's international."

Tumenbayar regarded her curiously. "It's surprising that I haven't heard of you."

"Well, it's my first time in Asia," she said. That, at least, was the truth.

The stone trader seemed to accept that. "Okay, so you wanted to see the moonstone."

"Yes."

"The truth is that ... I don't have it." He lifted his palms to the air.

Ainsley felt her heart sink into her shoes. "Why?"

"I sold it a month ago."

Her eyes flicked over to his bag. "Then why did you bring that?"

The geological engineer stretched out, tried to appear casual. "No reason."

Ainsley knew what happened: This guy had changed his mind about selling the gemstone on the way over. Now he was going to try to renegotiate, build up its value, before changing his mind back. He was amateur.

"Open the bag and show it to us," said Yalgesh.

"No."

The driver grew insistent. "Open the bag, Tumenbayar."

"No—"

Suddenly Yalgesh snatched the bag off the chair, leapt off his stool, and ran to the far side of a table of four sunburned Australian men. They wore navy blue polo shirts and were nursing tall pints of lager.

"What've ya got there, mate," said one.

"Yalgesh!" shouted Tumenbayar, "don't open that—"

Ainsley watched as Yalgesh unzipped the bag and thrust his hand into it. His eyes lit up.

Alarmed, the Australians swiveled their heads back and forth, trying to suss out what was happening.

Tumenbayar launched himself across their table. The Australians leapt backwards, the drinks flying, glasses breaking, beer splattering.

"Give me it!" he shouted.

Just as the gemstone trader reached him, Yalgesh pitched the bag halfway across the room—

—into Ainsley's hands.

It was a great toss, well aimed. She suddenly found herself holding Tumenbayar's bag.

A short distance away, the two men had crashed to the floor and were rolling around, grappling, squeezing, slapping one another. It was ugly. Neither looked like he'd ever set foot inside a wrestling ring. It went from a struggle Yalgesh was keeping

Ainsley unzipped the bag and peered inside. Something was shining. She reached into the sack and felt around. She found a cylindrical object. It was long, cool, and hard.

She slowly pulled it out.

It was the moonstone.

She gasped at the gem. Not because of the color, which was fairly whitish and cloudy, but because of the cut. The long facets were beautifully delineated. Somebody in the nineteenth century had really taken the time to get it right.

Ainsley wasn't any expert in the East Asian gemstone market, but on the Western market, the piece was moderately valuable to a dealer. She guessed that somebody could probably get fifteen hundred dollars for it.

But according to Gantig, its civic value to the people of Zhakorum was enormous. Therefore, to Excovane, its hidden value was astronomical.

But Tumenbayar didn't know about any of that. To him, it was just a fairly nice moonstone.

On the floor, the two rival traders were finally pulled apart by restaurant staff. Each man got to his feet, straightened himself out. A busboy arrived with a mop and started cleaning the floor.

The four Australians whose table had been destroyed glared at Tumenbayar. "What was that about, mate?" one said.

"I'm very sorry," said Tumenbayar.

"I'm sorry too," said Yalgesh, "for *his* behavior."

The geological engineer dropped his head. "I lost control. I apologize. I will buy more beer."

That was all he needed to say, evidently, because the Australians picked up their stools and settled themselves at the table again. The waiter brought them a fresh round of lagers, and Tumenbayar handed him a fistful of tugriks. Ainsley guessed that fights were regular here, nothing for bystanders to get worked up about. Collateral damage was shrugged off.

On her stool, Ainsley placed the moonstone in the middle of their table and sat quietly. When Tumenbayar saw it, he seemed to deflate.

He sat down at the table and sighed. "So we will have a different conversation than I expected," he said.

"You lied to me," she said.

"I did."

She looked down at the moonstone. "It's a good cut. Very pretty."

"Yes, it is."

"Where did you get it?"

He shook his head and said nothing. That was what she'd expected. Traders never reveal their sources, because that could mean getting cut out of future deals. Tumenbayar wasn't a total amateur.

"I won't ask you to lie again," she said. "I just want to ask you one thing. Is this enough?"

Ainsley removed a pile of currency from her bag and slid

it across the table. She'd counted it out while he was out of the pub. It was half a million tugriks, which amounted to a little less than two hundred dollars. She was guessing that the mere sight of cash would be enough to turn him. In her experience, this little gambit worked quite well on venal people. They always reached for the money. They couldn't really help themselves.

Tumenbayar picked up the cash. Counted it. Then he set it back down again, crossed his arms, and thought about it.

Yalgesh stood on the opposite side of the table, just behind Ainsley. "Take the money, man."

"Why?" said Tumenbayar.

The driver started speaking in Mongolian. He was halfway fluent, but Ainsley could tell that he wasn't native. In fact, she could almost understand the conversation—Yalgesh seemed to be giving Tumenbayar a brief talk about opportunity costs.

Then again, she didn't know how much effort Tumenbayar usually went through to sell his gemstones. It was possible, but unlikely, that he received potential buyers here every week. In which case he would turn her down.

The gemstone trader caught her eyes. He tapped his finger on the table. "I want more."

She'd been expecting this. Ainsley reached into her pocket and removed another roll of currency. She slid it across the table to him. That was another half million tugriks. All together it was just under four hundred dollars.

"It's not enough," he said.

"It's more than enough."

"I can get three million tugriks for this."

Ainsley started to sweat. He was right. Though she was carrying a little more than that, she didn't want to hand that much over to him. It would leave her nearly bankrupt in the middle of Mongolia, and she had to save some for her return. She decided to pursue a different route.

"How many days a week do you work here, Tumenbayar?"

"I work six days a week."

"So you don't have many opportunities to travel."

"No," he said, "not anymore."

"So when do you sell these gemstones in your collection?"

He shrugged. "Whenever I can."

"Which is not very often."

"Well, buyers come to me."

"How many sales have you made in the last four months?"

Tumenbayar's eyes were glowing angry now. She realized that he was savvier than she'd given him credit for.

"I know what you're going to say, Miss—"

Ainsley cut him off. "Let me say it anyways. My offer will save you a lot of effort and expense in finding a potential buyer for this moonstone." She lifted her eyebrows in an expression of sympathy, as if she were letting him in on a secret that only they knew.

"But there's no reason for me to sell it right now."

"Do you really think there is a large number of collectors who would be willing to pay top dollar for that?"

"Yes."

"If so," she continued, "what are the chances that you will ever meet these people?" Ainsley held the engineer's eyes. "This isn't an emerald, a sapphire, a ruby, a diamond. This is just a moonstone. It's large, and it has an unusually attractive cut, but that's about it."

"No—"

"Don't deny it, Tumenbayar. Look." She lifted the moonstone up. "The color is pleasing but it's not clear. Clear stones get top dollar. And this end even has a slight green adularescence—"

"I don't know that word," he said.

"Adularescence?"

"Yes."

"It means sheen. The most valuable moonstones have a blue adul—um, sheen. And now look at this." Ainsley held the stone closer to him but didn't let go of it. "There is a pretty big centipede in the middle of the stone."

His brow furrowed as he studied it. "What is a centipede?"

"A tension crack. It looks like an insect with a lot of legs. Do you see it?"

The engineer squinted closely. Ainsley wasn't sure that Tumenbayar had ever really looked that closely at a gemstone, despite trading them. Maybe his clients weren't very educated in the field, or maybe they weren't very picky. She guessed that he probably sold to *nouveau riche* Chinese couples. There were a lot of Beijing wives who wanted pretty stones to put on the mantel above their new fireplaces.

"I think I see it," he said.

"But do you understand what I'm telling you?" said Ainsley.

The gemstone trader thought for a minute. "This client of yours—he regrets letting it go."

"Yes, he does."

"How much?"

"I can't measure his feelings."

"But he feels bad enough to hire you?"

"Apparently. He's what we call a hip pocket client."

"What is that?"

"Someone unimportant. I try to remember him while I'm looking for bigger deals. The octopus jade, for example, is worth at least twenty thousand dollars."

She was stacking her lies upon lies now.

"I see," said Tumenbayar.

A weird silence settled on the table. Ainsley decided to push for the sale. It was now or never.

"So one million tugriks," she said, glancing at the stack of currency. "That is double my initial offer. You can take it and save yourself a lot of stress. Or you can leave it. Which do you choose?"

Watching them, Yalgesh rolled an imaginary cigarette between his fingers and thumb. Ainsley could feel his anxiety. He really wanted his rival trader to get ripped off.

Tumenbayar turned his head to one side, a pained expression on his face. That meant that her tactics were working. Unfortunately, she knew, in many negotiations, one person must act as the aggressor and inflict a degree of pain upon the other. Ainsley was playing this role now.

Finally Tumenbayar laid his palms down on the table. He studied them for a long moment. Without looking up, he said:

"I accept."

Ainsley felt the relief wash across her. She'd been bearing the weight of this assignment for what felt like centuries. Now that the end was in sight, the world seemed lighter, airier, friendlier.

She reached her hand across the table. With obvious regret, the gemstone trader slowly grasped it. He held the handshake a moment longer than necessary, but his eyes couldn't meet hers.

Sighing, Tumenbayar pulled the tugriks off the table and stuffed them into his bag and zipped it shut. Ainsley took the moonstone and stowed it in her own bag and closed that too.

The deal was finished. Ainsley tried not to betray her happiness. With shining eyes, she looked back and forth at the two rival traders. "Do you guys want to have another beer?"

"No," said Tumenbayar, sliding off his stool, "I'm finished here. Thank you for your business." To Yalgesh he offered a narrowing of the eyes, and a small tip of the chin. Yalgesh tipped his chin in return. Ainsley imagined their rivalry would continue.

"I hope we can work together again sometime," she said.

The gemstone trader gave her half a smile, then moved across the pub and went out the door. It closed heavily behind him.

Ainsley exhaled and leaned back. She let her arms drop loosely at either side of her chair. She tipped her head backwards until she was looking at the ceiling.

"You got him," said Yalgesh.

"Boy, it feels good," she replied.

The fossils trader sat down next to her. "You're tough. If someone tried to bargain with me like that, I'd put my foot up their butt."

He kicked his foot into the air to emphasize his point. Laughing, Ainsley patted her face with a napkin. It came away damp. "Yalgesh, I hope nobody ever finds out how much Tumenbayar just potentially screwed his own company. That could cost him his job."

"Traders are like cockroaches. We always survive." Yalgesh giggled. "So where do you go now?"

"Back to Ulaanbataar. I'm finished."

"You want a ride?"

Ainsley looked at him. "Are you headed that way?"

"I could be. I don't have anywhere else to go. We can leave at eight in the morning."

"That would be great."

He lifted his phone. "Take a photo with me."

"Why?"

"Because you are a talented woman. And pretty. I want to remember you."

Ainsley reluctantly leaned her head towards his. They both looked at the phone in his outstretched hand while he snapped a photo.

"Thank you," he said.

The waiter brought two more beers. She lifted her glass. "To Tumenbayar."

"Cheers," said Yalgesh. They clinked glasses and drank. He watched her out of the corner of his eye.

CHAPTER THIRTY-FIVE

Deep in sleep, Ainsley didn't hear the dark figure creeping into her *ger*.

The night before, she'd rented a *ger* in the residential zone of Muk Tolgoi. The tent was one of twenty identical white domes, located close to the factory that she'd seen earlier that day, not even a three-minute drive down the road.

First, she'd taken advantage of the free showers, which were clean and spacious, even if they used recycled gray water. It smelled a bit rank, but she hadn't really cared. Ainsley herself had smelled like a month-old cat litter box. This had been her first chance to clean herself in almost a week.

There'd been no hairdryer, so she'd hurried back through the cold with wet tresses freezing against either side of her head. Inside her *ger*, she'd put the space heater on high and blasted it towards the single twin bed with its inflatable mattress. Then she'd thrown herself into the sheets, and honest to God it'd felt like the most luxurious thing Ainsley'd ever slept on.

Gripping the moonstone in hand, she'd plunged into a deep slumber.

Now, in the wee hours of the predawn, the dark figure stood at the foot of her bed.

"Ainsley," said the voice.

She jerked awake, rifling up like a shot in bed. "Who is that?"

The figure flipped on a headlamp. "It's me."

The bright light was shining directly on her. She held a hand over her eyes and squinted. "Yalgesh?"

"Yes," he said. "We have to leave."

She looked at her watch. "But it's only five-thirty. You said we were leaving at eight."

"Plans have changed. I think there's something going on."

"With who?"

"Tumenbayar."

That got her attention. "What are you talking about?"

"I don't think it's safe for you here. We need to go now."

Ainsley was still fuzzy-headed and didn't question him. She jumped out of bed and pulled on her shirt and her pants and her shoes and her jacket. Then she slung the bag over her shoulder.

Yalgesh stood there, looking at her.

"What?" she said.

He gestured to the bed. She turned. The moonstone was laying there on the blanket.

"I'm not good in the morning," she said, picking it up. Then she followed him outside.

The night winds were blowing cool from the north, and they walked down the road towards the factory.

"Tell what you know," she said.

"It's better if you don't know."

"Who did you talk to?"

"It's not important."

"But I would like to know. I'm trusting you."

Yalgesh fixed her with a stern look. "People here, at Excovane."

"But who?"

"Stop asking questions."

"Fine."

They walked in silence for a while. "Where is your jeep?" she said.

"Another question?"

"Come on," she said.

"It's at the factory."

"Why?"

"Because that is where I left it. Why do these questions not stop?"

Ainsley decided to shut her mouth. They arrived at the gravel parking area of the factory, where the jeep awaited them. Yalgesh shone his headlamp on the vehicle, then rushed over. "Oh no, no no no—"

Ainsley looked over. The tires were flat. He circled the vehicle and looked at the others. "Over here too."

"Can we pump them up again?"

"No," he said, "somebody cut them."

Ainsley crouched down at a tire and probed it with her finger. Sure enough, between the flaps of rubber, she found a long, clean, narrow slit. The product of a knife.

Yalgesh clutched the thinning hair on the side of his head. "I cannot believe this. I cannot believe this. Who could do this?"

"Is there another vehicle we can take?" she said.

"No, there isn't."

Ainsley stood there in the darkness, one hand clenched tight, the other resting on the hood of the jeep. "Could we ask somebody? Or buy one?"

"I don't think so." Then Yalgesh looked up. "I have an idea, but it is very difficult. I don't know if you want to do it."

"What?"

Yalgesh pointed to his left. "Yesterday did you see the horses there?"

"Yes," Ainsley replied hesitantly.

"You could take one and just ... go. Ride away."

The idea hit Ainsley like a bag of topsoil to the stomach. "I could steal a horse and ride away."

"Yes, you could."

"Right now?"

"Yes. There are so many horses, nobody cares."

Ainsley heard her voice pitch higher. "But where would I go? I can't ride a horse to Ulaanbataar."

"If you can get off the Muk Holgoi property," Yalgesh said, "I can meet you at the ruins of Baruun-hara. Do you know it?"

"No."

"It's used to be an archaeological site. Now it's empty."

This scheme sounded horrible, but she decided to listen. "How far is this Baruun-hara?"

"From the exit gate, it's maybe"—he wavered his hand back and forth—"I don't know, thirty kilometers."

"That's all?"

"It's not far on horse."

"How long will it take?"

Yalgesh thought for a moment. "I am not expert, but probably a few hours. If the horse runs, maybe two hours. If the horse walks, maybe six or seven."

"And how far is the exit gate from here?"

"Another two hours."

"So if I leave now I can be there by maybe ten o'clock am."

He nodded. "Then you wait for me there. Maybe I can get

one of the official vehicles but it's going to take a little time. So maybe I arrive at noon, maybe later."

Ainsley weighed her options. This could all be a big setup. The safe thing to do would be to diplomatically thank Yalgesh for his help, return to her *ger*, go back to sleep, and find a different ride in a few hours.

But Yalgesh had helped her immensely, and there was no evidence that he had anything but her best interest in mind. Plus his own tires had been slashed, which would cost him hundreds of dollars. The most obvious explanation was that Tumenbayar had had second thoughts about the sale and had resorted to very desperate measures to get it back.

Still, nothing could take away the fact that Ainsley now had the moonstone. And she had to admit that there was wisdom in simply getting the gemstone off the property as quickly as possible.

While she was thinking about it, a large Excovane security truck came roaring down the road, its white-and-red roof lights flashing. Ainsley felt a small tingle of horror pass through her body. After all, Gantig had warned her that the mining company had sent someone to look for her. She'd assumed that they didn't have her name—but it was impossible to know.

Maybe coming to Muk Holgoi had been playing with fire.

She and Yalgesh both waited as the vehicle passed. Then Ainsley made up her mind.

"I'll do it," she said.

"By horse?"

She drew a deep breath. "Yes. I hate horses but I feel like I have to get off this property as fast as possible."

"I'll help you find one," Yalgesh said. "Let's go quickly now."

"Do you want some money for the repair?"

"No, not until we leave to Ulaanbataar."

"I thought you were all about money," she said.

He smirked. "Maybe you have misjudged me, Ainsley."

She wondered what exactly he meant by that as she trailed him out of the gravel parking lot.

CHAPTER THIRTY-SIX

Ainsley followed the driver to the area near the factory where the herd of horses had been standing that afternoon.

"Hopefully they're still here," he said.

"Where would they go?"

"They go wherever they want," he replied. "They're free."

"So I'm going to literally steal a horse," said Ainsley.

The driver sighed. "I know in your country a horse is a luxury. But here a horse is like a cheap bicycle. It even costs the same."

She thought about it. "So it's like I'm borrowing a cheap bicycle for a while."

"And someone else will borrow it after you."

That was a good rationalization. Because horses were common here, taking a horse was a much smaller violation than it would be elsewhere. It fell into that gray area between theft and community property. Plus, if he was shrugging it off, then Ainsley shouldn't be too worried.

Meanwhile, the eastern horizon had begun to glow a deep purple. Ainsley could make out the dark shadow of the fossil trader as he walked in front of her. The dark shapes on the ground revealed themselves as rocks.

Then she saw a different shape. A short, stocky figure, with four legs and a long mane.

It was a horse. Standing alone.

Yalgesh approached the animal calmly, whispering quietly. He stroked it on the neck, the side, the haunch. Its tail swished. The horse wore a bit and a pair of reins was tied around its neck, but it had no saddle.

"This one looks good," said Yalgesh. "Come, I'll help you up."

Ainsley felt her legs turn wobbly, and she clutched her bag to her side. "I can't ride that one."

"Why?"

She pointed. "There's no saddle."

Yalgesh shrugged sympathetically. "You don't have any other choice."

They faced each other in the field, the layer of green turf beneath their shoes. The horse neighed impatiently.

"I really can't ride a horse," Ainsley answered.

He sighed impatiently. "And why not?"

"Because a horse threw me when I was a kid."

It was the truth. She'd been bucked off the back of a pony at summer camp back in middle school, and spent the next two months with her arm in a sling. Since then, she'd avoided the animals like the plague. Riding one bareback across a Mongolian landscape held about as much appeal as getting flayed with a barbed wire whip.

"You have to," he said.

"I can't," she said.

Yalgesh released the reins. "Then I'm going to fix my car."

The driver turned to walk back to the parking lot. The lights of the factory had winked on behind him, and Ainsley could hear the sounds of machinery starting up.

The tension had built up inside of her like a cone of lava. Ainsley knew she couldn't contain it.

The words erupted out of her throat before she even realized it.

"Will you help me get up?" she said.

Yalgesh stopped, came back to her, and put one arm across her shoulders. He gave her a side squeeze. "I'm happy. You will do well."

"I don't think so," she said.

In the growing light, Ainsley could see that the horse stood a little shorter than she did. A big mane of shaggy black hair hung from its neck like the tangle of an aging rock star put out to pasture.

She faced the animal's left side. She felt Yalgesh put his hands under her armpits. "Okay, one, two, and three—"

With his assist, Ainsley crouched, jumped, swung her right leg over the horse's back, and found herself suddenly astride the animal.

Yalgesh handed her the reins. "How does it feel?"

The gray mare stood calmly between her legs. "It feels okay."

"Do you have any questions?"

"How do I control it?"

"With your legs. Make a small kick and she will go."

"And to stop?"

"Pull back on these." He handed her the reins. "Also they will take you left and right. It's not hard. You don't have to run."

Ainsley felt her stomach fluttering. "So we meet in the ruins of Baruun-hara?"

The driver pointed to the west. "Just follow the road, and leave the property through the gate we came in. Then go to the mountain range."

"Is there a sign to find the site?"

He shook his head. "No signs. But there is a small mirror, hanging from a string." Yalgesh illustrated with his hands, making a twisting motion. "It turns in the wind. So you will see it flashing in the sun."

That was a remarkably low-tech solution to the problem of communication. Ainsley guessed that Mongolians had been using mirrors for centuries to mark territory on the steppe. She could only think of one problem.

"What if it's cloudy?" she said.

"This is Mongolia. It's never cloudy." Yalgesh patted the animal on the barrel. "See you later this afternoon."

He reached up with his hand to Ainsley, and she shook it. "Be careful," he said.

Then the fossils trader turned and walked away. Ainsley sat, alone on the horse, watching him go.

When he was out of sight, she took a deep breath. Then she lightly kicked either side the horse's barreled ribcage with her heels.

The animal sprang forward into a fast walk. Using the reins, she tugged it around until they were heading towards the road.

CHAPTER THIRTY-SEVEN

Two hours later, the day had dawned—and it was cloudy.

Ainsley had steered the horse a few hundred meters to the side of the road. One reason was that the horse seemed a little skittish of the rumbling of the trucks and maintenance vehicles driving by. Another reason was that Ainsley knew the drivers were noticing her. An American woman riding alone here was like an innocent white mouse moving across a field of rattlesnakes.

The horse moved at a steady trot, with only a bit of guidance needed—a tug to the left here, a pull on the reins there. Ainsley bounced on its back, occasionally high enough to land on the croup. Still, keeping her legs locked on the flanks made it mostly manageable.

So far, the only danger Ainsley faced was getting a sore butt. She was starting to wonder why she'd been so frightened of horses for so long.

As she moved on, the factory, the collections of vehicles, the heaps of geologic waste—all of it had gradually fallen away behind her. It almost felt as if she were out on the open steppe.

Finally she glimpsed the fence, a thin horizontal metallic line on the horizon. She could see the guard booth beneath the arched gate too. From here, it was the size of her pinky nail.

Ainsley stopped the animal and mulled her options. She doubted that the guard at the gate would take kindly to her riding a horse off the Muk Holgoi property. Plus, if it was true that Tumenbayar was looking for her—or if Excovane itself had learned her name and was looking for her—management might stop her on the way out.

The other option was to skirt the fence and hope for somewhere to pass over, under, or through.

She decided on the second option. The guard booth was at least a kilometer and a half away, too far for them to sight her, at least without binoculars. So Ainsley pointed the horse to the right, towards a distant portion of the fence, and spurred the animal in the ribs with her heels.

The gray mare began moving again. Twenty minutes of trotting later, and she arrived at the limit of Excovane property.

Ainsley studied the fence. It was an ordinary chain-link number, almost head high, with poles located every six or seven meters. The squares had been rotated forty-five degrees into a diamond pattern. She felt her spirits drop. Only wire cutters would peel that thing apart, and she wasn't exactly toting a pair of those across the open steppe.

In other words, it was an ordinary fence, the same type that had circled her elementary school playground as a kid. The type Ainsley had vaulted countless times in her rough-and-tumble tomboy youth. She wondered why Muk Holgoi had even bothered to erect it in the first place in this vast empty country. Perhaps to keep herders off the land.

Unsure of where to go, Ainsley tugged the horse to the right and began following the fence. She grew frustrated.

From atop the animal, she could look straight down onto the other side of the fence. So close, yet so far.

One gap in the fence. That was all she needed.

The small speck of the guard booth disappeared from sight behind her. Ainsley couldn't see or hear any trucks on the road either. She was invisible at this point.

She cursed Excovane under her breath. They'd maintained the fence well. Not even one portion that had been bent down, or torn apart.

Then Ainsley felt the ground grow slightly steeper beneath the horse's hooves. It wasn't her imagination; the grade had increased slightly. The hard-packed dirt had given way to loose sand.

Then she noticed that the fence was growing shorter.

Ainsley finally put two-and-two together. The fence wasn't actually growing shorter. It was getting buried by blowing sand.

When the fence was less than a meter high, Ainsley jumped off the animal. Reins in hand, she walked the horse up to the fence and measured it. The top of the fence reached the animal's elbow, that little knobby joint where the horse's leg joins the shoulder.

That was high enough. The horse could make it.

Ainsley easily stepped over the low fence. Then she turned and tugged on the reins.

"Come on," she said, "jump."

The gray mare didn't move. Ainsley pulled harder on the reins. The horse yanked its head back.

"Look how easy it is! I did it! You can do it too!"

The horse whinnied angrily. It didn't respond well to the hard sell, or the guilt trip.

There was only one possible solution. Ainsley vaulted back to the other side of the fence, then patted the horse on the muzzle.

"You," she said, "are going to jump this fence."

The horse's left eye looked sideways at her. Ainsley squinted back.

"It's not hard. You can almost step over it. Plus, I believe in you. Okay?"

The horse whinnied again.

Ainsley interpreted that as a yes. She leapt up, belly-flopped onto the animal's back, and swung her right leg around its rump. Then she scrambled up to a sitting position, took the reins, wheeled the animal around, walked about fifteen meters out, and turned the horse back towards the fence. She leaned down to the horse's left ear.

"You and me. One, two, three—"

She spurred the horse in the ribcage. It took off trotting towards the fence. As they approached—

—the horse suddenly stopped dead in its tracks.

"You are *not* holding up your end of the agreement, you bastard!" cried Ainsley.

She circled the horse back around to the same starting place. She whispered a few more sweet nothings into the animal's ear, stroked its crest, patted its withers. Then spurred it again with her feet.

The mare broke into another fast trot. And then it stopped again, just shy of the fence.

"Goddamnit," Ainsley said.

She circled the horse around for a third attempt. Ainsley knew she'd have to break the animal into a canter. That was smoother and faster than a trot.

Back at the starting point, Ainsley took a deep breath. She tensed her abdominals, then, mustering all her strength, kicked her heels into the mare's ribs.

"Go!" she shouted.

The horse went into another trot. Ainsley viciously kicked it a second time, and a third. The horse leapt forward like a scalded cat. Ainsley's legs locked around the flanks as her torso leaned backwards from the sudden acceleration.

This was a canter.

The fence grew larger. Ten meters, five meters. Ainsley spurred the horse again with her heels. She slapped its rump.

"Yah yah yah!" she shouted.

Two meters—

One meter—

The liftoff was so smooth she barely noticed that the horse had made the leap.

Then ... *boom*.

The horse touched down the ground on the other side. Airborne for a brief moment, Ainsley came down hard. She bounced, and the rebound sent her back up into the air—

—flying—

—she let go of the reins, her body pinwheeling through the air, tumbling, falling—

—until she landed flat on her back.

In loose sand.

Ainsley lay there in shock for a moment, just breathing. Finally she lifted her head. The horse was a short distance away, standing calmly as if nothing had happened.

She lifted her arms and looked at them in amazement.

They were intact.

Ainsley rolled onto her side and pulled herself to a sitting position. She waited for pain. Nothing. She'd been *so convinced* that she was going to hurt herself. That accident back in junior high had been a single piece of bad luck. Now she'd bounced off a horse again ... and lived to tell the tale. True, she might have a sore butt later, but nothing felt broken.

Junior high was a distant memory.

A good feeling stirred in the depths of her stomach like a little furry creature coming out of a deep sleep.

Ainsley Walker stood up. She wasn't scared to ride a horse anymore.

BARUUN-HARA

As Ainsley slowly crossed into the Gobi, she discovered that a desert didn't necessarily have to be made of sand.

She knew the dictionary definition of a "desert"—a region of the world that received less than 250 millimeters of precipitation each year.

But her mental images of deserts came mostly through media, the same ones we all have. Classic epics about English explorers in the Arabian peninsula, cartoons about the coyote and the road runner. As a child, she'd even travelled to Arizona with her father, before he'd passed on, and remembered seeing the desert there.

All of it carried a single color in her memory.

Brown.

But this desert, the Gobi, wasn't brown, or orange, or tan, or anything remotely close to that.

It was *green*.

The truth is that only a small percentage of the Gobi desert is composed of sand. Instead, grasslands make up the vast majority of it.

Atop her trotting horse, Ainsley marveled at the wide, flat

pan of scrubland, a plain carpeted by sporadic humps of low green grasses. Here and there, bleached rocks dotted the landscape like white soccer balls abandoned on a tattered pitch after a game.

It felt like crossing an enormous putting green.

The Muk Holgoi mining complex was situated on the northern edge of the Gobi, and the mountain range that Yalgesh had indicated was a bit further to the south. There wasn't a road in sight connecting the two. It wasn't needed. A vehicle could drive almost anywhere. A person could crawl, cartwheel, or somersault across the landscape.

The Gobi was open and free.

A movement to the left caught Ainsley's eye. A group of two-humped Bactrian camels were grazing. Her breath caught in her throat. These were the same animals that, centuries ago, pulled the caravans down the Silk Road. And she was passing them as casually as she might cruise past a hamburger joint in a strip mall back home.

Ainsley remembered reading about the Gobi, back during her first night in Ulaanbataar. She recalled seeing that the Gobi hadn't always been dry. Millions of years ago, it used to boast wet oases.

That's why dinosaurs had gone there.

Roy Chapman Andrews, the famous American explorer and zoologist, had found the first Proceratops dinosaur skull in the Gobi, back in the 1920s. Andrews' findings had been groundbreaking. He'd been the first, for example, to verify that dinosaurs laid eggs. He'd also found evidence of the ways that dinosaurs died—killed by sandstorms, or wounded by other dinosaurs while protecting their nests. There have even been enormous dinosaur footprints fossilized in the rocks.

In effect, this desert was a dinosaur cemetery.

But Ainsley didn't give a pterodactyl's ass about paleontology. She was focused on getting the moonstone back to the person who'd hired her.

To Gantig.

Ainsley felt the oblong gemstone in her pocket and wondered how he would react when he saw it. She imagined that he'd be surprised. He probably hadn't expected her to find it at all, even though he'd commissioned this wild goose chase.

The morning wore on. The clopping of the horse's feet, the slow back-and-forth of its gait, lulled Ainsley into a state of drowsiness. Her eyes slowly closed.

When she opened her eyes, she saw a basketball net. Right there in the middle of the open grasslands—a backboard and net, mounted forlornly on a wooden pole. She stopped the horse to look at it.

Her best guess was that a nomadic family must've built it, then left it behind after moving on. In this landscape, it looked as surreal as a melting clock or an elephant on leg-stilts.

Then she caught a flash of light in the corner of her eye.

It had come from the mountains. She kicked the horse; it started moving again. She kept her eyes fixed upon the range, waiting.

Another flash. There.

It had come from a small saddle, set between a pair of arabesque rock formations.

Baruun-hara.

Ainsley tugged the horse towards the site, the tension growing in her stomach. She'd been forced to make a last-minute decision about whether a fossils trader she'd known for barely twenty-four hours was telling the truth. She'd chosen to believe him.

If he'd been lying to her, she was in for a real problem.

———

An hour later, Ainsley arrived at the ruins on foot. She was leading her horse by the reins.

The old gray mare ain't what she used to be—maybe she'd been underfed, maybe she hadn't been used to carrying a human on her back. Whatever the reason, she'd pooped out.

No matter. Ainsley enjoyed the feeling of adventure on her feet, even in this brown, desolate portion of the mountainous desert. And there was life here, she'd learned, but you had to look for it. To the left, a gecko squeaked and skittered across the path. To the right, a black-tailed gazelle leapt quietly amongst the outcroppings. Up above, a herd of argali sheep sprinted along the steep slopes, running from an invisible predator. Ainsley admired their long, heavy, corkscrew-shaped horns that seemed to weigh nearly as much as their bodies.

By now, the sun was almost directly overhead. A stiff breeze snapped against Ainsley's face. She'd left nearly six hours ago and the water that Yalgesh had given her was halfway gone.

Then Ainsley finally spotted it.

A small mirror, no bigger than one in a makeup compact. It was hanging by a thin nylon string from a wooden plank that had been jerry rigged inside the crook of a boulder. The object twirled and twisted in the wind, sending its reflection around the world.

"All right, Yalgesh," she said, "I'm here."

She looked for a place to tie the horse's reins, but there wasn't any. Just some sparse brown ground cover and some low boulders. Therefore, she had two options. One, she could stand here dumbly holding onto the horse's reins like a child with a balloon. Two, she could release the animal.

Ainsley chose the second. The horse was tired anyways

and wouldn't exactly be galloping away. She dropped of the reins and patted the animal on the neck.

"Why don't you hang out," she said. "I might need you again."

The horse lowered its head, moseyed away, and nibbled at a few stray twigs on the ground.

"I'm serious," she said. "Don't pretend like you didn't hear me."

The gray mare wandered a bit further off. There was no controlling an animal used to foraging for grass on the open steppe.

Ainsley shrugged. She couldn't blame the animal for being hungry. She turned around, walked past the hanging mirror, stepped through the saddle formed by the boulders, rounded a corner—

—and stopped.

She found herself at the edge of a wide but shallow pit.

The site was about twenty meters across, thirty meters long, and a meter deep. In the ground were the faint remains of a partly excavated stone foundation. They formed a long rectangle divided by a low wall in the middle. A pair of deep holes had been dug on either side of the wall. The small mound of fresh earth on either side of each hole indicated it had been excavated recently.

This was Haruun-Bara.

Ainsley stood there, confused. The classic Mongolian Empire had been totally mobile, hadn't left any permanent structures at all. Maybe this was one of those fabled permanent sites that Harriet had mentioned, a military garrison. That would make sense, positioned here in the saddle between two mountains. Or maybe it dated from a civilization that predated Genghis Khan.

Whatever this place was, it hadn't been attended to in a while. And she had it all to herself, at least for now.

Ainsley crouched down and leapt into the site, a small cloud of dust blooming around her shoes when she hit the bottom. She walked around the foundation wall, admiring the care with which each stone had been cleaned, its shape revealed. Nearby lay a short collapsible shovel, a rusted trowel, and an old black tarp, all balled together and stuffed into a nook.

She didn't need to be an archaeologist to know that Haruun-Bara had a lot of secrets.

Ainsley stood there, listening to the wind whistling through the boulders, the distant caw of a crow. In the distance, a vulture wheeled around in the sky, coasting on vents. She felt shivers go down to her feet.

This site was eerie.

And if Yalgesh didn't come, she would be totally screwed.

Then she heard a low *whompa whompa whompa*. It was coming from the north. Ainsley pulled herself out of the excavation pit, climbed a small boulder, and shielded her eyes with her hand.

Flying towards her, from the direction of Muk Holgoi, was a small dot.

It was a helicopter.

Ainsley stood there frozen in fear, the black dot growing larger against the blue sky, the sound of its turbine growing higher in pitch. She forced herself to remain calm. It was possible that it *wasn't* coming after her, that someone on the mining base had decided to take a casual, meandering joyride over the Gobi on a gorgeous early afternoon.

But it wasn't likely.

And the way the helicopter was moving in a straight line, directly towards her location, suggested that the pilot knew exactly where to go.

Ainsley was frozen with fear. Her legs felt as if they'd grown a pair of complex root systems. The helicopter was

coming fast—Muk Holgoi was only a few kilometers away—
and soon she could make out the shape of the sides.

Somebody from Excovane was looking for her. And it
wasn't bound to be a friendly encounter. Nobody takes a helicopter to have a friendly cup of tea.

Maybe word had gotten out about the moonstone. Maybe
it was Tumenbayar. Maybe it was Yalgesh.

Either way, Ainsley didn't want to find out. She knew that
she had to hide herself.

She leapt off the boulder and scanned the area. There was
nowhere to conceal herself, short of crouching. She was
exposed on this small mountain.

Then she remembered the holes in the pit.

Ainsley took a few quick steps back to the excavation,
climbed down, and ran to the nearest hole. She peered inside.
With little direct overhead light, she couldn't make out
anything.

She took a deep breath and leapt inside.

CHAPTER THIRTY-NINE

It was a short drop. Ainsley hit the ground, rolled, then leapt to her feet.

She found herself in a subterranean storehouse. Crude shelves had been carved out of the stone on two sides of the room. Piles of gray rocks were heaped in one corner. Overhead, the opening in the ceiling was low enough that she could touch it with outstretched hands. The thick scent of decay surrounded her.

Then she saw it.

A sarcophagus. Made of stone, the box was as long as a human body. Its undecorated sides were thick and rough-hewn. There was no lid.

She went over and peered inside. Inside were two skeletons, wrapped in a final embrace.

Ainsley clapped her hands over her face and stumbled backwards. She backed up against one wall and felt something brush her arm.

She looked to her left. It was another skeleton, this one draped in tattered rags of what used to be clothing.

Ainsley screamed and pushed it away and ran back into

the center of the room. She looked more closely at the strange piles of rocks in the corner. Those weren't rocks at all.

They were piles of decomposing bones.

This hadn't been a military garrison at all.

Haruun-Bara had been a burial site.

Ainsley steadied herself. She took a deep breath, wiped her nose on her sleeve. Then she lifted her face towards the opening overhead. She could hear the *whomp-whomp-whomp* of the helicopter. It was circling the saddle. She could see the helmeted figures inside peering down at her.

She bit her lower lip until it almost bled. It was her fault for coming here, for taking this stupid assignment. It'd been one risky decision after another—and now she was hiding in an ancient mountainside cemetery in Mongolia as a billion-dollar mining operation sent helicopters looking for her and the gemstone that she carried.

It was too late to bail out. She was in too deep. Ainsley had to see this case all the way through.

But this little subterranean mausoleum was too much. Ainsley felt the walls closing in on her. The truth was that she'd never handled death well, not since losing her father to a cancer that she hadn't even been old enough to pronounce. For years afterwards, she'd suffered night terrors, panic attacks, dreams of death. But she'd pulled herself out of it.

Her father's death had caused Ainsley to dedicate herself to pushing every day to its maximum. To wringing the lifeblood out of each minute. She wouldn't stop for death, or even give it the time of day, because she knew that it would kindly stop for her, someday.

The *whompa whompa* grew faint and died away. Now Ainsley could escape this place.

She jumped up, grabbed the edge of the overhead opening, and summoned every ounce of her upper-body strength to pull herself up and out of the burial chamber.

A moment later, Ainsley lay sprawled on the ground of the excavation site, feeling the sun on her face, catching her breath. That had been the mother of all pullups, and she was relieved to have succeeded on the first attempt, because she didn't know if she'd had another in her.

The helicopter was a black dot in the sky, retreating to Muk Holgoi in the north.

Had it seen her? It was impossible to know.

Ainsley went back to the boulder and looked down on the flat expanse of the desert that she'd just crossed that morning.

Then she saw something that took her breath away. A caravan of three vehicles crossing the Gobi.

Towards her.

That was definitely not Yalgesh. He was a party of one, a lone wolf. But Ainsley knew that he'd ratted her out. She felt it in her bones.

The more she thought about it, the clearer it became. The scenario played out like a movie in her mind: Yalgesh had spent the night talking with Tumenbayar. Once Tumenbayar had been appraised of the full value of the moonstone—how it'd been the stumbling block for Muk Holgoi's billion-dollar expansion plans—they had spoken to Tumnebayar's Australian paymasters and arranged some kind of reward for their cooperation. Yalgesh probably hadn't been able to arrange everything in a single night, since he'd been scheduled to leave with Ainsley by eight in the morning, so he'd slashed his own tires, and made up a bullshit story about her needing to escape on horseback, which bought both of them more time.

It made perfect sense in another way: Yalgesh had probably expected that Ainsley would get caught at the exit gate.

He hadn't expected her to jump the horse over the fence, much less arrive to the ruins of Haruun-Bara.

Ainsley, however, made a habit of surprising those who underestimated her.

Now she watched the tiny vehicles zooming towards her across the flat green carpet. Her best guess was that the helicopter had spotted her just before she'd jumped into the burial chamber. They'd most likely alerted the powers-that-be at Muk Holgoi, who'd already dispatched their security.

Ainsley felt a pit open in her stomach. Private security forces had reputations as gunslingers. They were rough around the edges, and in a country that was already pretty rough around the edges, she was pretty sure they wouldn't be offering any massages.

Of course, this was all speculation. Ainsley could be wrong about all of it.

But that wasn't likely.

She knew that she needed to leave, and the sooner the better. She looked around for the gray mare.

There—a hundred meters below, on the southern side of the mountain. It was the opposite side from the way she'd arrived. That was perfect. Ainsley would find a way down, quietly ride around the small mountain range, avoiding the cars that were arriving on the north side, and head back up towards.

She ran over to the nook with the black tarp and pulled it out. A rat screeched and leapt out of the tarp. Ainsley yelped, dropped it, then picked it up again. Nothing else seemed to be living inside. She unfolded the tarp, shook it out, watching the rat pellets fly, then folded it again. It was gross but she needed something to serve as a saddle.

She glimpsed something plastic in the dark recesses of the nook.

She reached in. It was a liter of water. And another. And

another. And finally another. This was a godsend. Four separate liters of water, evidently stashed by the last archaeological team to work here. Ainsley stuffed them into her bag. It was so full that it would barely close.

I'm going to be all right, Ainsley said to herself, as she began descending towards the horse. *I'm going to be all right*.

If she repeated it enough times, it might come true.

CHAPTER FORTY

Eight hours of riding later, and Ainsley's backside felt like a piece of beef carpaccio.

Descending from Haruun-bara, she'd caught up to the gray mare, then led it by the reins down the southern slope of the small mountain. She'd tossed the tarp over its back, jumped onto it, and quickly turned the animal to the west.

They'd picked their way towards the end of the small mountain range, clinging to what few afternoon shadows could be found in the small foothills. After an hour of riding, Ainsley turned around and looked at the archaeological site.

She couldn't be sure, but she thought she saw figures moving atop the saddle. Ainsley hoped that they weren't scanning the area with binoculars, but they probably were. If they could afford to send out a helicopter, they could afford a pair of binoculars.

Excovane was going to find her. And they were going to find the moonstone.

Ainsley was determined not to let that happen.

———

The hours crawled by like a curious infant.

The brown peaks of the mountain range shrank down to orange hills, and then melted into the vast putting green of the Gobi.

Ainsley judged that the time had come. She tugged the horse's head to the right, back towards the north, and plunged across the open range. A vast plain of green turf stretched nearly as far as the eye could see. It was a hallucinogenic billiards table, kilometers of green felt. Somewhere to the east, beyond the edge of the horizon, lay Muk Holgoi.

Ainsley spurred the horse with her feet from a walk into a trot. After a while, she spurred it to a smooth canter. That gait was more than she could handle. Even with the tarp under her butt, she was afraid of sliding off the animal due to the back-and-forth motion. Plus she worried that a canter would tire the animal out—and this horse was her only ticket out of the region.

So she brought the animal back down to a stiff trot. The bouncing was ferocious on her spine and rear end, but she would tolerate it.

The horse itself, however, had begun acting buggy. As the afternoon wore on, the animal began whinnying, stomping, and prancing—often for no reason at all. At times, it veered wildly off course, forcing her to correct it. Ainsley had assumed all Mongolian ponies were sturdy creatures made stoic by long winters.

That was not the case. Her gray mare had a mild case of the heebie-jeebies.

A distant speck passed, a kilometer or two away. It was a vehicle. She was too far to catch it, or wave it down, but Ainsley felt reassured knowing that she wasn't totally alone on this vast carpet. She held out hope that she would encounter another vehicle.

For now, Ainsley was alone. And more than that, she had

no visual points of reference—no trees, no houses, no electric poles, nothing.

Soon her eyes played tricks on her brain. What looked to be a low hill a hundred meters ahead was actually a mountain range at least a day's ride away. What seemed to be a gargantuan boulder far off was actually a rock coming up fast. Golden pools of light on the earth blended with purple-streaked shadows and flowed into beautiful psychedelic blankets.

Back home, she'd be making an appointment with an optometrist. Here, it was a new way of seeing.

Finally, with the sun sinking ever lower, Ainsley made the decision to stop. She was going to have to spend the night here, literally in the middle of nowhere, with nothing except a tarp.

She stopped the horse, released the reins, and slid off its back onto the ground. She swept her arm around the plain. "Look, an all-night buffet. Just for you."

The horse lowered its head to the grass and began eating.

She patted its neck. "Don't wander too far tonight, or I'll be mad."

Ainsley opened the black tarp, spread it on the ground, and sat down cross-legged in the center of it. The habits of civilization. She rifled through her bag, hoping to find some stray bit of food. An overlooked protein bar? A forgotten piece of jerky?

Nothing.

She sighed and shut the bag. It was sad but she wasn't too concerned. A person could live without food for weeks. It wouldn't be the end of her.

On the other hand, water was vital. And fortunately she had that.

Ainsley realized that she was thirsty. She lifted a liter

bottle to her mouth and finished it. One down, three to go. It was dry out here. It was easy to forget that it was a desert.

She watched the sun smash into the horizon. Fear swarmed inside her torso like angry bees. She took several deep breaths, forcing herself to ignore them. Giving into fear wouldn't do her any good.

Ainsley lay down on the tarp, pulled either side of it across her body, and—using her bag as a pillow—shut her eyes.

She lay like that for a very long time.

She was sleeping in the Gobi Desert. At night. Wrapped in a sheet of plastic.

Alone.

CHAPTER FORTY-ONE

Late that night, Elbegdorj Batsuuri had approached Ainsley in a dream.

He'd stood up from a chair and walked towards her, hand out. She'd put her own hand out—and watched it go straight through his body. He'd dissolved instantly.

Then the sound of distant yipping yanked her back to reality.

Ainsley's eyes flew open. She was still wrapped in the black tarp, laying on the floor of the green desert. The land was bathed in a dark purple glow, just enough for her eyes to make out shapes.

The yipping sounded again, now closer. Those were animals. It sounded like a pack of wild dogs. Ainsley was laying here, on the ground, wrapped in a plastic sheet.

She was a human taco, waiting to be devoured.

Ainsley bolted to her feet, folded the tarp, and stuffed it under her arm. Without the night's accumulated body heat, she began full-on shivering like a sewing machine. She slung her bag over her shoulder, tried to steady her chattering jaw, and scanned the predawn gloaming for the horse.

The gray mare was nowhere to be found. Ainsley hoped that it hadn't wandered too far. Being torn apart by a pack of wild dogs wasn't the way that she wanted to go out.

Ainsley couldn't call the horse—it didn't have a name, and it wouldn't listen to her anyways. And doing so would attract attention.

So she walked. She wandered the cold, predawn desert, hearing the rowdy dogs nearby. The dark purple glow in the sky slowly transformed into a red that suffused the air and the ground. Forms resolved themselves.

And then she saw it.

The gray mare was standing about a hundred meters away, grazing happily. Ainsley wondered if it had been eating the whole night.

Behind Ainsley, the sound of the dogs changed to a high-pitched yipping. Something about it set the hair on her arms on end.

She turned. In the sunrise, the pack was visible now, maybe twelve in total. They looked about half a kilometer off.

And they were running—*directly towards her*.

Ainsley felt a primitive shiver zip down her pelvis and thighs.

She took off like a shot, running at a full sprint towards the gray mare, her arms pulling at invisible handrails, the way her track coach had taught her years ago. She'd been an all-state track star in high school and the muscle memory still lived somewhere deep within her.

Fifty meters...

She felt her bag bouncing against her back, the wind shear in her face. The sweat popping out on her forehead and upper lip.

Twenty meters...

The dogs had grown closer now, their cries changed to *ka-ka-ka-ka-ka*—

Ten meters...

Ainsley slowed her stride—

Five meters...

She gripped the tarp tightly—

Two meters...

She launched herself off her left foot—

—and landed square on the back of the surprised mare.

"Go!" she screamed, kicking it in the ribs.

The horse bolted like a shot, breaking straight into a three-beat canter.

Good thing too, because the dogs were upon them an instant later, snarling, leaping. Their reddish fur was mangy, their snouts long like hyenas.

Ainsley locked her legs around the barrel of the animal's body, leaned forward and wrapped her arms around its neck, and held on for dear life.

A dog jumped against the horse's shoulder—and the mare broke into an all-out four-beat gallop. Ainsley was terrified. The ground beneath the animal's hooves was a blur, its head fiercely bobbing up and down. She would be breaking speed limits if this were a residential street back home.

The wild dogs were so close that she could smell their horrid scent of musk and feces. She buried her nose in her sleeve.

Then she felt one of their mouths nip at her heel. Shrieking, she kicked at the cur. Another nipped at the horse's rear left leg, causing it to break its stride.

"Get off, you bastards!" Ainsley shouted.

But the dogs kept coming. One by one, the canines threw themselves at the horse, at Ainsley's legs, nipping, biting, snapping. She kicked each cur away.

This went on seemingly forever. Ainsley wasn't even sure that the dogs knew what they would do if they ever brought down a human on a horse, but she didn't want to find out.

The horse kept on steaming ahead, and the dogs eventually tired out. The pack fell away and soon shrank into distant points on the turf behind her.

They gray mare slowed to a trot. Ainsley sat up straight.

"I want to apologize for anything I said earlier that might've offended you," she said. "This was incredible."

The horse slowed from a trot to a walk. Then it violently pitched its head up and down.

"Hey now, watch it," said Ainsley.

Without warning, the animal suddenly kicked up its back legs. Ainsley felt its force drive her forward into its mane.

"Calm down," she said, struggling to keep upright.

Then the horse kicked up its front legs, throwing Ainsley backwards. Her thighs locked tight around its ribs.

"What is your problem—"

The horse kicked her forwards and backwards, Ainsley pitching around like a jack-in-the-box. This horse had become a bucking bronco that was trying to toss her.

And then it happened. Ainsley felt the animal's coat, slick with sweat, slip from between her tightly-clenched legs—

Her body lifted through the air—

Boom.

Ainsley hit the ground, hard, on her left side. She felt a stone under her arm, then the weight of her body landing on the arm, pressing on it.

Snapping it.

She rolled over on the ground onto her back. She lay there, breathing in the loamy scent of the soil surrounding her. Nearby, the gray mare was standing calmly.

It happened again.

Ainsley sat up, tried to lift her left arm—

A sharp pain radiated from her left forearm up to her shoulder and down the left side of her chest. It was so intense that she squinched her face into a grimace.

When the pain subsided, she opened her eyes.

This was bad. Very bad.

Ainsley looked down at her arm. From the outside, it seemed normal. No blood, no scrapes, no horrific angle. But she couldn't move it.

Then the next wave of pain hit her, without warning. This one was even worse. It sent waves of dizziness spiraling through her head. She felt nausea sweep violently across her torso.

When it had passed, she opened her eyes again. Her mouth was hanging open, her breath panting.

This was serious. Her forearm was fractured, maybe even broken. She was alone on the edge of the Gobi Desert with two bottles of water and a hostile horse. Somewhere nearby was a pack of wild dogs searching for her. Somewhere further, the security forces of a major international mining operation were searching for her.

And she had no help coming, from any quarter.

It couldn't possibly get any worse.

Ainsley felt the sobs begin—weakly at first, then more strongly. She had no strength to resist them. Her chest heaved, her lungs wracked with emotion. She lifted her face to the sky, the hot tears tracking down both cheeks. The howls that came from her throat sounded foreign to her.

She didn't even notice the pain in her arm anymore, because everything was pain. Mongolia was pain. Horses were pain. Gemstones were pain. Life was pain.

Ainsley opened her eyes. That was the First Noble Truth. *Life is suffering.*

The Second Noble Truth: *Suffering is caused by desire.*

The Third Noble Truth: *To escape suffering, end desire.*

She pulled out the moonstone with her good hand, the translucent cylinder cool in her palm. Ainsley looked at it.

"I understand now," she said, "but I need help finishing this journey."

CHAPTER FORTY-TWO

Later that morning, Ainsley sat astride the gray mare once again, trying to ignore the pain building on the left side of her body.

Her left arm hung at an unnatural angle at her side. A sudden wave of pain caused her face to grimace slightly, and her right hand squeezed the reins tightly.

The sun was obscured behind a haze that had drifting across the landscape. It was a wide fog that had seemingly rolled out of nowhere. It enveloped Ainsley and drained all the remaining vitality out of her.

The horse continued its slow plodding forward.

Clop clop, clop clop.

The fog swelled thick and dense. Ainsley's skin was clammy to the touch. She absentmindedly rubbed her left arm, then yelped in pain.

Clop clop, clop clop.

Soon she felt sleepiness stealing into her head. She grew sleepy. Her eyes fluttered shut.

Then her eyes flew open. Her body was tipping to the right. With a second to spare, she caught herself from falling.

"Dammit," she said aloud.

The fog eddied and swirled around her, wrapping her in its cold embrace. The gray mare whinnied.

The drowsiness crept into her eye sockets once again. There was no keeping them open.

Her eyes fluttered closed again. Her body slumped over.

And then she fell off the mare.

Falling to the right, Ainsley landed on the grass. The horse walked a few meters, then stopped.

She lay on the grass, still. She'd reached her limits. This was where Ainsley Walker had to stop. Whatever happened, happened. Fate was a cruel mistress.

She rolled over onto her back, the pain washing over her in horrific waves. A small moan escaped her lips. She stared up into the swirling mists overhead.

There was a silhouette of a bird. It was moving in slow circles.

She watched it for a minute. That wasn't just any bird. That looked like a vulture. Ainsley felt herself starting to cry. If this were a high school yearbook, the wild animals of the Gobi had just voted her Most Likely To End Up Dead.

Then the bird dove down through the fog, straight towards Ainsley. She covered her face with her right arm.

But the bird didn't attack. Instead, it landed on the ground nearby.

She looked at the creature. It was large, its curved beak designed for optimal tearing of flesh. And its two huge wings were covered in spectacular golden feathers.

That wasn't a vulture. That was an eagle.

It looked at her, spread its wings out wide, and issued a single bloodcurdling shriek.

Despite her pain, Ainsley scrambled backwards as best she could. The bird made no attempt to attack her. Then she noticed the two thin strips of leather attached to its legs.

It was an eagle-in-training.

Behind her, a man's voice sounded. It was muted by the fog. Ainsley twisted around.

It took her a while to recognize him. The brocade black coat, the red hat lined with brown-and-white fox fur, turned up oddly on either side. The long red tassel hanging down his back. The thick brown leather glove on his right forearm, extending all the way up to the elbow.

It was the Kazakh eagle hunter.

Ainsley sank back into the earth. She was utterly at his mercy. She had run out of fuel, couldn't so much as lift a finger to defend herself.

She lay there, staring straight overhead. His soft footsteps drew closer. Then his round, friendly face appeared over her.

The Kazakh eagle hunter said a couple of words. Ainsley couldn't respond. She felt the nozzle of a flask pressed to her lips. Water slowly dribbled into her mouth.

Then a salty piece of food appeared on her tongue. It was jerky. She lay there, feeling it slowly melt onto her tongue.

The Kazakh crouched down next to the eagle, luring it back onto his arm. The bird finally assented. It hopped onto the glove, its butcher-knife talons gripping the worn leather. The man stroked the eagle gently on his back, then slipped the tiny aviator's leather helmet over the bird's face.

The Kazakh stood up and held out his hand to Ainsley. Taking a deep breath, she gripped it. He pulled her to her feet.

The hunter said something. Ainsley didn't understand. He said it again.

Then she was hit by a pain so intense that she felt her knees give way. She felt herself falling. She felt the earth against the side of her face.

Then she didn't feel anything at all.

———

Ainsley awoke to her face buried in soft fur, and her body swaying gently.

She lifted her head. She was astride the gray mare, pitched forward onto its mane, her arms hanging down either side of its neck. The Kazakh must've thrown her onto the animal's back while she was unconscious. She decided to forgive him for that.

A few steps ahead, the hunter was leading the horse by the reins. On his arm was perched the golden eagle, its brown plumage twisting as its head scanned the desert for prey.

Ainsley pulled herself up to a sitting position. Her left arm was in excruciating pain. She needed medical attention. She needed food. She needed a lot of things.

"Where are we going?" she said.

The Kazakh turned around, walking backwards now. On his arm, the eagle's golden eyes bore into her like the sharp gaze of a suspicious old man.

"Eh?" he said. Ainsley knew that *eh*. It was the one truly universal word, the sound that carried the same meaning across all cultures of the world.

What?

"Where are we going?" she repeated.

She knew the hunter wouldn't understand, but she didn't care. Ainsley needed to feel like she was communicating with somebody.

The Kazakh pointed at her, then pointed at himself. He made an eating gesture, then a sleeping gesture.

"To eat and sleep," she said.

He nodded.

"But where?" She swung a finger around to indicate direction.

He pointed to the north. She looked ahead, expecting to see a range of hills, or a distant river. But there was nothing to the north except more of the same.

Ainsley pitched forward onto the horse's mane and closed her eyes.

TSILDIJIIN

CHAPTER FORTY-THREE

A loud roar of a crowd, and Ainsley jackknifed up to a sitting position.

She was in a primitive bed. A rough woolen blanket had been placed over the lower portion of her body. Her upper body had been propped at a slight angle against a stack of hard pillows.

Ainsley waited for her eyes to refocus, then looked around. She was in a *ger*. On the other side of the space were two beds, both of which were empty.

In the middle of the tent stood a table on which were stacked many medical supplies. She recognized gauze, antiseptic, tongue depressors.

Then she realized that was in a medical tent.

She looked down. Her lower left arm had been wrapped in a rudimentary splint. Seven cords of wood cinched to her arm by with leather cords, beneath which a thin towel had been wrapped around her skin.

This was a home job—crude, simple. Still, someone had taken care of her.

She wanted to know who.

The crowd roared outside the walls of the *ger*. This was driving her nuts. Ainsley needed to know where she'd been taken. She needed to know right now.

She kicked off the woolen blanket, swung her legs over the edge of the bed, and stood up. Wobbly, she teetered to the doorway of the *ger* and parted the flap and stuck her head out.

A group of two hundred spectators were standing around a patch of grass. Two floodlights powered by portable generators illuminated a small field in the center. Ainsley hobbled over, feeling every one of the horse's stiff trots in her bottom. She peered over the shoulders.

In the center of the grass were two men, their large bodies packed with both muscle and fat. They were naked except for traditional brown leather boots, bright blue Speedos, and red sleeves. They would've looked ridiculous, except for the fact that neither one was aware of their ridiculousness.

The two men weren't equally matched. One was larger than the other, but both were circling one another in a crouch, arms out, fingers twinkling.

It was a wrestling match.

Then Ainsley recognized the bigger of the two. His face was round and youthful, his eyes intense but mischievous.

It was Honey Bear.

A loud shout caught her attention. Nearby, a woman with her back to Ainsley had started clapping and hopping up and down. She was shouting the words *Honey Bear*. Ainsley peered at her. Something about her looked familiar.

Then she saw the knee-high pink Wellington boots.

It was Harriet, the naturalist.

The Englishwoman turned and noticed Ainsley. "Hey! You're awake!"

She hugged Ainsley, taking care to avoid her left arm. Ainsley drank the woman in with her eyes. Harriet was wearing the same clothing, the same sloppy ponytail, the same wild look in her eyes.

"My God, it's good to see you," said Ainsley.

Harriet put an arm around her. "I didn't know if you were going to wake up, so I came outside to watch Honey Bear."

"You took care of me?"

Harriet pointed to Ainsley's arm. "That's my handiwork—such as it is."

Ainsley was momentarily at a loss for words. "Did Erdene ever come back?"

"No."

Ainsley nodded. She had a sneaking suspicion that Erdene wouldn't be a woman of her word.

"Did you see Honey Bear?" said Harriet.

They both turned their attention to the match. The teenage wrestler had locked arms with his opponent. In one brusque move, he forced the man to the ground. Then Honey Bear straightened up and threw his arms into the dark sky, his prodigious belly hanging from his torso like a sack of yak milk.

"I'd say he's doing well," said Ainsley. She peered around. "Where am I, Harriet? What is this?"

Harriet answered matter-of-factly. "A small regional *naadam*. It's a festival. There are *naadams* all over the country in the summer. There's wrestling, archery, horse racing."

Ainsley nearly retched at the third item. She'd had more than enough of horseback riding. "I have so many questions. Like, how did I *get* here?"

Harriet looked perplexed. "You don't remember?"

"No."

"The Kazakh eagle hunter brought you. He found you out on the steppe. You were unconscious."

"Why did he choose this place?"

"Maybe because he knew that I would be here. And

Honey Bear. We came together." She gestured to Ainsley's arm. "So what happened?"

Ainsley hung her head. "I was thrown off a horse. Then I was chased by a pack of wild wolves."

"Oh goodness." Harriet lowered her voice. "Why were you riding a horse? Something happened to the motorbike?"

Ainsley chewed on her lip. "I crashed it in a river."

"Dear God, you are a *dangerous* woman."

"Harriet, are you mad at me?"

The English naturalist looked at her oddly. "Why would I be? You didn't steal anything from me."

"Wait, I didn't *steal* the bike—"

Harriet held up two fingers. "You're right. I stand corrected. You forced an involuntary sale."

Ainsley laughed. "Exactly."

"Did you find the moonstone?"

"Yes."

Harriet's eyes grew wide. She hooked her hand around Ainsley's good arm. "I want to hear everything. The nurse will arrive soon to set your arm."

The naturalist gently led Ainsley back towards the medical tent.

————

An hour later, Ainsley was seated in the bed, watching the nurse use a stone pestle to crush herbs in a bowl.

The nurse was not even eighteen, her round face still full of baby fat. She wore a modern blue long-sleeve top with traditional black tunic pants below. A thick headband kept the hair out of her face.

"What's her name?" said Ainsley.

"Amina," said Harriet. She was standing next to Ainsley. "We discussed your arm. She says it's probably fractured."

"So she's going to set it."

Harriet nodded. "Right now."

The young nurse walked over. "Hello, nice to meet you."

Ainsley's eyebrows leapt off her face. "You speak English?"

"I speak little. Please you stand."

Ainsley did so. Amina led her to the table in the center of the *ger*, where the she gently removed the makeshift stabilizer. Ainsley winced, gritting her teeth, as bolts of pain shot through the left side of her body. The nurse had given her some ibuprofen but it was useless in the face of this pain.

Amina slid a thin medical sleeve onto Ainsley's arm, then snipped five holes for the fingers. Then she wrapped the entire arm in cotton gauze.

A tea kettle was heating up on a stove. The nurse poured some water from the kettle into the bowl of herbs, tore open a small packet of powder, and poured it into the water. Then she stirred the concoction until it was a thick greenish paste.

Amina glanced at the arm. "Keep it no move."

Ainsley remained still as the nurse opened her laptop and pulled up a video. Ainsley craned her neck to see the screen. Two hands were setting a cast on an arm while a narrator described the process in Russian. The nurse watched the video with one finger on her lip.

Ainsley glanced at Harriet with alarm. "Do you believe this? She's watching a how-to video."

"Well, the orthopedic surgeon had to leave early tonight," said the Englishwoman.

"Don't be sarcastic. This is my arm."

Harriet shrugged. "This is the best they can do."

On the table was a small stack of precut strips of cloth. Amina selected the one on top, dipped it in the bowl, then wrapped it gently around the wrist. The scent of the poultice whisked Ainsley back to kindergarten art class.

Amina continued wetting and applying several more

strips, repeating the action up and down Ainsley's forearm, until her entire limb was covered in a hardening shell of plastered cloth.

It was a primitive cast.

"Thank you," said Ainsley, tapping the plaster with her other hand.

"No touch," said Amina. "Wait for dry."

Ainsley stood, the cast resting on the table, shifting her weight. Meanwhile, Harriet crashed backwards onto one of the beds. "I am absolutely knackered."

"Please don't fall asleep."

"Why not?"

"I need to call Gantig. Can you find me a sat phone?"

"Do you still have his number?"

"Of course."

Harriet sat up. "Then you are in luck because we have a sat phone."

"Can you bring it here? And bring my bag too."

The Englishwoman rummaged around in a drawer, pulled out a sat phone, and brought it over. It was a simple black Iridium 9575, and it looked like a child's walkie-talkie. But this could dial a lot more than a backyard tree fort.

Then she retrieved Ainsley's bag and set it on the table.

"Can you unzip it?" said Ainsley.

Harriet did so. Ainsley rummaged around inside with her one good hand until she found the paper with Gantig's number. It had smudged.

"Dial this," she said.

Harriet squinted. "I can't read it."

"Just try."

Harriet pointed to a number. "Is that a 6 or an 8?"

"It's a six."

Harriet dialed. Ainsley held the phone up to her ear. A gruff Mongolian voice answered.

"Hello? Gantig?"

The man disconnected. She handed the phone back to Harriet. "It's an eight."

Harriet redialed. Ainsley put it back to her ear. She had no plans other than to say, *I found your goddamned gemstone, tell me where to bring it.*

This time, Gantig answered. "Hello?"

"Hey, it's Ainsley. I have the moonstone."

There was a pause. "No way."

"Yes way. Why are you so surprised? Did you think I was dead?"

There was a pause. "Honestly, I thought you gave up."

She was miffed. "I always do what I say."

"I believe you now. Tell me where you've been."

Ainsley heard the words tumble out of her mouth. She explained everything—the arrival in Zhakorum; the encounter with Harriet; the three days with Tungdik, Norgema, and Honey Bear; the journey to Muk Holgoi with Yalgesh, the fossils trader; the tense negotiation with Tumen-bayar; the gaining of the moonstone; the escape on horse-back; the failed meeting at Haruun-Bara; the solo horseback ride across the Gobi; the broken arm; the rescue by the Kazakh eagle hunter.

When she'd finished, there was silence. "Are you still there?"

"Yeah, I'm here," Gantig said, "but I can't believe what you're telling me."

She cradled the phone between her chin and shoulder and used her free hand to fondle the moonstone. "Well, believe it."

"Okay, listen," he said. "I need you to bring the moon-stone to me in Zhakorum. And I need it fast."

"Why?"

"The villagers are supposed to sign the contract with Excovane at noon tomorrow."

Ainsley looked at the clock. It was seven o'clock am.

"So I have twenty-nine hours to get there."

"Yes. Where are you right now?"

"I don't know." She put the phone against her shoulder. "Harriet, where are we again?"

"The Tsildijiin *naadam*."

Ainsley returned the phone to her ear. "The Tsildijiin *naadam*."

"Oh, Tsildijiin isn't that far. It's maybe ten hours. Can you find a ride?"

"I don't know."

At that moment, a loud whoop sounded. She heard someone come through the front flaps of the *ger*. Ainsley turned her head.

It was Honey Bear. He had changed out of his wrestling outfit and into a white t-shirt, red tearaway track pants, and a pair of running shoes.

When he spotted her, his expressive face screwed itself up into a rictus of anger.

Then he charged like a rhino.

"I'm going to have to call you back," she said.

CHAPTER FORTY-FOUR

The teenager was across the *ger* in three strides. He stopped just short of Ainsley and pulled himself to his full height.

She lifted her face upwards. Honey Bear was a full head taller. He glowered down at her, his nostrils flaring in and out. His face was contorted like a demented gargoyle jutting out from the eaves of a cathedral. His fists were clenched.

Ainsley felt a lump form in her throat. This kid could break her in two.

Harriet slipped between them. "Now now, let's play nice."

Then the English naturalist said a few words to the hulking boy in Mongolian. He answered in a rat-a-tat-tat of indecipherable words. Harriet replied calmly.

The teenager looked over Harriet's shoulder. "But Ainsley take my motorbike."

"I paid you for it," said Ainsley. "Didn't you get the money?"

"No!" he said.

Ainsley's body went cold. No wonder this mountain of a teenager was steaming mad.

Then a ridiculous grin broke out across his cheerful

pumpkin face. "I just kidding! I have the money. And now ... I say thank you!"

The enormous teenager pushed Harriet out of the way and enveloped Ainsley in a suffocating crush. It felt like being smothered by half a ton of gelatin and smelled like the underbelly of a wild ox.

"Thank you," she said, twisting away, "but why?"

The mountain-sized boy released her. "Because I buy motorbike number *two*!"

"Oh really?" she said.

"Yes! Come! I show you!"

Harriet intercepted him. "Wait, hold on—Amina has to put a sling on her arm first."

The nurse came over with a pair of thin cotton straps. She wound them around the cast, looped them up around Ainsley's shoulder, and then clipped them together. Now it was supported.

"Okay, go now," Amina said.

Ainsley gingerly lifted her arm, testing it, then followed Honey Bear outside.

————

The sun was dawning on the *naadam*, and Ainsley got a better glimpse of the thousand-plus crowd in the light of day.

She was surprised. She'd expected a huge flock of tourists, toting baseball caps and digital cameras on straps around their necks. Reportedly, they swarmed the horse races and wrestling contests around Ulaanbataar.

But this place, Tsildijiin, was different. Far from any center of population, this *naadam* had drawn the locals. Ainsley moved through the sea of country people, the windbreakers and traditional *deels*, the dirty faces and gnarled hands. Half-empty bottles of vodka glinted in the morning light. Everywhere she saw groups of men eating legs of mutton, lounging on the grass, laughing at rough jokes.

At the east end of the festival were fifty heavy bags for archery, arranged in a long row with empty expanse of the green steppe behind them. Ainsley guessed that was for safety. At the west end were the attendees' *gers*, at least a hundred, fanning out across the land.

In the middle of the gathering were a few long rows of hand-made benches that had been arranged at a perpendicular angle, forming half of a small arena. On the grass in front of the benches, several wrestlers dressed in Speedos and boots were stretching their short, thick arms.

Ainsley looked around. "This feels like a party."

"It's a summer festival," said Harriet. "The people drink for days."

Honey Bear was easy to follow in the crowd. He stood out like an engorged watermelon in a field of baby carrots.

They followed him to a *ger*. Around the back was parked a brand-new gleaming Suzuki V-Strom 1000.

The large teenager grinned. "It's mine!"

Ainsley admired the bike. It was a dual sport model, equally good for city riding or off-roading. Two large aluminum panniers hung from either side. The cobalt-blue-and-pearl finish looked beautiful. It almost certainly had a lot of features that were invisible to the eye, like traction control and anti-lock brakes.

"It's very good!" she said.

"It's upgrade! You help!"

She gave him thumbs-up. "Very good! Very smart!"

Honey Bear's eyes widened with excitement, and a high-pitched giggle unspooled out of his mouth like a long, lacy pink ribbon.

The laughter, as always, was infectious. Both she and Harriet found themselves giggling in spite of themselves.

Ainsley walked over to Honey Bear and laid her hand on his arm. "Do you want to make more money?"

"Yes!" the teenage wrestler said. "I like money!"

"I need you to drive me to Zhakorum."

A quizzical look appeared on his face. "Zhakorum? Where that?"

"It's ten hours north. But I have to leave *right now*."

"How much pay?"

Ainsley pulled a random number out of the blue Mongolian sky. "Oh, I don't know. Let's say three hundred dollars."

"Three hundred dollars!" Then Honey Bear's pudgy face suddenly darkened. He shook his head. "But I have competition." He pointed towards the makeshift wrestling arena.

Ainsley struggled to remain calm. "What time?"

The boy counted on his fingers. "Twelve."

"At twelve o'clock?"

"Yes."

"We can leave after that."

The teenager looked confused. "No, I win. Always."

It was Ainsley's turn to be confused. Harriet explained. "The way it works is if the wrestler wins, he has to keep competing every two hours."

"For how long?"

"Days."

Ainsley rolled her eyes. This was unacceptable. She was under a time crunch.

"Honey Bear, can you lose?"

"No." He chopped a hand through the air. "I don't lose."

Ainsley sighed. If she couldn't find another ride—which was likely—then her only option was to watch the games and hope for Honey Bear to be defeated.

"Fine," she said, "I'll wait."

CHAPTER FORTY-FIVE

At noon, Ainsley found herself sitting in the second row of the benches, tapping her foot impatiently, squinting in the bright light of midday. The yellow sun arched over the field like a wrestler preparing an elbow drop.

Honey Bear stood on the grass, his back to the stands. He was wearing the boots, the tiny underwear, and a comically small jacket. He was stretching his arms over his head. When he bent forward to touch his feet, Ainsley averted her gaze.

"What are the odds he's going to win?" she said.

Next to her, Harriet reached into a sack, pulled out two strips of jerky, and handed one to Ainsley. "I only know wildlife. I'm not a wrestling expert."

Ainsley chewed on the dried meat. It tasted gamey and rough. "Well, I was just wondering."

The Englishwoman sighed. "Let's handicap this. He's enormous and young and, let's be blunt, a little stupid. It seems to me that someone more experienced or more intelligent could defeat him."

Ainsley's eyes scanned the thirty other wrestlers on the field. "But there's nobody bigger."

Harriet shook her head. "No, there isn't. Do you know he's bigger than some of the bears I've tracked? That's not a joke."

The opponent arrived. It was a young man in his twenties, considerably slimmer, wearing a black Adidas track suit. When he glanced at Honey Bear, a frightened look passed across his face.

Aw hell, Ainsley thought.

The boy removed his track suit. He was wearing roughly the same garb—cowboy boots, yellow Speedo, and tiny black jacket. After some stretching, they faced one another.

"Here they go," said Ainsley.

Honey Bear pounded his chest twice, pursed his lips, and put out his hands. His opponent did the same. They grasped one another's wrists. A referee stood nearby, watching.

Then they began grappling. There was no whistle, no ceremony, no marks or lines on the ground. Just two humans standing in an open field who gripped hands, nodded and began to fight.

"So how do they win?" said Ainsley.

"The first person to touch the ground loses," Harriet replied.

Both wrestlers circled around, leaning into one another, hands on each other's shoulders and waists, each looking for an opportunity. Honey Bear's hulking legs and chunky bottom jutted out like a Botero sculpture.

"It seems like an even match so far," said Ainsley.

No sooner had the words left her mouth than Honey Bear made his move. He seized his opponent, one hand squeezing the right waist, the other on the left shoulder.

Then flipped the man ass-over-teakettle.

In the blink of an eye, his opponent was flat on his back in the grass.

Honey Bear turned to the crowd and threw his arms into

the air. His face was electric, alive, flush with the joy of victory. A few people clapped.

Ainsley dropped her own face into her hands. This was going to be a long afternoon.

———

Two hours later, more people had gathered for the next match, probably because the competition grew better as the day went on. The makeshift bleachers were filled, and a line of spectators stood behind them.

Ainsley sat on the bench, watching Honey Bear stalk around the grass. He looked happy and confident.

Harriet laid a hand on her forearm. "Don't worry, I have a feeling about this one."

"Why?"

"Look at his opponent."

A heavily muscled older man stepped onto the turf, already stripped down to the standard uniform, his body glistening with oil. His round face was possessed by an unmistakable seriousness. True, he was smaller than Honey Bear, with a lower percentage of body fat, but he carried himself with an impressive economy of movement.

"I think that's our man," said Ainsley.

"You'd better hope."

Ainsley fingered the moonstone, which was riding in the pocket of her jacket. She had less than twenty-four hours to get it back to Zhakorum.

The two fighters faced off. Taking one another's wrists, they began to grapple. Ainsley saw that this opponent was more experienced than the last. He countered Honey Bear's turns expertly.

A minute passed. Neither one could get a lead on the

other. Two minutes passed. They were locked in a death match.

"Something has to give," said Harriet.

Honey Bear stepped his right leg forward, planted it, and exerted all of his strength downwards on his opponent's back. The opponent quickly planted his own left foot and resisted.

Honey Bear shouted with the exertion. The opponent's face was contorted, his teeth gritted. Ainsley imagined that his back must be near breaking.

Making a final effort, Honey Bear simply pushed his entire bulk onto his opponent. The man, his legs already stretched wide, toppled backwards, and Honey Bear fell on top of him. The teenager rolled off, arms stretched out in victory. His opponent appeared to be unconscious.

"How graceful," said Harriet drily.

Ainsley stood up. "This calls for drastic measures, Harriet. Follow me."

Harriet looked at her, astonished. To where?"

"The medical tent. I might need you to interpret for me."

————

An hour later, Ainsley found Honey Bear sitting in a folding chair next to the wrestling grounds. The plastic seat was begging for mercy beneath his bulk. The boy was looking at his phone, which seemed tiny in his mitts.

"Hello," she said, crouching next to him.

"Hi," he said, not looking up. Like teenagers all over the world, he was absorbed in his phone.

"You're a really good wrestler."

"You welcome." His thick index finger absently probed a nostril.

"You're supposed to say *thank you*," she said.

Honey Bear didn't reply. Ainsley handed him a clear

thermos filled with a yellow liquid. "I brought you something."

His eyes went towards the item. "What is?"

"Lemonade. I thought you might be thirsty before your next match."

The boy's meaty paw took the bottle and lifted it to his face. He began sucking at the nozzle. His eyes never left the screen.

"Say thank you," she said.

"You welcome."

Ainsley decided not to make anything of it. "You're still going to drive me to Zhakorum, right?"

"Yeah."

He hadn't been listening. She knew that. "Okay, good luck at four o'clock."

Ainsley stood up, clapped him on the shoulder, and walked over to Harriet, who had watched the exchange from a short distance away.

"I don't want to hear it," said Ainsley.

Harriet shook her head. "You're a bad woman."

———

By four o'clock, Honey Bear was attempting to warm up for his next match. It wasn't going well. He yawned twice, bent over and put his hands on his knees, then finally sat down on the grass. He shook his head oddly.

Ainsley and Harriet sat in the bleachers, watching.

"Ainsley, how much did you put in there?"

"Just a quarter of the pill," said Ainsley. "Enough to weaken him. He has to be awake to drive the motorcycle."

Ainsley felt bad about this betrayal. She knew she was going to whatever circle of hell is reserved for those who sabotage teenage athletes. And it was the second time she was hurting him for her own benefit. She tried to console herself with the thought that Honey Bear was young, that he had many other *naadams* to look forward to.

His opponent arrived. This one was a man in his twenties, fairly big—mostly fat—and looked like a decent fighter. Ainsley figured he must have something special if he'd made it this far in the competition.

"Go Honey Bear!" Harriet shouted, clapping.

"Please don't," said Ainsley.

"Well, we should lift his spirits, right? It's not every day he gets dosed with a quarter of a benzodiazepine an hour before a match."

Yawning, Honey Bear clasped wrists with his opponent. From here, Ainsley could see the sleepiness in his eyes.

As they began grappling, Honey Bear was slow to react. The opponent wasted no time in sussing that out. The opponent quickly stepped to the left, hooked his leg around the boy's ankle, and pushed him backwards. Sluggish, unable to stop himself, Honey Bear fell backwards onto the grass.

He covered his face in shame.

"Next time, Honey Bear!" Harriet shouted. Then she gathered her things and turned to Ainsley. "Meet us at his bike in twenty minutes."

CHAPTER FORTY-SIX

As Honey Bear jumped on the ignition, the Suzuki's engine roared to life.

Seated behind him, Ainsley tightened her grip on the strap that encircled Honey Bear's enormous waist. Sitting in this position normally meant she would grip the small bars on either side of the seat. But because her left arm was in a sling, she had to improvise a different method of riding.

Harriet had found a long piece of canvas, cut it into a strip, and tied it around the wrestler's torso. Ainsley could either hold onto the end of it or, even better, slip her good forearm between the canvas strip and his back.

She reached her good arm over Honey Bear's shoulder and thrust a map in front of his nose.

"You know where to go, right?"

He yawned. "I go north."

"To Zhakorum."

"Okay."

Harriet slipped Ainsley's bag around her shoulder cross-wise, then gave her a kiss on the cheek.

"Take care of yourself," she said. "You still have it, right?"

Ainsley disengaged her hand from the strap and reached into her pocket and produced the moonstone.

"Yes."

Harriet looked relieved. "Just checking. I hope all your effort will be worth it."

"Me too. What are you going to do?"

Harriet blew air out of her mouth. "I don't know. It's too late in the season to start tracking wolves again."

"Well, look me up someday."

"If I make it back to civilization."

Harriet squeezed her arm, smiling. Then she jabbed Honey Bear in the ribs. His head jerked up.

"Wake up! You have to drive!"

"Sorry!" he said. "I so sleepy!"

Harriet gave Ainsley a look that said, *Keep an eye on him*. Ainsley felt another stab of guilt. It was her fault for dosing him with a quarter of a sedative shortly before asking him to drive her for ten hours.

The teenager popped the clutch, hit the gas, and the motorcycle lurched forward. As they accelerated, Ainsley's head lolled backward. She squeezed the seat between her legs. Then she gripped the canvas strap tight towards her chest.

As they left the *naadam*, the steppe opened up again, yet another flat expanse of green. The sun was angling to the left, which meant they were headed north.

She slipped her forearm between the strap and Honey Bear's fat back. Her shoulders relaxed.

They were on their way to Zhakorum.

———

Four hours later, with the sun a hand's width from the horizon, Ainsley stared stupidly at back of Honey Bear's t-shirt.

This ride was already boring her, and they weren't even halfway yet. Her nose twitched. His wrestling stench was strong enough to make her eyes water. She leaned back, keeping her face as far away from his body as possible.

The teenage wrestler had found a road, not much more than a narrow strip of gravel. The center was a continuous line of potholes, more or less, so Honey Bear avoided it by keeping the wheels aligned on the ridge that ran alongside it. It required a decent amount of attention—she wouldn't let him zone out—but it was still fairly easy riding.

Ainsley thought about where they might sleep that night. There wasn't much to think about. It would be another night on open grass. She didn't like the prospect at all, even though she'd swapped the black tarp for a thick blanket, currently folded beneath her bottom.

A jolt brought Ainsley's attention back to the road. The motorcycle had slipped off the ridge. They were now in the pothole-riddled middle portion.

"Honey Bear—"

He jerked his head up. She felt his right foot stamp down on the rear brake, saw his hand twist the throttle.

The bike began fishtailing on the gravel.

"Get control!" she screamed.

"I try!" he shouted.

Then the front end of the bike hit a pothole. It wasn't a big one, but large enough to send them sideways.

In the blink of an eye, Ainsley found herself, Honey Bear, and the bike falling to the right. She hit the gravel on her right side, rolled to her left—

—and gasped as Honey Bear landed squarely on her exposed right arm.

They skidded to a stop. The wrestler rolled away. Ainsley sat up and felt more pain radiating up to her right shoulder.

"Oh God," she said, "not the other one."

"I sorry, I did bad."

The motorcycle was a few meters away, wheels still spinning. Honey Bear went and picked it up and kicked the stand, propping it up. He inspected the wheels.

The teenager clapped his hands. "Motorbike is okay! And you?"

Ainsley winced as she tried to lift her right arm. "I think you maybe just broke my other arm," she said.

"I sorry. What we do?"

Ainsley sighed. "We spend the night here."

"Here?"

"Yes, right here."

———

Half an hour later, night had fallen. Honey Bear had made a small fire, over which he'd cooked some chunks of lamb they'd brought from the Tsildijiin *naadam*.

Ainsley's right arm hadn't improved. In fact, she discovered that she couldn't lift it at all.

"Honey Bear, can you give me the food?"

"Okay."

He handed her a stick of lamb.

"No, I need you to put the food in my mouth."

The wrestler grunted. He sat cross-legged next to her, then used his fat fingers to stuff a piece of hot lamb into her mouth.

Ainsley chewed and swallowed. "Good job."

"I sorry, Ainsley."

"Show me how sorry. Give me another."

The teenager fed her for a while that way. Suddenly Ainsley felt sleep stealing upon her. Her eyes looked at the blanket on the ground.

"Honey Bear, can you help me get ready to go to sleep?"

"Okay, I help. What you want?"

With great effort, Ainsley rose to her feet, walked over to the blanket, and kicked it out across the ground. Then she kicked her bag onto the blanket. Finally she laid down on her back, resting her head on the bag.

"Cover me."

The teenage wrestler lifted both sides of the blanket and placed them gently over her body. Once again, Ainsley felt like a human taco. She looked at the teenager standing over her and was struck with intense pangs of guilt. First she'd forced the sale of his motorcycle, then she'd drugged him. And still he was still helping her.

His landing on her good arm was cosmic justice.

"It is comfortable?" he said.

"No," she sighed, "but that's okay."

"Maybe I help—"

She shook her head. "You're not going to understand this, but I'm paying for my sins right now."

The wrestler went back to the fire and sat down. "What is a sin?"

"It's when you do something wrong."

"Like on exam?"

Unburdening herself to this kid would going to be harder than it seemed, so Ainsley abandoned the effort. "Yeah, it's like that."

They both lapsed into silence. Soon the sun extinguished itself, and Honey Bear slumped over onto the ground. He began to snore.

Ainsley stared up into the galaxy and listened to her own breathing, waiting for morning to come.

CHAPTER FORTY-SEVEN

At five thirty, the eastern side of the sky turned a deep indigo, and Ainsley struggled to her feet.

Not a lick of sleep, and her right arm ached as though an elephant had sat on it. She didn't know if it was broken, but she did know that she couldn't grasp or squeeze anything in her right hand. A persistent dull pain throbbed through her arm.

Two useless arms.

She staggered over to Honey Bear, who was slumbering on his side on the ground. Ainsley nudged him in the ribs with the toe of her shoe.

"Wake up," she said.

He muttered something unintelligible. Maybe he was still feeling the effects of the drug.

She kicked him a little harder.

"Hey—we have six more hours of driving, and I have to be there by noon."

Honey Bear rubbed his eyes. "But I still sleepy."

"Let's go," she said. "And we have to figure out how I can hang on."

————

Twenty minutes later, they were blazing down the gravel road again, Ainsley tied to Honey Bear's back.

Literally.

First they'd mounted the motorbike together. The teenager had wrapped the canvas strip around her lower back, then pulled it around his own waist.

"Ready?" he'd said.

"Yes."

He'd cinched it tight, and Ainsley found herself pressed completely against the young wrestler's spine. It was a wall of subcutaneous fat that smelled worse than a young bull elephant in musth.

Now they were tearing along the ridge on the side of the road, Ainsley's face pressed sideways against his back, her two arms cradled carefully below her ribcage. She gritted her teeth in pain.

"You okay?" the boy shouted.

"Go faster," she shouted back.

Honey Bear slowly rolled on the throttle with his right hand. Ainsley squinched her eyes shut and prayed for this journey to finally be over.

————

Six hours later, Honey Bear brought the motorcycle to a halt at the crest of a hill. Ainsley peered around him.

Below them lay the village of Zhakorum.

No breaks all morning, and her bladder was aching. Ainsley had no idea how she was going to take care of that once she dismounted. She didn't want to think about it either.

"Where we go?" he said.

Even from this distance, she recognized the group of people amassed in the middle of the white cubes. An unusually large collection of vehicles glinted in the sun.

"Go to the center of the village."

"They pay me there?"

"Yes, they will. What time is it?"

The wrestler lifted his wrist. His watch read five minutes to twelve. In Ainsley's long history of narrow arrivals, this was going to be her narrowest.

"Go!" she said.

Honey Bear peeled out, down the curving road, and at exactly noon they entered the village.

CHAPTER FORTY-EIGHT

As they drew closer, Ainsley could see a large group gathered in the middle of the village. In the center of the group stood a figure, talking. It was too distant to make out his face, but she could see that the figure wore a dark suit. That was probably an Excovane representative.

Behind the figure sat three men at a long folding table, on which was draped a long tablecloth with the Excovane insignia. Those were Excovane executives.

Her heart skipped a beat. This was the official signing ceremony.

Honey Bear stopped the motorbike a safe distance away from the group. Several heads turned, mouths gaped open. Ainsley imagined that it wasn't every day that the locals saw a teenager wrestler carrying an American woman tied to his back.

Two figures separated from the crowd, and came running over.

It was Gantig and Erdene. Both were dressed in business-wear—Gantig in a white collar shirt, tie, and slacks, Erdene in a modest dark blue dress.

Honey Bear uncinched the canvas strap, and Ainsley was freed. Legs weak from the ride, she slipped off the motorbike, feeling like a newborn deer taking its first steps.

"You made it!" said Erdene. Her expression was more surprised than happy. Ainsley sensed a bit of resentment.

"Of course she did," said Gantig, "she's Ainsley Walker. How are you?"

Grinning, Gantig reached out to shake her hand. Ainsley was barely able to extend it. She winced as he pumped it twice.

"Are you being sarcastic?" she said.

His eyes flitted around while he looked for an answer. "Maybe I am. I mean, I wasn't totally sold on your reputation."

"I hope that's changed," she said.

"Yes," he said, "it definitely has."

Erdene's eyes darted towards Ainsley's bag. "Do you have the moonstone?"

"I do."

Gantig's eyes grew passionate. "Give it to me. We need it, like, *now*."

"Hold on—" said Ainsley.

"This is the signing ceremony! We can't wait another minute."

The moonstone felt heavy in her pocket. Ainsley lifted her palms in a gesture of peace. "I understand. But two things first. One, I need the rest of my fee."

Gantig didn't miss a beat. He reached into his coat, produced an envelope, and thrust it towards her.

"Take it out and count it for me," she said.

Sighing, the young Mongolian opened the envelope and slowly counted out twenty-five one hundred dollar bills. It was a little less than the first amount he'd given her, but Ainsley decided not to complain. She'd never signed a contract with his father; dead men usually have trouble signing papers. Also, it was still good money for such a short amount of time.

"Okay, now put it in my bag," she said.

Gantig pushed the envelope into her bag. "What else?"

She nodded towards Honey Bear. The young wrestler stood nearby, as quiet as an elephant, eyes rounded. He was all ears. "This young man needs some money."

"For what?" said Gantig.

"For driving me here. You said it was ten hours from Tsildijiin."

The young man sighed. "How much does this kid want?"

"Three hundred dollars!" said Honey Bear. He lifted three pudgy fingers.

"No," said Ainsley, "we agreed on *four* hundred dollars."

The teenager quickly caught on. "Sorry—four hundred dollars!"

Gantig rolled his eyes, then nodded to Erdene, who ran back towards the group. "She's going to get it."

While they waited, Ainsley and Gantig stood there, the awkwardness growing between them like a poisonous plant. Neither knew what to say. Maybe because there was too much to say, or maybe because there wasn't anything left to say at all.

Ainsley peered over his shoulder at the group. She heard the speaker's deep baritone, but she couldn't get a glimpse of him.

"Listen," she said, "I was so emotional when I left Ulaanbataar that... I forgot to tell you how sorry I was to discover your dad ... you know, the way that I did. I hope you accomplish his life goal here."

Gantig fixed her with a long, curious look that caused her to immediately regret ever bringing it up. At that moment Erdene returned and handed Honey Bear a small stack of cash. His eyes lit up like a pair of electric bulbs.

"You have what you asked for, Miss Walker," said Erdene, uncommonly formal. "Now give us the moonstone."

Ainsley unzipped her right coat pocket. Erdene and Gantig fixed their eyes on it. She slowly removed the gemstone and handed it over.

"As promised, here is the moonstone. I hope the people of Zhakorum treasure it."

Erdene took the cylindrical gemstone and admired it. "It is more beautiful than I expected."

She handed the moonstone to Gantig, who held it up to the sun. A low whistle escaped his mouth. "It is opaque."

Ainsley ran a light finger along one of the long rectangular facets. "The value is really in the cut. Nobody does hexagons like this. It's very unusual."

He handed the moonstone back to Erdene, who wrapped it in her bag and carried it towards the meeting.

Gantig planted his feet wide apart and looked at her in the eye. His mouth was twisted and his eyes were focused coolly upon her.

"What's the matter?" she said.

He managed a stiff, robotic smile. "Thank you for your help, Ainsley."

She noticed that Gantig held himself in a strange manner. He seemed to be blocking her way. Ainsley glanced over his shoulder at the gathering. "Can I watch?"

"No, that's not a good idea," said Gantig.

"Why not?"

"You won't understand it."

"There are Australians there," she said.

He shook his head. "The people of the village are very sensitive."

That was a weird excuse. After everything she'd been

through, she felt that she'd earned the right at least to stand at the side and watch the proceedings, even if she couldn't understand all of it.

"Come on," Ainsley said.

"I'm sorry, it's better if you don't," he replied. "But my driver will take care of you for the rest of the afternoon."

He stuck his fingers in his mouth and made a short, sharp whistle. Nearby, the driver with the salt-and-pepper hair was leaning against a small cabin. He leapt to attention.

Gantig said something to the man in Mongolian. The man went around the shack, and the sound of an engine started up. A black Mercedes SUV came rolling around and parked next to them, engine idling.

"He'll take you up to the monastery," said Gantig.

"I already went there with Erdene."

"You can go again," Gantig said. "We'll let you know when we're ready to return to Ulaanbataar."

Gantig opened the back door and waited, his hand resting on the handle. His eyes said everything.

Sensing defeat, Ainsley climbed into the backseat.

"Thank you for all your help," he said. "I mean it."

Then he closed the door.

The driver began to accelerate. Ainsley watched the small structures of Zhakorum whizzing by the window.

She couldn't let herself get railroaded out of the village like this.

"Excuse me," she said, leaning forward towards the driver, "I need you to stop the car."

In the rearview mirror, the driver looked back at her. She could tell that he didn't understand her.

Ainsley made a puking face, covering her mouth with her right hand. Then she pointed outside the car. "Stop," she said.

That was enough. He halted the SUV. Ainsley opened the door, leapt outside—

—and began running back to the village.

The driver honked the horn. Ainsley ignored him. The vehicle circled around and slowly followed behind her.

No matter.

Soon she was back in the windswept village. Keeping away from the main street, she picked her way over the tufts of grass, around the puddles of mud, past the concrete-block shacks.

Ainsley saw the small museum that she'd visited at the beginning of this journey. The guard wasn't present.

The door was unlocked, and Ainsley darted inside. The single room was empty. All the treasures had been swept off the shelving. The corner where the Buddha statue had stood was empty.

Ainsley went back outside. The Mercedes waited in front of the door. The window was rolled down, and the face of the driver looked at her. He pointed at the backseat.

She wagged her finger no, then began running back towards the gathering.

The group was still circled around the speaker. As she arrived, Erdene caught sight of her and tried to intercept her.

"No, please, you shouldn't be here—"

Ainsley straight-armed the tour guide and proceeded to the outside edge of the group. The same baritone was pleading with the crowd. She stood her toes and struggled to see over the shoulders of the crowd.

Finally, between the heads, she glimpsed the speaker—

—and the breath was instantly sucked out of her lungs.

It was Elbegdorj Batsuuri.

Gantig's father.

CHAPTER FORTY-NINE

Ainsley's knees went shaky, and her vision turned blurry.

Gantig's father wasn't dead at all. He was very much alive, talking in front of her, right there, in the flesh. In public.

Either he'd survived his poisoning—or he'd never been poisoned at all.

Ainsley felt the anger running through her like a jousting sword. As Elbegdorj spoke, she felt the angry fire growing hotter in her belly. He'd duped her. Gantig had duped her. Even Erdene had duped her.

Gantig stood near his father, a couple steps behind, ever the dutiful son. Then he noticed Ainsley in the crowd, and a look of panic flashed across his face. He went to his father and whispered in his ear. He pointed at Ainsley in the crowd.

Elbegdorj paused the speech. When he saw Ainsley, his face brightened. "Ainsley Walker," he said, "please come up here. I want to talk about you."

The entire crowd, all two hundred odd people, turned to look at her. She felt her face reddening.

Still, she wanted to help the people of this village, because she knew how things usually turned out for uneducated country people who made deals with multinational corporations.

Seething, she moved slowly through the parted crowd, arriving in the center. Gantig guided her toward a position behind his father, in front of the Excovane executives. Ainsley recognized them as the same men who had been in the restaurant with Elbegdorj, two weeks earlier in Ulaanbataar. One nodded at her. She looked away.

"You're not supposed to be here," Gantig whispered through a forced smile.

Her smile was equally forced. "Neither is your father," she whispered back. "Were you going to pin your father's death on me?"

His grin grew so big and brittle that she was afraid it was going to crack his face in half. "No, we faked a poisoning."

"Why?"

He kept his voice low. "To change the narrative. We were losing against Excovane and we needed to get public opinion on our side."

Ainsley struggled to understand this. It was manipulative. It was brazen. But in Mongolia, maybe such outlandish events changed public opinion. A Mongolian business oligarch would know better than she would.

She looked at Elbegdorj, who was speaking again to the crowd.

"Then why did you have *me* discover him?" she said.

Gantig stood with hands folded behind his back. He spoke casually, out of the side of his mouth. "It was a mistake. My father honestly forgot you were coming over. He was distracted at the restaurant the night before."

That much was true. Ainsley remembered that he'd been in an obviously tense meeting. She remembered Gantig grabbing his father's attention for a few precious seconds just before he walked out. She remembered that it'd been clear that the older man had had more important things on his mind than chatting with a fish-out-of-water American hired to attempt a long-shot recovery of a missing moonstone.

"So somebody else was supposed to discover him," she said.

"Yes."

"Who?"

"It doesn't matter."

"You weren't trying to frame me?"

Gantig gave her a magnificent side-eye. "What would be the purpose of that?"

At that moment, Elbegdorj pointed at her. There was a smattering of applause.

"What did he just say?" she whispered.

"He said that you found the moonstone, and that the people should show their gratitude."

The smile plastered on her face, Ainsley lifted a hand and waved to the villagers.

Then Gantig's father gestured to Erdene, who stepped forward and handed him the gemstone. He lifted it up before them. The cylindrical moonstone shone in the midday sun.

The people fell silent. It wasn't reverential silence, but more confusion. Ainsley figured that none of them had ever seen the moonstone, maybe not even photos of it. Maybe they would need time to process the recovery.

Then Elbegdorj walked over to the Buddha statue, which had been rolled out to the center of the road for just this occasion. With great ceremony, he angled the moonstone into the hexagonal space in the forehead—and pushed it in.

It entered cleanly. Ainsley breathed a sigh of relief that she hadn't been duped once again.

Then he stepped back and made a grand gesture.

But the people of Zhakorum didn't react. Nobody spoke, nobody moved, nobody clapped. The villagers just stood there like a herd of cows. Ainsley scanned the faces. They wore no expressions. Maybe the moonstone was such a distant memory at this point—more than a century had passed—that they were too stunned to react. Maybe they didn't know the story of Cholsaiban's sacrifice.

Or—worst of all—maybe they just didn't care.

Elbegdorj said another few words. He pointed at the Buddha, the moonstone shining in its forehead. Still no reaction.

"Why don't they say anything?" she whispered.

"I don't know," Gantig said. His jaw clenched and his nostrils flared.

Behind her, the three Excovane executives exchanged glances with one another. En masse, the three Australians stood up and walked to a long table that was covered in white plastic.

Without a word, the three men yanked the plastic cover off the table. Ainsley gaped. It was loaded with an array of meats, cheeses, and bottles of vodka. There was enough to feed everybody present—at least twice.

"Excovane," said an executive, "would like to thank you in advance for signing the contract!"

He nodded to a Mongolian man, wearing a red polo shirt bearing the Excovane logo, who translated loudly to the crowd.

The people of Zhakorum broke out into a cheer—then rushed the table.

Ainsley, Gantig, Erdene, and Elbegdorj all stepped aside to avoid the stampede. The villagers descended upon the food and drink like a pack of wolves upon a fresh kill.

Elbegdorj placed a large hand on her good shoulder. "I'm sorry, Ainsley. We were going to tell you, but—"

His velvety baritone was full of regret.

"When?" she said.

"After we secured the villagers' cooperation."

Ainsley glanced at the feeding frenzy. "Well, you didn't. Look at them. Your public relations stunt didn't get you any sympathy either. Neither did the moonstone."

Elbegdorj looked crestfallen, wounded. His shoulders stooped. He seemed to be aging right in front of her. She regretted saying it. It all came out sharper than she'd meant it to.

Erdene gently steered Ainsley away. "I think it's time we return to Ulaanbataar."

"You lied to me," said Ainsley.

"Well, you lied to me too. You said your name was Karin."

"Can I guess another one of your lies?"

"Okay."

"Gantig's not really your cousin."

The tiniest crack of a smile. "He's my boyfriend."

"I knew it. And you didn't go back to Ulaanbaatar for a funeral."

"No, I just wanted to see him."

A frustrated breath blew out of Ainsley's mouth. "Well, I guess we all lie."

"But it was all for a good cause."

"Yes," said Ainsley, "it was."

They climbed into the back of the waiting Mercedes. Before she closed the door, Ainsley took a final look at the scene. The people of Zhakorum gorging themselves. The three Excovane executives lighting cigars for one another. Elbegdorj sitting on the ground, face in hands, while his son crouched beside him, hand on his father's arm.

And nearby sat the Buddha, the moonstone in its forehead forgotten.

"You and Gantig overestimated how much the villagers of Zhakorum wanted the moonstone," said Ainsley. "They really don't care."

"Maybe," she said.

A half-smile appeared on Ainsley's face. "Maybe you should've given them a table of food."

"Knowing them, it's more the vodka."

Ainsley studied the concrete shacks, the rutted road, the cold mountain range. Zhakorum didn't know it, but it lay on the cusp of a new era, something bigger. "What's going to happen to this village? And to this region?"

Erdene looked pensive. "I don't know. But whatever happens, at least it will be our choice. At least we have that now, in Mongolia."

"At least you have that," agreed Ainsley.

She closed the door, and Erdene said something to the driver. The vehicle began to pull away.

As the village receded into the distance, Ainsley looked quietly out of the window, until her eyes slowly closed shut.

PLOTWORKS PUBLISHING

Visit Plotworks Publishing to follow Ainsley Walker on another exciting gemstone travel mystery—*The Uruguay Amethyst*!

Turn the page for a sneak peek—

THE

URUGUAY AMETHYST

AN AINSLEY WALKER
GEMSTONE TRAVEL MYSTERY

J.A. JERNAY

THE URUGUAY AMETHYST

Ainsley pulled the backseat door closed. Her driver's eyes looked at her in the rearview mirror.

"Where can I take you?" Oswaldo asked in Spanish.

"Back to Tabarez," she said.

He nodded, and they pulled away from the curb. Ainsley studied him in the mirror. His jaw was set firmly. She decided to see what she could learn from him.

"Do you like working for Tabarez?" she said.

"Yes," he said. Nothing else.

Of course he wouldn't comment on his employer. She decided to stick to facts.

"Oswaldo, after lunch I will need you to help me take a very large package to this address." She handed him the paper with Bernabé's address. "Can you find this place?"

He read the address and nodded. Not a word. Ainsley was beginning to wonder if he was a bit simple.

The car was slicing down La Rambla, and Ainsley contented herself with staring out the window, at the blurring breakwall and at the choppy brown water of the delta. The sky was bright blue and the clouds puffy and white and a chill wind was blowing again.

It was mesmerizing. She wrapped her coat around herself more tightly and snuggled in.

Then she woke up to Oswaldo touching her knee. The vehicle had stopped. She was outside Tabarez's house.

Ainsley emerged from the vehicle and buttoned the top collar of her coat. "It's so cold here," she said.

Oswaldo didn't respond. Conversationally, there was no difference between her driver and a piece of drywall. She decided to just issue him orders instead. It would save both of them a lot of trouble.

"Stay here until I return."

He lit a cigarette and looked straight ahead.

Slinging her purse over her shoulder, Ainsley walked alone towards the house. Her stomach was twisting itself into anxious knots. Partly because of El Árbol Negro, partly because she was so hungry.

And nervous. She was about to enjoy homemade ñoquis in a private dining room with an extremely wealthy and attractive man who may or may not have refused to sleep with her, even after she'd thrown herself at him. Why did she have to black out on that night of all nights? And now he was going to sell her a famous amethyst after telling her its secret history.

This felt too good to be true.

The copper gate was rolled wide open. Ainsley cocked her head. That was strange, given the value of the contents inside the mansion.

She stepped through the open gate onto the driveway, then moved into the manicured yard. It made her heart sing again. She touched the bougainvillea, listened to the branches clacking in the breeze from the estuary.

Then she rang the front doorbell and waited. The slab of

wood before her was exquisite. Spirals and whorls had been dug into its surface, like the enormous thumbprint of a criminal.

There was no response. That was weird. Heinrik was the epitome of the efficient manservant. He should've been there in a flash.

She rang the doorbell again, then turned and surveyed the landscaping. Water was trickling from some unseen fountain. She couldn't find it. An invisible bird sang crookedly from the branches of a tall ash. She couldn't find that either. A sinking feeling filled her stomach.

Had she been lied to? Had Tabarez cast her aside that quickly? Had he decided to keep El Árbol Negro? She'd heard the old cliché of how Latin people lived for the moment, but this expulsion was quicker than she'd expected. She felt anger sprouting from her back like a bouquet of hot orange flames.

Upset, she turned back to the door. If he wouldn't answer the door, she would invite herself inside. She gripped the doorknob and turned it. The slab of wood swung open easily, as though it weighed ten pounds instead of twenty times that much. Of course Tabarez had made sure that the hinges were well-oiled.

She entered the foyer and noticed a large object, wrapped in black plastic, resting immediately next to the door.

El Árbol Negro.

With her fingertips she traced its lovely branches beneath the plastic. So beautiful. She noticed a dolly sitting next to it. How thoughtful.

Remembering her host's orders, she kicked off her shoes, then crept around the edges of the carpet. The house was completely silent.

"José Ignacio?" she shouted. "Heinrik?"

Still no response. She crept up the stairs to the second

floor sitting room where she had last seen him, in his white robe, strumming his instrument.

As she rose to the landing, she caught her breath.

José Ignacio was still sitting on the sofa in the sumptuous second floor sala. The guitar was laying next to him. His head was tilted back, and his eyes were shut. A thin smile decorated his mouth.

Another thin smile, this one quite a bit redder, and eight inches across, decorated his throat.

José Ignacio Tabarez was not going to be dining with her this afternoon.

He was dead.

Visit Plotworks Publishing to follow Ainsley Walker on all her exciting adventures!

Then explore a new series by J.A. Jernay—the Cosmo Bennett Mapping Thrillers!

Turn the page for another sneak peek—

J.A. JERNAY

BOUNDARY

A COSMO BENNETT MAPPING THRILLER

FROM *THE AUTHOR OF THE AINSLEY WALKER GEMSTONE TRAVEL MYSTERY SERIES*

BOUNDARY

Cosmo and his assistant Noah shuffled down the dirt shoulder of the boulevard in the midday heat, sweating and miserable.

Each was lost in his own thoughts. Cosmo dreamed of hitting a heavy punching bag at his gymnasium. Noah dreamed of passing level nineteen of Operation Earlobe, an obscure RPG he'd abandoned last semester.

The morning's meeting had been a complete bust.

"I don't think we should continue," said Cosmo finally.

Noah didn't respond, but Cosmo took no notice. He continued: "I don't think anybody here takes our task seriously. I don't think this propaganda map was as influential as they say. I don't think this map has driven the civil unrest. I think social media and centuries of tribal warfare are more to blame for the unrest than anything else."

He looked over at Noah, waiting for a response. "What about you?"

The graduate assistant came back from his reverie. "Huh?"

"Did you hear anything I said?"

"No."

"I was just saying this is pointless and we should go home."

"I don't have a problem with that."

They arrived at Vida e Caffe. It was a chain café, with hundreds of similar franchises scattered across the southern half of the African continent. The branding was modern and inviting. A hundred people sat beneath umbrellas at small tables on the large outdoor patio.

An arm was waving at them. It was Christopher, their fixer, a cup of tea on a ceramic saucer in front of him. Two other cups awaited them.

"Hello sirs," he said. "I ordered us all a rooibos. It's a vanilla tea that is extraordinary."

Cosmo and Noah pulled out the chairs and sat down. The driver quickly sussed out that something was wrong.

"It was a bad meeting?" he said quietly.

"Yes," said Cosmo, "there was no progress made."

"I'm very sorry."

Cosmo sighed. "I think we have to leave."

The fixer looked confused. "But you just sat down—"

"The country," he clarified. "We have to leave Fabajouti. We can't seem to do any good here."

Christopher looked crestfallen. "I do understand your frustration."

Noah said, "If it's okay with you, we'd probably like to just get in the car and go back to the hotel."

The fixer rediscovered his manners. "Of course, as you wish—"

"But we'd love to try the tea first—" added Cosmo.

"You two enjoy the rooibos," said Christopher, "while I fetch the car. The parking lot is very jammed and it will take quite a while to remove. I've already paid the bill."

Before they could object, the driver had shot to his feet.

He clapped Cosmo on the shoulder and left the patio. They watched him cross the boulevard to an off-street parking area that was crammed tightly with vehicles. On his approach, the attendant began shifting other vehicles.

Noah sipped the tea. "This does taste really good. I don't drink enough tea."

"I like tea," said Cosmo. He sipped from the cup. "This one is good."

"What's your favorite?" asked Noah.

"Maybe pu'er."

"That one's bitter, right?"

"Yeah. It's fermented."

"What about Earl Grey?"

"A cliché."

"I think I'm more of a fruity tea guy," said Noah.

Cosmo nodded. "Yeah, they have their charms."

"You ever try chamomile?"

"It's good for sleeping," said Cosmo, "but otherwise it's—"

His comment was cut short by a massive fireball that erupted from the parking lot across the street.

————

In a split second, Cosmo and Noah instinctively rolled off their chairs and onto the ground beneath their table. Their eyes met. Each was filled with terror.

Then the shock of the overpressure hit. Cosmo felt the force of the blast wave hit the left side of his body. The highly compressed air rattled the left side of his skull. It even sent his lips and cheeks flapping to the right.

The initial sound of the explosion was deafening, but that was soon replaced by a symphony of falling destruction. A thousand pieces of metal, plastic, glass, and upholstery rained down upon the boulevard, the grass, the other cars.

A shower of tiny shrapnel hit on the patio of the cafe. One hit Noah in the hand and sizzled his flesh. He shook it off.

They waited another few seconds for the shrapnel rain to end. Then Cosmo and Noah lifted their heads.

The patio of the café was transformed into pandemonium. The patrons started to pull themselves up from the ground and flee out to the street and in the opposite direction. The street itself was coming alive with panicked people running in every direction.

"What the actual—" said Noah.

"Christopher!" interrupted Cosmo. "What about Christopher?"

He scrambled up to his feet. Without waiting for Noah, he sprinted out of the café and across the boulevard, weaving through the stopped cars. The air was acrid with chemicals and the heat had somehow intensified even further.

The parking lot was a field of wreckage. The bomb had exploded in the middle of the space, shredding every vehicle and person within twenty meters. Pieces of concrete and metal and glass had been blown across the scene.

"Christopher!" he shouted again. "Christopher! Don't do this!"

He saw a shoe with a foot still in it. He saw a red string of guts entangled in a hubcap. A wave of nausea gripped his stomach. He covered his nose with his t-shirt and backed away.

He tripped backwards over a piece of metal, stumbled, and fell to the ground.

That's when he saw it.

A long strip of shredded fabric. A yellow-and-green printed tropical shirt.

It was bloody and torn.

Cosmo turned his head and retched onto the asphalt. All the tea he'd just drank came out.

He somehow pulled himself to his feet and staggered back to the café. Noah was waiting at the far corner, on the sidewalk, pacing frantically.

"So?"

"I found him," said Cosmo. He forced the next words out. "A little bit."

Noah's face went white. "Oh my God."

Cosmo didn't say anything. He just gripped Noah by the upper arm. "Walk with me. And don't look back."

———

The pair moved briskly down the boulevard, away from the scene. People were running past them, mouths open, eyes full of fear, but Cosmo maintained a steady pace. His face betrayed an intense desire to appear as normal as possible.

"So we're just going to leave the scene?" said Noah.

"Yep."

"Why?"

"Don't make me answer that, Noah."

"I think we should talk to the police, cooperate, tell them everything—"

"In a different country," Cosmo replied, "in a different scenario, you'd be right. But not here, not now."

Noah looked back over his shoulder at the scene.

"Look straight ahead," Cosmo said through his teeth, "and listen to me. Our Mercedes is gone. Christopher is ... gone."

"Shit—"

"And I'm going to suggest something else that could blow your mind."

"What?"

"It's possible that we were the intended target."

"That's insane."

"Is it?"

"How do you know?"

"I don't. But it's a possibility. Here's another one. It's possible that we are going to be used as scapegoats. We were the last people seen eating with Christopher. Do you want to be put in a Fabajouti jail on suspicion of a crime?"

They walked for another half minute in silence. Behind them, the chaos grew distant.

"Where are we going?" Noah said finally.

"Back to the hotel."

"And then?"

"We're leaving, like we planned."

"We're not going home, are we?" said Noah.

Cosmo's mouth grew hard and his jaw jutted out. He stared straight forward at an invisible point on the horizon. "No, we're not."